Nightfall

Nightfall

Book One
The Tyke McGrath Series

by

William Woodall

Jeremiah Press · *Antoine, Arkansas*

Jeremiah Press
PO Box 3
Antoine, AR 71922

This is a work of fiction. Any resemblance to actual persons, places, or events is purely coincidental.

First published by Jeremiah Press on 11/12/2013

Printed in the United States of America.

This book is printed on acid-free paper.

ISBN: 978-0-9833298-5-5

For Mickael,

Christian, scientist, and warrior

They shall beat their swords into plowshares,
And their spears into pruning hooks;
Nation shall not lift up sword against nation,
Neither shall they learn war any more.
- Micah 4:3

Quotable Quotes

"Cherish the time that you have, and be glad for the days you've been given. They don't last forever, and they'll pass by faster than you think."

"God is good, in this as in all things. When your time of testing comes, trust in His love and do whatever it may be that He asks of you, even if you can't see the reason why."

"There are really only two kinds of problems in the world. There's the kind you can do something about, and then there's the kind you can't do anything about. If you can do something about it, then quit worrying and go do it. If you can't do anything, then worrying won't help you in that case either. Worry is nothing but fear, and fear is nothing but lack of faith."

"One way or another the world will die for lack of love, and if there's anything to be saved from the ruins then it'll only be love that saves us."

"There's no such thing as a normal life. Every person in the world has his own burdens and issues, most of which you'd never guess."

"Your circumstances are only as hard as you think they are. If you focus on all the things you don't have then yeah, your life will be pretty miserable. But it doesn't have to be that way."

"He knew all these things, and up till now he would always have said he believed them. But when it came to the point of decision and his own back was up against the wall, he found that things were quite different."

"Sometimes we have to make sacrifices for the people we love, even ones that break our hearts and cost us dearly."

"Human beings always have a choice."

"So if we're only like the curve in a waterfall, and there's not a shred of matter that we could ever put a finger on and say that that's really us, then what are we?"

"Slogans and cheap lines were easy to repeat, but in real life the decision was far from simple. Sometimes he feared the world was doomed in one way or another no matter what anybody did or didn't do."

Contents

Important Characters

Micah McGrath: *Mike is a 23-year old student working on his PhD in astronomy, and has no idea of what is about to befall him.*

Josiah Wilder- *Joey is 25 years old, Mike's best friend, and his roommate at school. He is studying to be a psychologist.*

Philip Carpenter- *Once known as Cameron, Philip is Joey's adopted brother and the leader of the Avengers. He is 20 years old.*

Joan Carpenter- *Joan is Philip's wife, an Avenger herself, and a former spy for the Confederate Army. She is also 20 years old.*

Annabelle Rusk- *Joan's 19-year-old sister. Annabelle is a mathematical genius and every inch a Victorian lady.*

Lieutenant Luke Bartow- *Commander of the Tampa NADF office, Luke is cold and ruthless. But he does have a conscience.*

Luther Anderson- *An Avenger, and also an intelligence agent with the NADF office in Asheville, North Carolina.*

Damon Doucet- *Matthieu Doucet's great-grandson, an avid pilot and former leader of the Avengers. Damon is 65.*

Katrina Doucet- *Damon's daughter, she is 15 years old and the last living member of the Doucet family.*

Tycho McGrath- *Mike and Annabelle's son. Tyke is only 4 years old when the story ends, but his part is critical.*

Chapter One
Friday, April 25, 2036

At the worst possible moment, the power died.

The lab instantly went pitch dark, causing the tip of Micah McGrath's screwdriver to slip just the tiniest bit. Metal touched metal, and before he knew it one of the capacitors had discharged its built-up load right into the circuit board he'd been trying to fix.

Mike cursed and slammed his fist on the table in sheer frustration; what *else* could go wrong today? He didn't have *time* for things like this; he was supposed to have his dissertation finished in only three more weeks.

After a few seconds the university's emergency generator kicked in and the lights flickered back on. Then Mike promptly forgot about power glitches and burnt-out circuit boards, and his eyes widened in shocked surprise.

The tachometer was gone.

Mike knitted his brows and stared at the empty spot where the machine had been sitting just a few seconds ago. He rubbed his eyes to make sure he wasn't seeing things, but there was no doubt about it. The thing had definitely vanished.

He didn't know quite what to think about this unexpected development; in spite of all his efforts to fix it, the tachometer hadn't actually worked in years. And even if it had, he'd certainly never switched it on or set the controls for it to do anything. There was no reason he could think of why it shouldn't still be sitting there on the workbench.

His first thought was to wonder if the discharge from the capacitor might have inadvertently activated some obscure function, even though that seemed highly unlikely. Anytime the tachometer was operational it was always surrounded by a silvery bubble of energy several feet across, and he certainly would have noticed if anything like *that* had appeared.

But then again, Mike would have been the first to admit that he didn't really understand the blasted thing very well.

The machine was designed to capture and manipulate tachyons; those ghostly, faster-than-light particles which supposedly contained the power to foresee the future before it happened, and perhaps even to travel there.

True, Mike had never actually witnessed any of those things personally, but he'd heard plenty of stories from people who had. It was a fascinating subject, and when the time came to pick a research topic for his dissertation, there'd never been the slightest doubt that he'd choose to study tachyons. Never mind the fact that not everybody even believed they existed; Mike was determined to be the one who finally proved it to the world.

Dr. Bevels had smiled and called it "a learning experience", but that was okay; Mike was confident he'd show them all someday. He might only be twenty-three years old, but then again some of the greatest Nobel Prize winners in history had been in their early twenties. Mike himself was on track to become the youngest Ph.D. graduate in the history of the university, and surely that had to say *something* good about his prospects, didn't it?

He would never have admitted to harboring such grandiose thoughts, of course, but they were awfully nice to think about now and then.

He glanced at the clock and saw that it was already 4:15; close enough to call it a day if he liked. He normally stayed in the lab at least till five, but the inexplicable disappearance of the tachometer was a mystery he felt too mentally tired to tackle at the end of such a long day. Not to mention the fact that he'd skipped lunch and his stomach was beginning to suggest pretty urgently that it was high time to get something to eat. Maybe he could come back in the morning with a fresh mind and think of some new ideas.

He shut down his laptop and turned off the lights before locking the door and putting the keys in his pocket. When everything was in order, he tiredly climbed the stairs from the basement and walked outside to where his Jeep was parked in front of the athletics building. The science center and several other structures on campus were closed for renovations at the moment, which meant Mike had been assigned this little niche in the gym instead. It was adequate, perhaps, but certainly not very glamorous.

His "lab" had actually been somebody's office before Mike moved in, but he'd done his best to make it work as a research space, shoving the desk up against one wall and moving in a lab bench from the science building. He'd even hung a portrait of Tycho Brahe above the desk, the father of modern astronomy and one of his particular heroes. Heaven knows he needed some inspiration and encouragement now and then.

There were more people than usual gathered in scattered groups outside, but Mike was too preoccupied with his own thoughts to pay much attention to that. He fired up the Jeep, intending to drive home, find something to eat, and then do absolutely nothing for the rest of the evening.

He heard police sirens wailing somewhere off to the north, and wondered idly what was going on. He supposed he'd hear about it soon enough, if it mattered.

He drove slowly down the quiet street next to the university, and other than the traffic lights not working there didn't seem to be anything out of the ordinary. Just a typical springtime afternoon. An old lady weeding her azaleas waved at him, and he smiled and waved back. He passed the fire station and the white-columned library, then the bank and his favorite coffee shop and the big red-brick Victorian courthouse on the town square. Almost home!

The house he shared with his best friend Joey Wilder was built on the side of a hill maybe half a block past the courthouse, where Third Street ran steeply down to cross the railroad tracks. But then as Mike swung into the front yard, he noticed an anomaly. There was a small crowd of people standing in front of the church across the street, but it was what they were staring at that immediately caught his attention and left him every bit as speechless as they were.

Just past the church, the street ended. Where it had once swept on down the hill to the tracks, now it just. . . stopped. And where the street used to be, now there were only trees. Large ones, that looked as if they'd been there since the day the world began.

That was shocking enough, but when Mike raised his eyes swiftly to look out over the treetops, he was in for an even greater shock. Where there had once been railroad tracks and factories and houses scattered thickly as far as he could see across the valley, now there was nothing. No tracks, no houses, no streets. Just an unbroken canopy of green that stretched all the way to the horizon.

Mike broke his stupefaction and walked slowly the last hundred feet or so to the end of the pavement, reaching out to touch the trunk of a massive oak tree that stood right in the middle of where the street should have been. The bark was rough and solid. Then he knelt down and touched the edge of the pavement, and found that it cut off as sharply as if someone had sliced it with a gigantic razor blade and left only this side behind.

The cut extended smoothly in both directions from where he knelt. To the east, it crossed the parking lot between the church and where the Family Life Center should have been, and then it passed quickly behind the church itself and out of Mike's sight. In the other direction it passed right through his own back yard, almost clipping off the corner of his house as a matter of fact. He could see a little bit farther in that direction, and it seemed that the razor's edge had a slight curve to it, though it was hard to be sure.

A dark suspicion flirted at the edge of his mind, but he dismissed the thought immediately. It *couldn't* be.

He gingerly took a step past the end of the street, and then another. Soon he was standing amongst an almost silent forest of trees that whispered tranquilly in the breeze. They were unusually large and thick, but otherwise no different than any other trees he'd ever seen.

Except for the fact that they hadn't been there when he left the house that morning, of course. The trunks were widely spaced and the forest floor was level enough to drive a small car through, if the driver were careful.

After a few seconds he quit gaping at the trees and walked swiftly back up the hill to his own front door. As soon as he got inside the house, he found Joey fiddling with the little battery-powered radio they kept for emergencies.

"Where have you been, Mike? Have you seen what's going on out there?" Joey asked. He was almost exactly two years older than Mike himself, but they'd known each other ever since Mike could remember.

"Yeah, I see it. I don't believe it, but I definitely see it. Have you heard anything on the radio?" Mike asked.

"No, I couldn't find any batteries for it. All the ones I've tried are already dead," Joey said. For some reason Mike had never been able to force himself to throw away old batteries, and as a result almost every shelf and drawer in the house contained at least a few of them. Joey had complained about it times without number.

"I guess I better run go get some, then. I'll be back in a little while. One of us better stay here and keep an eye on the house, though, don't you think?" he asked, and Joey shrugged.

He grabbed a chocolate chip granola bar from the kitchen before running back outside to where the Jeep was parked. He usually walked or rode his bike around town, partly to save gas and partly to get some exercise, but at the moment he cared more about speed than anything else.

He didn't head directly for the store, though. As soon as he was out on the street, he began following the razor-edge to the west. There were places where it had sliced right through the middle of houses or buildings, with the other half disappearing like magic, with no trace of rubble or destruction. Except in a few cases, where the remainder of the structure had collapsed from the stress and fallen into the trees that crowded right up to the line. After a while, he also noted that the tree branches were cut off in a similar fashion; not even so much as a twig crossed the boundary.

People were gathered all along his route, staring at the trees with attitudes that ranged anywhere from mild curiosity to dumbfounded amazement. No one seemed panicky or hysterical, and some were even laughing and socializing, as if the whole thing were some kind of huge joke.

The line crossed right behind the National Guard armory and the post office, cut through some more houses and streets, then clipped the corner of the old cemetery. Then Mike saw some major damage; the blue jean factory and the junior high school had been sliced in half, and both of them had mostly collapsed. Thank God school had already been over for the day.

The line continued on into another residential area where Mike couldn't follow, but he drove quickly to Pine Street and picked it up again. It ran right through the middle of the Arby's drive-thru, and then plunged back (again) into residential areas.

Mike doggedly followed the line as far as he could. It ran right behind the university football stadium, and sliced off the main highway out of town exactly where Pizza Hut should have been. That was a bad scene; someone in a black Lexus had smashed into the trees when the highway disappeared in front of her, and two other cars had piled up behind the first one. There was no ambulance to be seen; nothing but the smashed Lexus, and three bewildered-looking cops who kept glancing at the trees.

Mike made an illegal U-turn and drove urgently back to his lab, parking the Jeep right by the front door. The group of students from earlier had disappeared, which suited him just as well. The fewer witnesses there were, the better.

As soon as he got inside the gym he heard the sound of someone playing basketball, apparently unaware of what was going on. He rushed downstairs to his little cubbyhole and unlocked the door, almost stubbing his toe in his haste to get inside. There was a city map in his desk drawer, and he quickly unfolded it on the workbench next to where the tachometer had been. Then he took a pencil and carefully marked every location where he'd seen the razor cut pass.

He noticed immediately that it was an almost perfect circle, and with shaking hands he drew three separate diameter lines with a ruler so as to find the center point.

The lines met right where his lab stood.

A cold knot of fear threatened to cut off his breath when he saw that, because there could be only one explanation for everything he'd seen. Namely, the tachometer must have been activated somehow by the discharge of the capacitor, and then dragged the entire central core of Arkadelphia to some unknown point in the future.

Never mind that it hadn't been switched on, or that an ocean of trees looked nothing like any kind of future Mike had ever anticipated, or that he'd never imagined the tachometer could swallow an area big enough to engulf nearly a whole town. Those were incidentals which could be explained later. In the meantime, there wasn't a shred of doubt in his mind about what had actually happened.

You've really done it now, boy, he thought to himself.

Even worse, he knew it wouldn't be long before other people started connecting the dots and reaching similar conclusions. Oh, they might not know exactly what happened, true, but it wouldn't take a genius to figure out who was responsible for it, as soon as somebody noticed whose lab was at the exact center of the circle. His research wasn't a secret, and neither was the location of his lab. One of the few things he liked about working in the gym instead of in the science building was the extra peace and privacy, but that wouldn't mean a thing once the whole town was looking for him. And he was sure they soon would be.

He quickly gathered up his own research notes along with Dr. Garza's original lab manuals. He didn't dare leave anything at the lab to be confiscated or destroyed, and least of all *those*. He even took the laptop, although he felt guilty about that. It technically belonged to the university, not to him, and he wasn't actually supposed to leave campus with it. He was careful to make sure no one saw him removing items from the building, since that would only focus attention on him that much faster.

He finished loading up and calmly drove away, thinking hard. Most people in town probably didn't really comprehend what had happened yet, and some of them might not even know. Things still seemed bizarrely normal at the moment. But Mike could guess what was coming within the next few weeks, if a world of trees were really all there was in this future time. Food and clean water would run out quickly, and when that happened, it was only a matter of time until cholera or dysentery reared its ugly head. And with no medicine to speak of. . . He shuddered.

Without wasting another second, he drove immediately to the bank. The lobby was already closed, of course, but the drive through was still open. He pulled up to the window and stopped, breathing a sigh of relief when he saw the girl at the computer. It was Allison, and he knew her well enough that she might do him a favor. He smiled and waved at her so she could see his face, and she smiled back when she recognized him. He pushed the call button and noted with satisfaction that the bank must have had a generator, since the machine was still working. Thank God for small blessings.

Mike quickly wrote a check for 2419.85, which was every nickel he had in his account.

Allison took the check and sent the cash and his driver's license back out, which he took with trembling hands. Somehow he managed to smile again and thank Allison before he left. He stuffed the cash in his pocket and then drove directly to the grocery store. If trouble were coming then he wasn't taking any chances.

It was busier than it should have been at that time of day, which worried him; apparently word was getting around and people were starting to get uneasy. The bread and milk sections were practically wiped out already, he noticed, but those weren't the kinds of things Mike had in mind anyway.

He grabbed a shopping cart and filled it as quickly as he could with anything that wouldn't spoil, especially canned goods. Then he filled two more. Not just with food, either; he quickly cleaned out everything useful he could find in the pharmacy section, too, including all the antibiotics and bandages, all the painkillers, and all the major vitamins. As an afterthought, he grabbed two handfuls of lighters, six bottles of chlorine bleach, and anything else he could think of that was useful and couldn't be replaced. The checkout lady gave him an amused look when he got to the cash register.

"You think the end of the world is comin', honey?" she asked with a chuckle.

"No, ma'am, just making sure," he said. That only made her laugh again, as he hoped it would. It took a while to pay for everything and get it loaded in the back of the Jeep, but there was still one more stop to make before he dared go home. His usual sporting goods store was gone, but there was a hole-in-the-wall gun shop downtown, and as soon as he got there Mike bought every .22 bullet they had. He got some raised eyebrows for that, but he couldn't have cared less.

He didn't park in the front yard when he got home as he usually would have. Instead, he backed into the garage to unload his supplies.

"Where have you *been,* dude? Don't you know-" Joey began, coming out of the kitchen door into the garage. Then he saw the mountain of grocery bags and trailed off.

"Uh, do you know something you're not telling me?" he finally asked.

"I'm not sure. Help me carry all this stuff inside and then we'll talk about it and try to figure things out. But first let's lock all the doors, and the windows too for that matter," Mike added as an afterthought.

"Whatever you say, buddy," Joey said, with a shrug that indicated he clearly believed Mike had lost his mind.

They quickly locked every door and window, even drawing the blinds and drapes. Joey was mostly quiet during all this, even when Mike started taking food down to the basement instead of the kitchen, but when he saw the case of bullets that must have been too much for him to keep silent about.

"Hold on a minute, dude. Seriously, what's going on? If you're gonna come home and start acting like it's world war three you should at least tell me what's up," he said.

"You're absolutely right, but let's finish putting this stuff away first. As soon as that's done I'll tell you everything, I promise,"

Mike said. Joey looked like he wanted to argue about it some more, but then seemed to change his mind.

"All right, then," he finally said. And he was as good as his word; he worked as fast as Mike did to get all the groceries hauled down to the basement and hidden carefully behind the old furnace. Not just the food and supplies, either, but Mike's computer and lab notes, also. Only when everything was safely stashed away did they both sit down at the kitchen table and partially relax.

Chapter Two

It was dim in the kitchen with the blinds drawn, so Joey quietly lit an oil lamp and put it on the table between them. The light cast dusky shadows across his face and made him look like a mummified corpse. Mike thrust the hideous image out of his mind

"So, are you going to explain now?" Joey asked.

"I'm not sure where to start," Mike said.

"Well, the beginning is always a good place," Joey pointed out.

"Well. . . I think I might've accidentally activated the tachometer," Mike said.

"I didn't think it worked," Joey said.

"I didn't think so either, but can you think of any other explanation for all this? You see the way the street cuts off like somebody sliced it with a knife, don't you? It goes on like that all the way around town, it even cuts right through buildings and houses sometimes, in certain places. It makes a perfect ring just a hair bigger than a mile and a half wide. Everything inside the circle is exactly the way it always was, but outside that there's nothing but trees. I followed it all the way around before I came home," Mike said.

"Okay, I admit that's suggestive, but it doesn't *prove* anything," Joey said.

"No, but there's more. My lab is at the exact center of the circle, and I know I accidentally discharged the capacitor this afternoon at the exact same time the power died. And besides that the tachometer itself disappeared. What other conclusion could you draw from all that?" Mike said bleakly.

Joey digested that thought.

"I don't know, Mikey. I can see how maybe you might have accidentally switched it on when you discharged the capacitor. But I never heard of the tachometer covering such a big area as this," he said.

"Me neither, and I can't imagine any time in the future when there wouldn't be anything but trees, either. This is more like a million years ago," Mike said.

"But it can't be. The tachometer doesn't work backwards," Joey pointed out.

"Not that we *know* of, anyway," Mike said.

"No, it's scientifically impossible; you know that as well as I do. We've got to be somewhere in the future, if that's what actually happened," Joey insisted.

"Okay, so maybe we skipped ahead ten million years and there are no human beings left on the whole planet," Mike said.

"Don't get so far ahead of yourself, Mikey. We can't know what year it is unless we go out there past the ring and find some kind of hard evidence. Which I'm sure we will, sooner or later. It's not like we won't have time," Joey said wryly.

"Yeah, you're definitely right about that," Mike admitted. If there were anything certain about the entire situation, it was the brutal fact that there was no going back. Once you skipped ahead with the tachometer, you were stuck there forever. Time was the one thing they had no shortage of.

"In the meantime, all we can do is deal with what we see. I'm guessing that's why you bought all those supplies?" Joey asked.

"Yeah. It's all stuff we could either use or trade later on, if we had to. Things could get nasty around here in a hurry if people start running out of food and water," Mike agreed.

"So what are the six gallons of Clorox for? Any special reason?" Joey asked.

"Yeah there is. We can use it to sanitize water to make it safe to drink. It won't taste too good, but it'll get the job done," Mike explained.

"All right, I guess I can understand that. But what about the ten bottles of cinnamon and the fifty pounds of sugar? Planning on baking a really big cake?" Joey asked.

"No, those are for keeping food safe, and like I said maybe for trading later on when everybody else runs out, which they will sooner or later," Mike said.

"And the .22 shells? I assume those are for hunting?" Joey asked.

"Yeah, mostly. But also just in case we need to defend ourselves," Mike said darkly.

"I really don't think anybody will come after us with torches and dogs, Mikey," Joey said. He was trying to lighten the mood, which Mike appreciated, but he didn't agree with his assessment of the danger level.

"They might. Things are hectic right now and maybe nobody's had a chance to think it through very much, but they will. They'll notice that this little slice of town that's left is a perfect circle, and it'll cross somebody's mind to see where the center is. And once they do that, it won't be long before somebody puts two and two together and figures out one of the astronomy students was doing experimental research down there in the gym. I don't know if Dr. Bevels is still in town or not, but he wasn't the only one who knew about it. People will talk, and then they might just start to wonder if maybe Mike McGrath was on to something with his silly little tachyon machine, after all. Then what do you think they'll do?" Mike asked.

"They'll come looking for you, to see if you know anything," Joey guessed.

"Bingo. And then what will I tell them?" Mike asked.

"The truth, maybe? You didn't mean any harm. Nobody ever thought you were doing anything dangerous," Joey pointed out, and Mike gave him a withering look.

"Do you think that will matter, when people start going hungry and getting sick? They won't want to hear excuses when that happens. They'll want answers, and they'll want all this to be undone, and if they can't have that, then they'll want vengeance. You of all people should know how folks think in a disaster," Mike said, and that was unquestionably true. Joey was a psychology major, and a pretty sharp one, too.

"Nothing to say to that?" Mike asked pointedly, when the other boy didn't answer.

"No. . . I guess you're right," Joey admitted, and then they were both silent for a few seconds after that.

"I don't guess you remembered to get any batteries for the radio, did you? We might hear something on the university station, at least," Joey finally asked.

"No, I forgot," Mike admitted, feeling supremely stupid. He'd been tied up in a million knots, of course, but that was no excuse.

"Well, it's too late to do anything about it now. We'll get some in the morning, if they're still selling them, that is. How *did* you get all that stuff, anyway? It must have cost a fortune," Joey said.

"I used what I had in the bank," Mike admitted, and Joey raised an eyebrow.

"All of it?" he asked.

"Yeah. . . I wasn't sure if I could even get access to it after today, so I figured I better grab it while I could. Besides that, I figure it probably won't be worth the paper it's printed on within a couple days or so. I wanted to get what we needed to maybe save our necks while I still had the chance," Mike said.

"I don't know, Mikey. It'll be hard to get by even in a little place like this without some form of money to simplify trade. You might end up feeling kind of silly if everybody goes right on using the same old cash as always and then you're broke except for fifty pounds of sugar and a case of lard," Joey said.

"If that's the worst problem I have to deal with then I'll be happy to eat sugar and lard for the next six months. Besides, if that's the way it plays out then we can always sell the stuff, probably for a lot more than I paid for it. I'd be glad to waste all the money in the bank, if I knew it would undo all this," Mike said sadly.

"It's okay, buddy. You didn't know. Nobody can blame you for this," Joey said, and Mike laughed a little.

"Oh, there are all different kinds of ways of being to blame, you know. *I didn't mean to* isn't much of a defense," Mike said.

"Well. . . Let's not worry about that right now, okay? There's nothing you can do about it at this point, anyway," Joey said.

"No, I guess not," Mike admitted.

"The only thing that matters right now is what we'll do tonight and tomorrow. Everything else can wait," Joey said, and Mike realized the comment was sensible. With an effort, he pulled himself out of his momentary funk and refocused on the present.

"Well, we have enough food to last us for a month or so if we're careful with it. I still have a little bit of cash, if it's worth anything. There's enough clean water in the water heater to do for drinking for a while, and we have plenty of bullets for the .22 if it comes to *that*. The Jeep has almost a full tank of gas, even though we don't really need to go anywhere for a while. I think it'd be best if we stayed put and kept all the doors and windows locked for now. We have oil for the lamps and wood for the fireplace; I'm not sure what else we need at this point," Mike said. Joey nodded all the while, and finally smiled.

"See, there you go. We're all set," he agreed.

"Are you not worried at all about what's going to happen or the fact that we're stuck in this weird place for the rest of our lives or anything like that?" Mike asked.

"What good would it do to worry about it?" Joey pointed out reasonably.

"I just don't see how you can be so calm about everything," Mike said.

"Mikey, there are really only two kinds of problems in the world. There's the kind you can do something about, and then there's the kind you can't do anything about. If you can do something about it, then quit worrying and go do it. If you *can't* do anything, then worrying won't help you in that case either. Worry is nothing but fear, and fear is nothing but lack of faith. We can't do a thing about being stuck here and nobody knows what the future will bring. We've done everything a reasonable person could do at this point, so I'm not going to worry, and you shouldn't either," Joey said.

"I guess so," Mike finally agreed. He sometimes envied Joey for his untroubled tranquility. He'd never found it that easy, himself.

They spent a quiet evening, Joey reading by candlelight and Mike pretending to do likewise, even though he was too preoccupied to pay much attention. They both went to bed early, and Mike was asleep almost as soon as his head touched the pillow.

He woke up in the middle of the night to the sound of an explosion, followed by gunfire and a blood-curdling scream. It must have been far away because the sound was faint, but it was piercing nevertheless.

He jumped out of bed and grabbed his jeans from the floor, quickly slipping them on before he ran outside into the hall. Joey was already there.

"What was *that?*" he hissed in the darkness.

"I don't know. It sounded like machine guns," Mike began, and then he was cut off by another explosion, louder than the first one. He crept quickly to the window at the end of the hall to part the curtains and see what he could see, but cautiously so as not to show any movement.

It was almost pitch dark outside, with all the street lights off. The only illumination came from starlight, faint and far. And yet, even that was enough for him to glimpse darker shadows here and there, moving between the buildings. They looked like soldiers carrying assault rifles, but he couldn't have said for sure.

Then the night was lit up suddenly by the orange glare of a bomb blast somewhere downtown, and for a second he glimpsed the soldiers perfectly. Somewhere in the distance, he heard more screams.

His mouth grew dry and his heart was pounding as he pulled the curtains shut and turned back to Joey.

"Did we lock all the doors and windows today? *All* of them?" he asked urgently.

"Yeah, I think so. What did you see?" Joey asked, whispering as if someone might overhear them.

"Bombs, and a bunch of soldiers roaming around everywhere," Mike said, also whispering.

"Friendly or not?" Joey asked.

"I'd tend to say not, if they're the ones blowing things up. But I don't know for sure, and I don't want to find out the hard way, either," Mike said.

"We'd better go check the locks one more time, then, just in case. I'd feel a lot better if we did," Joey said.

"Yeah, me too," Mike agreed, and they quickly did so. Only when they'd double checked the last one in the house did Mike relax even a tiny bit.

"Do you think it's safe to stay here?" Joey asked. They were standing in the kitchen by the arch that led into the living room, and the sound of bombs and gunfire hadn't let up for a second.

"Where else would we go?" Mike asked.

"Well, I don't know. We could take the Jeep and go hide out in the woods, if we had to," Joey said.

Mike considered it, and then shook his head.

"I think we're better off if we sit tight for now. If we head down to the basement then we ought to have pretty good shelter," Mike said, nodding his head vaguely in that direction.

That was right before someone kicked the front door in.

There was no order to freeze, no attempt by the intruders to identify themselves, nothing like that; only a flurry of bullets that barely missed Mike and Joey and left holes in the living room wall big enough to put a fist through.

Mike was no fool; he ran for the Jeep as fast as his feet could take him, ducking low and hoping the soldiers wouldn't realize what he was doing in the pitch darkness of the house. Apparently they didn't, because he made it to the garage without getting a hole in his head. Joey was right behind him, and half a second after he reached the driver's seat he had the engine started. There was more gunfire from inside the house, and he hit the gas without even switching on the headlights. The Jeep shot out into the driveway, and Mike fought the wheel to make a hard right turn across the yard and down the hill onto Third Street. He knocked down the picket fence beside the curb and heard more bullets whizzing far above his head before they finally hit the edge of the pavement and slipped into the deeper darkness of the trees.

"What *happened* back there?" Joey yelled.

"Shut up! We'll figure it out later!" Mike said.

He switched on the fog lights to give him just enough illumination to see his way between the huge trunks, if he paid close attention. But it was nerve-wracking, especially when he didn't know if a posse of homicidal maniacs were hot on their trail or not. He didn't dare turn on his bright lights for fear of giving away their position, even though it slowed them down.

But eventually the adrenaline rush began to wear off, and several hours later he found himself creeping through a thicker-than-usual patch of trees maybe three or four miles south of town. There'd been several times already when he'd had to stop and back up to avoid obstacles even the Jeep couldn't get past, and every delay made him want to chew his fingernails down to the elbow. Finally they came to a wide creek that looked like it might take some serious maneuvering to get across, and Joey spoke up.

"Don't you think we're far enough from town to be safe by now? We sure wouldn't want to get stuck in *that* mess," he pointed out.

"Yeah, I guess you're right," Mike agreed reluctantly, and parked the Jeep under a big heavy-limbed magnolia tree that he hoped might keep it hidden from prying eyes. It was the best concealment they could hope to find on such short notice. Then they kicked the seats back and tried to sleep, but the distant sound of sporadic explosions and gunfire still coming from town made that awfully hard to do.

"Why would they be shooting machine guns at people?" Mike finally asked aloud. He didn't really expect Joey to know the answer; he was more or less talking to himself. But the whole thing was so senseless and inexplicable, his mind wouldn't leave it alone.

"I don't know, but there's nothing we can find out till morning. Let it alone and go to sleep, Mikey," Joey muttered.

That was easier said than done, and for a long time Mike lay wakeful in his seat. But eventually, sheer exhaustion closed his eyes for a few hours.

Chapter Three

The sun was well up by the time he woke, and Mike wearily rolled over in his seat with a deep yawn. It was cold for April, and he started the Jeep so they could run the heater at least for a little while. He felt like he'd slept on a block of ice all night.

"Are you awake, Joey?" Mike asked, looking over at the other seat. Joey was curled up in a ball, trying to stay warm himself. But he stirred when Mike called his name.

"Yeah, I am now," he said, sitting up to stretch.

"Come on, let's get up and go see if we can see anything," Mike said.

"Hold on a few minutes till the heater warms up. I'm freezing," Joey said.

"Yeah, me too," Mike admitted.

Eventually the heater had been on long enough that they stopped shivering, and then Mike killed the engine to save gas.

He quickly grabbed his binoculars from the back seat and stepped outside onto the wet ground, not waiting to see if Joey followed. He could still hear occasional gunfire from the direction of town even though the bombing seemed to be over, and the very first thing he wanted to do was to get a closer look and maybe figure out what in blue blazes was going on.

The woods were much too thick for him to see anything from ground level, of course, but the huge magnolia tree had given him an idea about that. It grew on a slight rise, and from the top he just *might* be able to see something.

He'd run off from the house last night with no shoes on, but the magnolia bark was fairly smooth against the soles of his bare feet when he started climbing. Before long he'd made it as close to the top as he dared, and he braced himself against the trunk so he could have both hands free. Then he broke off two or three branches so he could see out through the dense foliage.

"Can you see anything?" Joey asked, climbing up beside him.

"Just a second," Mike said, still trying to get himself situated well enough so he wouldn't fall out of the tree if he let go. The only thing he saw at the moment were several plumes of thick black smoke rising heavily on the morning air above what was left of the town. It looked ominous.

When he was finally able to lift the binoculars to his eyes, he immediately focused in on a scene of devastation. Almost every building was bombed or gutted by fire, and there was nary a living soul to be seen. For a second he stood staring at the town in shock.

"What *happened?*" he finally asked aloud.

"Let me see," Joey said, and Mike handed him the binoculars. From Joey's sharp intake of breath, he was every bit as stunned by the destruction as Mike had been.

"It looks like somebody destroyed everything on purpose," Joey said, and Mike had to agree.

"But who? And why? And where did they come from? It sure did look like we were alone in the middle of the woods, yesterday," Mike said, and of course there were no answers for any of those things.

"Do you think we should go back down and see if anybody needs some help?" Joey asked. He had an uneasy note in his voice, like he thought it might be their duty to go back to town but he sure didn't want to. Mike sympathized, since he felt exactly the same way himself. But while he hesitated, Joey spotted something.

"Hey, I see something," he said.

"What is it?" Mike asked.

"Um. . . looks like some more guys in army gear. They're just walking along the street hunting through houses and stuff, looks like," Joey said.

"Let me see," Mike asked.

"No, wait. . . looks like they found somebody. They-" he started, and then the binoculars slipped out of his hands, bouncing off branches and dropping all the way to the ground nearly sixty feet below.

"What? What happened?" Mike asked.

"They killed him," Joey whispered, eyes big.

"What?" Mike asked.

"They killed him, right there in the front yard," Joey said.

"This is crazy," Mike muttered.

"No, this is *way* beyond crazy, buddy. We passed the crazy mark a *long* time ago. But I think we better get away from here while we still can, or else *we'll* be the ones with bullets in our heads before long. Those dudes look like they mean business," Joey said.

He was right, of course. Mike's .22 deer rifle was still in the back seat, but there was no way they could hope to fight off trained soldiers with nothing but that. All they'd succeed in doing would be to get themselves killed too, without helping anybody else in the process.

"You're right. Let's go," Mike agreed.

They quickly climbed back down to the Jeep and retrieved the binoculars from where they'd fallen. Then Mike carefully backed out from under the magnolia limbs and started following the line of the creek, looking for a place where he thought they could cross it. They finally found one, being careful to get out and erase their tracks as much as possible afterward. Then it was simply more of the same, driving slowly through the empty woods. There was nothing to eat except an old can of beans and wieners left over from last deer season, and Mike wished a thousand times they hadn't been so quick to unload all those groceries.

"Do you even know what direction you're headed?" Joey asked after a while.

"Yeah, south," Mike said.

"Any particular reason?" Joey asked.

"No, not really. Just trying to get as far away as fast as I can. I figure we'll have to come out somewhere eventually," Mike said.

"You think?" Joey asked.

"Yeah. It stands to reason, you know; those soldiers had to come from *somewhere*. The trees can't go on forever," Mike said.

And indeed, late that afternoon they arrived abruptly at a chain link fence topped by razor wire. It vanished out of sight in both directions, and on the far side was a gravel access road.

"Well, now *that's* interesting," Mike said, stopping the Jeep and staring at it.

"I don't know that *interesting* is the word I'd use. I was thinking more along the lines of *awesome* and *thank you Jesus,*" Joey said.

"I could probably go along with those words, myself," Mike agreed.

"At least it means we're finally getting back to civilization," Joey said.

"Yeah, sort of," Mike said, thinking about the brutal destruction of the town. People who could do something like that in cold blood were nowhere near what he'd personally call civilized.

"So how do we get out, then?" Joey asked.

"Well, we've got some cutting dikes in the toolbox. I think we can make a big enough hole to drive the Jeep through," Mike said.

They got to work, taking turns with the cutter to give each other a break now and then when their hands started to cramp up. It didn't take all that long before they had a wide gap through the fence, and then Mike drove through.

"Maybe we should fix that hole a little bit so it's not quite so obvious, you think?" Joey asked, and Mike nodded. That turned out to be quite a bit harder than cutting it open had been, but eventually they were able to make it look semi-normal from a distance. Anyone who passed by and saw the place would know immediately that somebody had broken through, but hopefully no one would. The access road was grassy and overgrown, so it couldn't possibly be used all that often.

"Which way, do you think?" Joey asked.

"East," Mike said decisively.

"Why's that?" Joey asked.

"So the sun won't shine in my face," Mike said, and Joey laughed.

"That's a really scientific way to choose," he said.

"Can't think of any better reasons. Can you?" Mike asked.

"No, I guess not," Joey admitted.

So they headed east, and barely a hundred yards from the spot where they'd cut through the fence, they spotted a steel sign fixed to one of the posts. Mike stopped the Jeep to read it.

William T. Clark Containment Zone
North American Defense Forces
No Trespassing - Violators Will Be Shot on Sight

"What's *that* supposed to mean?" Joey asked, staring at the sign.

"I guess it means they're pretty serious about keeping people outside that fence," Mike said.

"Yeah, but *why?*" Joey said, and Mike shrugged.

"Don't know, buddy. You'd have to ask the North American Defense Forces, whoever *they* are," Mike said.

"Yeah, that's another thing. I've never heard of anybody called the North American Defense Forces," Joey said.

"Me neither, but I guess we'll find out soon enough," Mike said, and started driving again.

They made much better time on the road than they had in the woods, even as old and rutted as it was in places. About two hours later, they actually came to a gate that pierced the fence, and a T-junction with a paved road which seemed in slightly better condition than the one they'd been using.

"I say we turn here," Joey said, nodding at the new road.

"Yeah, I agree," Mike said, and did so.

About five miles later, they abruptly emerged at a junction with what looked like an interstate highway.

They both sat there for a few minutes, struggling to make sense of what they saw. Cars whizzed past in front of them at high speed; all of them strange models that Mike had never seen before, sleek and unfamiliar.

"Where *are* we?" he whispered under his breath.

The access ramps were blocked with ancient pieces of concrete, but of course the Jeep had no problem getting around those. Mike pulled out onto the freeway and continued eastward, trying to be as inconspicuous as possible. No easy task, under the circumstances. Heads were turning in every passing car, much as they might have done to stare at a Model T Ford back in Mike's day.

"Do you think this is a good idea? I mean, we stick out like sore thumbs, dude. We're the only Jeep on the road," Joey finally said.

"We won't have to worry about it for much longer if we don't find a gas station soon," Mike said.

Before long a big overhead sign appeared above the road, and for the first time Mike had a chance to get some confirmation of where they might be. *Rockport – Hot Springs – Ouachita National Park, I-34, Next 2 Exits* it read.

"This is *Rockport?*" Joey asked, staring across the ditch at what they could see of the town.

"Apparently. Changed a lot, hasn't it?" Mike said.

"You can say that again. I don't even recognize the place," Joey said.

"Well, at least now we know for sure where we are," Mike said.

"I'm a lot more concerned about *when* we are than *where* we are," Joey said.

There was a filling station right by the off-ramp, and Mike quickly pulled in to one of the bays. The Jeep was almost on empty. But as soon as he got out to fill the tank, he noticed an anomaly.

The station didn't sell gas at all. Instead, it sold hydrogen by the liter. Nor was that some kind of strange exception, either; they visited several other stations nearby and found that not a single one of them sold anything but hydrogen.

"That's truly weird," Mike commented, getting back in the Jeep after visiting the last one. The Jeep was still getting a lot of curious glances from people, and he quickly decided *that* needed to come to a halt as soon as possible. There was a parking garage just ahead, so he pulled inside and parked in the darkest corner he could find so they wouldn't be seen, and then killed the motor.

"We must have skipped ahead an awful lot of years. I mean, look at those weird cars, and the hydro-stations. Look at *Rockport*, for goodness sake. And since when did they have a Ouachita National Park, or an Interstate 34, or some cripey Containment Zone where they shoot people for trespassing? This is a *long* way out, buddy," Joey said.

"Well. . . I saw a library a while ago that looked like it was still open. Let's walk back down there and see if we can find out anything. It couldn't be more than a few blocks," Mike said.

"Might as well," Joey agreed.

So that's what they did, and the old red brick library building looked pleasantly ordinary amongst all the weirdness they'd seen lately.

"Do you think they'll let us go inside with no shoes on?" Joey asked, and Mike hesitated. There hadn't been a chance to pick up a pair of shoes yet. Nobody paid attention to things like that at filling stations or even on the sidewalk, but the library might be another story.

"Pull your pants legs down over your feet and maybe they won't notice. I've seen several people wearing them like that since we've been here," Mike said.

They both did so, and Mike curled up his toes the better to keep them hidden. The cuff of his jeans was barely long enough to drag the ground, even when he pulled them down as low as possible. Joey had an easier time since his legs were shorter. As soon as that was done they waited for a chance to cross the street, and then quickly climbed the front steps.

The place looked nothing like a library inside, or at least not the kind Mike was used to. Instead of endless shelves of dusty books, now there were only endless rows of dark gray cubicles. As they stood there staring at the place, unsure of what to do next, a lady at the front desk spotted them.

"Can I help you, gentlemen?" she asked, in the same warm and cultivated tone of every librarian Mike had ever encountered. If she noticed his toes sticking out then she didn't see fit to comment.

"Uh, yeah. We need to use a computer," he said. It seemed to be the only thing they *could* do in such a place, since there were no books.

"Make sure to sign in, and remember we'll be closing at seven," she said, handing him a reassuringly familiar clipboard with a sign-in sheet and a pen attached to a string. He quickly signed his name and Joey's, and then handed her the sheet back.

"Number fourteen," she said, nodding her head toward one of the cubicles. Mike thanked her absently and went to the specified cubicle, shutting the door behind them. There was nothing inside except a chair and a black shelf; no computer or anything remotely resembling one.

"Do you think she gave us one where the computer was missing?" Joey asked, sounding puzzled.

"Surely not," Mike said, sitting down uncertainly.

Immediately a touch-screen keyboard lit up in the middle of the shelf, and a holographic display screen appeared in the air in front of him, automatically adjusting itself whenever he turned his head so as to be most comfortable for his eyes.

"That's the coolest thing I've ever seen," he marveled.

"The amazing wonders of modern technology," Joey said dryly.

"Yeah, yeah, I know; stuff like that is trivial and we've got bigger fish to fry. Chill out a minute and we'll get down to business," Mike said. Then he started typing on the screen. The keyboard felt flat and strange under his fingertips, though he supposed it probably kept dirt and spills from getting down into the guts of the thing.

Where am I? he typed, although he didn't know if the computer was smart enough to understand such a question or not. Apparently it was, because he quickly got his answer back.

You are at the Hot Spring County Public Library, located at 201 Main Street in Rockport, Arkansas.

Well, that was nothing they didn't already know. Now for the much more relevant and scary question.

What is today's date? he typed.

Today is Friday, April 26, 2136.

Mike felt a chill in the pit of his stomach and swallowed hard. Suspicions were one thing, but to have it confirmed in stark print was something else again. The tachometer had moved them ahead exactly a hundred years, right down to the very hour. He supposed a perfectly round number like that was reasonable, coming from a circuitry glitch. He could only thank God it hadn't been a thousand years, or even a million or a billion. At least here things were *somewhat* normal and familiar.

"I can't believe it," Joey said in a low voice.

Well, we better get used to the idea pretty quick, buddy boy, Mike thought to himself.

"That can't be right, Mike. It just *can't* be. What are we supposed to do in 2136? Everybody we know is gone by now. We've got no money, no ID that anybody would ever believe, a car we can't buy gas for and nowhere to go in the first place. What are we gonna do?" Joey demanded.

Mike fought down a rising sense of panic himself and tried to stay calm.

Then he thought of something that might save them after all.

Chapter Four

"This ought to be close to the time Cameron and Joan went to, shouldn't it?" he asked, and as soon as Joey heard that he visibly calmed down again. He and Cam were brothers, sort of; Joey's parents had unofficially adopted Cameron and his cousin Zach many years ago. Zach was still around, but Cam had followed his girlfriend Joan into the future when Joey was only a baby. Zach talked about him a lot, actually; that story was one of the main reasons Mike had gotten interested in tachyons in the first place.

"Yeah, you're right. They went to 2134," Joey said.

"Well, that's all to the good, if he's had two years to get settled in and adjusted. I'm sure they'd help us, or at least *you* anyway," Mike said.

"He knew your dad, too," Joey pointed out.

"Yeah, but you're his brother. That counts for more," Mike said.

"Maybe. He hasn't seen me in an awful long time," Joey said.

"A long time for *you*. It's only been two years for *him,*" Mike reminded him.

"Yeah. . . true. He'll actually be younger than I am now, with the years all switched around like this. He was eighteen when he left so

I guess he'd be twenty now. That's so weird," Joey said, shaking his head.

"Well, weird or not, do you know where he lives? I can't remember," Mike said.

"Wasn't it supposed to be somewhere in Florida?" Joey asked.

"Yeah, I think it was, now that you mention it," Mike agreed.

"Dang, that's a long way," Joey muttered.

"Yeah, I know, but I really can't think of any other options. Can you?" Mike asked.

"No, not really. I guess we better see if we can find him, then," Joey said, and then Mike turned his attention back to the computer.

Give me an address and phone number for Philip and Joan Carpenter in the state of Florida.

"I'm glad you remembered that other name he started using," Joey commented, looking at the screen.

"I only remember it because somebody at church told me one time that Philip means Horse, and thinking about a horse driving nails and sawing wood always used to make me laugh," Mike admitted, and Joey laughed.

"How come you never told me that story before?" he asked.

"I don't know; I was only a kid," Mike said, feeling foolish.

It wasn't long before the computer obligingly gave them an address on Hillsborough Avenue in Tampa, along with the phone number he'd asked for. Apparently there was only one matching reference, thankfully. Mike quickly saved the information on his cell phone, being careful to get everything exactly right.

"So how do we get there? The Jeep won't even make it twenty more miles on the gas we've got left," Joey said.

"I guess we could hitchhike," Mike said doubtfully. He didn't like the thought of it at all, but then what other choices did they have?

"They might come get us, if we call them. I know it's a lot to ask, but you never know," Joey suggested.

"I wouldn't even begin to know how to ask somebody for such a thing. Let alone a complete stranger," Mike asked.

"Well. . . what exactly did you plan on saying when we got to their doorstep?" Joey pointed out.

"I don't know, Joe," Mike said with a sigh, running his fingers through his hair tiredly and rubbing his eyes. He'd barely slept in the Jeep last night, and he'd been up at six a.m. the morning before to work on the tachometer. It was beginning to catch up with him.

There was a long pause, and then he shook his head.

"I guess we'll just have to tell them the truth and see what they say. Come on," Mike finally said, getting up from the computer. The screen vanished when he got up, and he couldn't help marveling again at such a cool (if minor) convenience. Probably everybody in 2136 took it completely for granted, but for Mike it was still fresh. Joey followed him to the front desk, where the librarian looked up with her bright smile again.

"Ma'am, is there a phone we could use?" he asked politely, and the lady furrowed her brows.

"You want to call somebody?" she asked uncertainly, as if she didn't know quite what to think of such a question. Her puzzlement confused him.

"Yes, please," he said.

"Just use the computer, honey. Type in the number and touch the call button," she said, as if she were explaining something only an idiot wouldn't already know. Her attitude made him feel like a fool, and he reddened slightly.

"Thanks," he mumbled under his breath, and headed back for the cubicle.

"You sure did put your foot in it that time," Joey said when they got back inside, and Mike could have sworn he thought the whole incident was funny.

"Shut up, Joey; you didn't know any more than I did," he said, disgruntled.

"Aw, ease up, dude; I was just joshing you a little," Joey said.

Mike grunted in reply, typing in the phone number just as the lady had told him. Sure enough, a discreet *call now* button appeared at the top of the keyboard, and when he touched it with his forefinger the familiar ringing tone of every call he'd ever made in his life filled the cubicle. The screen displayed a soothing psychedelic wave pattern while the call connected, and when it did the colors changed from blue to green. Mike had halfway thought he might get to see someone's actual face, but apparently not.

"Hello?" came a young woman's voice.

"Uh, is this Joan Carpenter?" Mike asked.

"Yes, it is. Who's this?" she asked.

"Ma'am, you don't know me, but my name's Micah McGrath, and I'm here with your husband's brother, Josiah Wilder," he began, fumblingly.

"I see. And what can I do for you, Mr. McGrath?" she asked.

"It's a long story, ma'am. You see, I'm an astronomy student and I was working on a machine called a tachometer, which I think you might be familiar with. But there was an accident and it ended up tossing both of us a hundred years into the future, and now. . ." he said, trailing off.

"So now you're stranded and don't know what to do, is that it?" she asked, but there was kindness in her voice.

"Yeah, that's pretty much it," he admitted.

"Where are you?" she asked.

"Rockport, Arkansas," he said, and at that a note of alarm came into her voice.

"Where did you come through?" she asked urgently.

"Uh, we were in Arkadelphia when we got here," he said.

"That's inside the Containment Zone," she whispered.

"Yeah, I noticed that. They-" he began, but she cut him off.

"Don't talk about it on the phone. They listen sometimes, if the computer picks up certain keywords. We'll be there to pick you up tomorrow afternoon, and in the meantime don't talk to *anyone*. You'll give yourselves away a hundred times by the things you don't know, and they may be searching for you already. Find a safe place to spend the night and call me again tomorrow at four o'clock from a different phone than you used this time. Do you understand?" she asked crisply, in the tones of one who was accustomed to giving orders.

"Yes, ma'am," he agreed.

"All right. We'll see you then," she said, and cut the connection. Joey was close enough to have heard the entire conversation, so there was no need to repeat it for him.

"What do you think she meant, they might be searching for us already?" he asked, and in spite of all his usual tranquility, there was a note of worry in his voice.

"I don't know, but I sure don't like the sound of it," Mike said.

"Me neither," Joey said.

They left the library not long afterward, walking casually along the street back toward the parking garage. It seemed like the most inconspicuous place they could pick to spend the night, since they didn't know where else to look. No one paid much attention to them on the sidewalk; they were both wearing jeans and t-shirts, which didn't seem to be all that unusual for clothing in 2136. There was *that* much to be thankful for, at least.

"You did say we've still got a little money, didn't you, Mikey? I'm awful hungry," Joey said after a while. They hadn't eaten anything since that can of beans and wieners several hours ago, and Mike felt like he could have eaten half a cow himself.

"I've still got about a hundred dollars, if you want to get a burger or something. I saw a stand just now," Mike said.

"Yeah, that sounds pretty good," Joey said.

They went to the hamburger stand and ordered two burgers and two cokes, but when Mike tried to pay the man he got laughed at.

"Keep your play money, kid. Come back when you've got some real cash," the man said, and shut the window in his face.

"What was *that* all about?" Joey asked when they got a little distance away.

"I guess he didn't think it was real," Mike said, staring at the twenty dollar bill in his hand.

"They must use different money now than we're used to. We should've thought of that," Joey said, and Mike sighed.

"I guess we'll just have to do without, then. It won't kill us to go a day without eating," he said.

"Maybe if we could find a coin dealer or a pawn shop or something like that, we might sell the money. Even if it's not worth anything at face value, it still might be worth something as antiques," Joey said.

"Worth a try," Mike said, shrugging.

They walked along the main drag until they found a pawn shop downtown, where Mike emptied his pockets on the counter.

"Can I get anything for this?" he asked, and the man behind the counter riffled through the bills and change for a few seconds.

"No, I don't deal with old money unless it's silver or gold. I'll take *that,* though, if you want to sell it," the man said, nodding at the necklace Mike wore. It was an 1897 silver sixpence from Queen Victoria's Diamond Jubilee, set in a coin holder and attached to a chain. It had been a gift from his mother several years ago, when he graduated from high school.

"I'll sell you the chain, but not the sixpence," Mike said quickly, stuffing the useless money back in his pocket. The man grumbled at that, but he weighed and tested the silver chain and ended up offering them what seemed like an incredible sum.

"We'll take it," Mike agreed, slipping the sixpence into his other pocket.

The man counted out the money, which seemed to be made of something resembling very thin and flexible plastic rather than paper. It was multicolored and speckled with silver holograms.

"Awfully pretty dollars they have nowadays," Joey commented after they got back outside.

"Yeah, no doubt. I never heard of any of these people on the faces, though. And since when did we become the North American Union?" Mike asked, reading from one of the bills.

"Beats me, buddy. But since we've got some spendable cash now, let's go back and see old sourpuss again. My stomach still has a date with that cheeseburger which was rudely interrupted," Joey said, and Mike laughed.

"You're on. Let's go," he said.

The man had no qualms about taking their money the second time, and Mike thought it had to be the juiciest and most delicious cheeseburger he'd ever tasted in his life. The Coke was another matter.

"Does the Coke taste funny to you?" Mike asked after a while.

"Yeah, a little. But then again who knows what they might be flavoring it with nowadays. It's still pretty good," Joey said.

They slept in the Jeep again that night, with the seats kicked back as far as they'd go for comfort. It was a thousand times better than the night before, if only because there were no screams or gunfire to snap them awake at all hours.

The next day was mostly tedious waiting, interrupted only by a vague worry over Joan's warning that "they" might be searching for them, whoever "they" might be. The only possibility Mike could think of was the soldiers they'd seen. But there was no sign of them or anyone else, so Mike listened to the radio for a while, trying to accustom himself to the odd music these people liked and maybe figure out something about how the world worked by listening to the news and comments from the announcers.

Most of the talk was blather, pure and simple; the kind of stuff that wouldn't have been out of place on the radio a hundred years ago, or even two hundred years ago for that matter. There was a fifty percent off sale at thus-and-such department store, and so-and-so was having a birthday next week, and so forth. But amongst the flood of inconsequential rubbish, he did manage to glean a few interesting nuggets of information.

There was apparently a war going on between China and India, for reasons that none of the announcers ever bothered to explain. The thing that seemed to interest them most about the whole affair was whether local jobs at an ammunition plant might be affected; as boring a topic as Mike could easily have imagined. He also gathered that there were now sixty-five states in the North American Union, though how and when that came about was still obscure. President Richards had just canceled a state visit to meet with the president of Brazoria (wherever *that* was), amid allegations of electronic spying, and a tornado in Kansas had killed three people the night before.

"Things sure have changed a lot," Mike muttered after a while. He'd said it before, but this strange new world kept surprising him in ways both great and small.

"Yeah, that tornado in Kansas thing; that's a real shocker," Joey said dryly.

"Ha ha, very funny. I was talking about all the other stuff. Sixty-five states now, and changing the name of the country, and all that jazz," Mike said.

"Sounds like mostly superficial stuff to me, honestly. But then again you know what they say. The more things change, the more they stay the same," Joey said.

"I guess," Mike agreed.

"It's getting close to four o'clock. Don't you think we should call Joan back?" Joey asked. Mike glanced at his watch and saw that it was 3:46; close enough that he probably ought to start looking for a phone.

"Yeah, come on," he said, getting out of the Jeep and heading back for the library.

"I thought she said not to call her back from the same phone as yesterday," Joey reminded him, when he saw where they were headed.

"Yeah, I know; we'll just have to pick a different cubicle. I don't know what else to do," Mike said.

There was a different girl at the help desk that day, so they quietly signed in under different names than before, and the girl incuriously sent them to cubicle number five this time. They still had no shoes; even the cheapest ones they'd seen had cost way more than they could afford. But that was all right; the cuffs-over-the-feet trick seemed to work pretty well.

As soon as the got inside the cubicle, Mike called.

"Hello, Mrs. Carpenter? You asked me to call you at four o'clock today," he began.

"Yeah, that's right. We'll be coming into town in about an hour. Where will you be?" she asked, getting right to the point. She sounded tired, but then again that wasn't too surprising after she'd just made such a long trip on short notice.

"We'll be inside the parking garage on Main Street near the library. I drive a gray Jeep," he said, and she chuckled.

"Yeah, I don't think we'll have any trouble spotting *that*. See you soon," she said, and that was that.

"Come on, let's go," Mike said, getting up from the computer.

They were almost back to the Jeep when Joey suddenly stopped moving.

"What's wrong, dude?" Mike asked, turning to look at him. He wasn't quite sure how it was possible to turn both pale and green at the same time, but somehow Joey had managed it. His forehead had broken out in sweat, and he was breathing hard.

"Just let me alone for a minute; I'll be all right," Joey said.

"You better come sit down for a while, at least," Mike said. The concrete wall of the garage was built in such a way that there was a knee-high ledge about a foot wide all along the bottom, and it didn't take much coaxing to get Joey to sit down on it.

"It hurts all over," Joey said, wrapping his arms around his body.

"Do you need me to take you to a hospital?" Mike asked, beginning to be really concerned.

He thought Joey started to say something else, but whatever it might have been, the words never made it past his lips. They were replaced almost instantly by an ear-splitting howl of agony, and then a sharp pop of displaced air as he disappeared.

Chapter Five

Mike scrambled backward instinctively and fell off the ledge onto the floor before catching himself. He glanced around wildly for Joey, heart pounding. The other boy was nowhere to be seen, and when Mike glanced at the spot where he'd been, he saw only a handful of gray dust sitting on the ledge.

He forced himself to calm down, and then approached the ledge cautiously. Nothing happened when he poked the dust with a pen, and immediately a thousand questions cropped up in his mind, clamoring for answers. Was that dust all that was left of Joey? If so, was there any way to fix him? Should he bury it somewhere? He wondered crazily if Joey might want him to scatter it back home on Coca Cola Lake instead.

At a loss for anything else to do, he quickly trotted to the Jeep to fetch an old envelope from the glove box, and then carefully collected the pile of dust inside. If that were really Joey's remains then he needed to make sure they didn't get lost.

He sat down in the driver's seat of the Jeep to wait for Cameron and Joan, still shell-shocked from the experience. How he'd explain Joey's disappearance he couldn't imagine, since he didn't have the slightest shred of an explanation for it himself.

It wasn't quite an hour later when a sleek silver car came rolling up beside him.

Philip and Joan Carpenter were an oddly matched couple, he couldn't help thinking. The top of her head barely reached his chest, and they differed in other ways, too. He was blond and muscular, she was dark-haired and slight; his eyes were bright blue and hers green as beech leaves.

He recognized Cameron from old pictures at Joey's house, but it was jarring to see him still so young. He couldn't possibly have been more than twenty, just like Joey had said he would be. Mike knew that it shouldn't have surprised him, logically speaking, but then again feelings aren't always logical. He was so used to thinking of Cam as an old middle-aged man that it was hard to accept reality at first.

In addition to wedding bands, they both wore the matching silver rings that marked them as Avengers; ones who had sworn an oath to God to fight evil in all its forms, to the utmost of their power. Mike knew quite a bit about that particular group, since Zach had been one too.

But he didn't have time to notice anything else, because just then the rear door opened and another girl got out who resembled Joan so much that they could only have been sisters.

"It's nice to finally meet you, Mike. I'm Joan, and this is my husband Philip and my sister Annabelle. Where's Joey?" she asked.

"I don't know. He disappeared," Mike said.

"What do you mean?" Philip asked.

"I don't know what happened. He was here one second, and then he screamed and vanished. I don't know what to think," Mike admitted.

"Where did it happen?" Philip asked.

"Right here, about forty-five minutes ago," Mike said, leading them to the very spot.

"There was nothing left behind? No other clues as to what happened?" Joan asked.

"Nothing but a handful of gray dust. I collected it in an envelope, just in case," Mike said.

"There was no one else around? Nobody following you? Nothing like that?" Philip asked.

"Not that I could tell. We were alone in the garage and he got sick all of a sudden, then screamed and vanished and left this little pile of dust behind. There was a little popping sound when he disappeared, like when you stick a needle in a balloon, and that was all. I haven't seen him since," Mike said.

"I see," Philip said, sounding just as baffled as Mike himself was.

"I hate to say it, boys, but we all know it's not safe to linger here too long. The NADF could show up at any time," Joan said, and Philip nodded reluctantly.

"You're right, babe. I'm just worried about Joey, that's all," Philip said.

"I know it. But we can't help him if we get ourselves killed or locked up in the meantime," Joan said.

"Come on, then. We'll finish talking about it in the car," Philip said, heading back toward the Jeep.

"Is there anything you need to take with you?" Joan asked.

"Maybe my deer rifle and my binoculars. Nothing else that I can think of," Mike admitted.

"All right, then. The Jeep won't do you much good anymore, I'm afraid; everything is powered with hydrocells now, not gas," she said.

"Yeah, we sort of figured that out," Mike said dryly.

"You might sell it to a classic car buff, I guess; it might actually be worth a good bit of money since it's in such good condition," Philip said.

"How would I go about doing that? Put an ad in the paper?" Mike asked.

"Yeah, something like that. I think it'll be all right if we leave it here in the meantime, though. We don't have much petty crime anymore these days," Philip said.

"I *would* take anything that has your name on it if I were you, and your license plate, too. If they track down the Jeep before you can get rid of it, that'll make it a lot harder to figure out who you are," Joan said, and Mike nodded.

He grabbed his title and registration papers from the glove box, and soon had the license plate off as well. Then he put everything he wanted to keep in the trunk of Philip and Joan's car. The Jeep sat there looking forlorn and abandoned, but Mike knew it was no time to get sentimental.

"All right, let's go," Philip said, and they all got back into the Carpenters' car. Mike and Annabelle had a car seat strapped in between them in the back, which made for a tight squeeze.

"How old is your baby?" Mike asked politely, glancing at the infant beside him.

"Ten months. His name is Christopher, but we usually call him Chris. Don't worry, though; he usually sleeps most of the time when he's in the car," Joan said.

"I'm sorry you had to make such a long trip, but thank you, though," Mike said.

"That's all right; it was kind of nice to make it back up to this neck of the woods for a little while, anyway. It's been a couple years since we had a chance to come back and visit," Philip said.

"Yeah, I was born and raised here myself. Don't think I've ever been more than two or three hours away from home in my whole life," Mike said with a little laugh.

That was a *slight* exaggeration, of course; he'd been to Dallas or Houston a few times, and even to Pensacola once, but those were only short-term vacations or shopping trips. He'd certainly never spent more than a few short days far from home. The idea that he was about to permanently abandon all his old haunts was kind of intimidating, actually, even though he would never have admitted such a thing.

Thankfully, Philip and Joan seemed not to notice.

"Yeah, I've been to your house a time or two. You weren't born yet, but your father did me a favor I'll never forget," Philip said, which only served to remind Mike that his parents were surely dead in this time. That wasn't something he wanted to think about too much, either.

Philip quickly maneuvered the car out of town and back onto the freeway, headed west. For a while that made Mike uneasy since it took them directly back toward the Containment Zone, and that was the last place on earth he wanted to be. The very thought of it made the hairs on the back of his neck stand up.

But Philip almost immediately took another exit which turned them sharply back eastward onto I-34, which hadn't even existed in Mike's day. He relaxed again as the Containment Zone receded into the background.

"Everything's so different," he finally said.

"What do you mean? The freeway?" Philip asked.

"Yeah, it wasn't here last thing I remember," Mike said, and Philip chuckled.

"There'll be a lot of things like that you'll have to get used to, I'm afraid. New roads are the least of it," he said.

"I feel like I don't know anything at all," Mike admitted.

"You'll learn faster than you think. But in the meantime try to remember there's no such thing as a stupid question. You need to ask about anything you don't know, so you can learn to fit in as soon as possible," Joan said.

"Okay, then. Here's my first stupid question. What exactly is the Containment Zone and why are they so determined to keep people out of it?" Mike asked.

"Well, it's a circle about thirty miles across, surrounded with razor wire. They're not really as serious about keeping people out as they used to be, though I don't doubt they'd still shoot you on sight if they caught you inside the fence. There was some kind of explosion right in the middle of Arkadelphia about a hundred years ago; a *huge* one. Everything was completely destroyed for miles in all directions. So they fenced it off after that and won't let anybody inside. They rerouted all the roads to pass around it and I've heard they won't even let planes fly overhead. So I guess *something* must still be going on in there, but your guess is as good as ours what it might be. They say it's because of high radiation levels, but I'm not sure I really believe that," Joan said.

"So then what's with the shooting trespassers on sight business, if that's all it is? Surely that's a bit much, don't you think?" Mike asked. There was a brief silence at that, and then Philip cleared his throat.

"You may find that the government here is a bit. . . harsher, than you're used to," he finally said.

"What do you mean?" Mike asked.

"I mean they don't look kindly on people who won't do what they're told. They really won't think twice about putting a bullet in your head if they think you're a threat of any kind. Or even just a scofflaw or a troublemaker, for that matter," Philip said.

"But that's. . ." Mike said, and then trailed off.

"Unfair? Immoral? Unconstitutional, even? Are those the words you were looking for?" Philip asked.

"Something like that," Mike said.

"Maybe it is. But you might be surprised what people will put up with and even applaud in the name of safety. It's a dangerous world we live in nowadays. In North America we still have a certain amount of peace and prosperity, and most people are willing to turn a blind eye to anything it might take to guarantee those things. Lots of other places are much worse, and however much people might fear the loss of liberty, they fear the loss of security even more," Philip said, and the disapproval was thick in his voice.

"You have to forgive Philip; he tends to get on a soapbox about this issue whenever anybody gives him half a chance," Joan said.

"And so I should. It's like Benjamin Franklin said; people who are willing to trade freedom for safety don't deserve either one," Philip said in righteous tones.

"See what I mean?" Joan asked, smiling a little.

"All right, I'll shut up for now. To be fair, ninety-nine percent of the time you won't even notice how heavy-handed they are," Philip said dryly.

"You really think they'll come after me?" Mike asked

"Did they actually see you inside the Containment Zone?" Philip asked.

"Yeah, they tried to shoot us. They bombed and shot up the whole town night before last, right after we first got here," Mike said.

"You brought the *whole town* with you?" Philip asked.

"Well, not the *whole* town. Only a circle about a mile and a half across," Mike said.

"I didn't think the tachometer could handle anything that big," Philip said.

"No, neither did I. But obviously it did," Mike said.

"And you say they bombed the place?" Philip asked.

"Yeah, bombed it, burned it, and killed anybody they could locate who was still alive," Mike said.

"Well, I'm not really surprised," Philip sighed.

"They saw me drive off into the woods in the Jeep. I don't think they could see very well; it was pretty dark that night. But I'm sure they know *somebody* slipped the noose," Mike said.

"I wouldn't doubt several people did, if they managed to run off into the woods in time or maybe hide somewhere the soldiers didn't think to look. But I'm sure the NADF knows that, too. They might do a mop-up operation to try to get rid of the survivors or they might not bother. It's hard to say, not knowing what their motive was," Philip said.

"I see," Mike said.

"It really just depends on how much of a threat they think you might be and how busy they are with other things, Mike. Hopefully they'll decide you're not worth the trouble," Joan said.

Somehow, that wasn't much comfort.

They talked about that and many other things during the long trip back to Florida. Mike had only been that way once before, on the way to Pensacola, and he'd forgotten how far it really was. He'd had far more than his fair share of sitting in the car by the time they got there, that was for sure. He also learned quite a lot about this future time he found himself in, some of it to his liking and some of it most definitely not. But at long last, after traveling more miles than he cared to think about, he finally found himself trudging up the concrete walkway in front of Philip and Joan's place in Tampa.

The house was a small stucco, painted a garish lemon yellow color. It looked awfully small, and when they got inside Mike soon found that that was an understatement. The house contained only three rooms; a combination living room and kitchen, a bathroom, and a single bedroom the exact size and shape of a cracker box. He wondered how three people plus a baby had ever managed to fit inside, and where they might squeeze in a fourth person he couldn't imagine. *Cramped* was too mild a word for it.

"It's not much, I know, but you're welcome to stay here as long as you need to," Joan said, watching him stare at the tiny living room.

"I was just wondering about sleeping arrangements, that's all," Mike said guiltily, not wanting her to think he was ungrateful.

"Annabelle sleeps on the couch, but you're welcome to take the recliner. I've slept in it lots of times myself. Or we can get you an air mattress to put on the floor; that might work better," Philip said, and Mike nodded.

And so it was. He settled in fairly quickly, and truth to tell he didn't mind the cramped conditions so much after he once got used to them. Philip and Joan barely had space enough to shut the bedroom door, and they had to crawl across the bed itself to reach the dresser drawer where the baby slept. Joan had padded the bottom of the drawer with quilt scraps to make him a bed, since there was no room for a crib anywhere.

But they made do, and even seemed happy, and one day Mike asked her how that was possible, considering how tough their circumstances seemed to be. Joan only laughed.

"Oh, Mikey; your circumstances are only as hard as you think they are. If you focus on all the things you don't have then yeah, your life will be pretty miserable. But it doesn't *have* to be that way. When Cam and I first got married, we decided to spend at least fifteen minutes before bed every night thanking God for all the things he's blessed us with. How could we not be happy, after He's done so much for us?" she said.

"That sounds like something my mother would say," Mike said.

"Then she was a wise woman," Joan said.

"Yeah, I guess she was," he agreed, playing with the silver sixpence in his pocket. He hadn't had time or money to get another chain for it yet, but he still liked to keep it close. It was a link to memory, and he found that he needed that during those first few days and weeks. He was lonely and homesick, and then there was the nagging worry over what might have happened to Joey and whether something similar might not catch up with *him* sooner or later. Let alone whether or not the Defense Forces might be searching for him or what they might do if they found him. All of it together was enough to keep him tied up in knots.

Philip and Joan both had jobs to go to during the week, he as a helper at a construction site and she as a nurse's aide. Annabelle had school at the University of South Florida three nights per week, but during the day she stayed home to babysit Christopher and help take care of the household chores. She never said much, but Mike had no one else to talk to and found himself telling her all kinds of things just for the sake of socializing with someone.

So he told her about his tachyon project, and his family back in Texas, and the ranch where he grew up and anything else that came to mind. Sometimes he took out the garbage or mowed the grass or did whatever else he could think of to make himself useful, since he found it hard to sit idly by and do nothing while everybody else had work to do.

Annabelle couldn't drive, it turned out, and Mike himself dared not, but she did like to go walking sometimes, to get out of the house for a while and give the baby some fresh air. There was a large park only a few blocks from the house, with an artificial lake and a paved walking trail around it, and that was one of her favorite haunts when the weather was nice.

Mike usually tagged along on these expeditions, if only for the company and the chance to see a little bit more of the future. He soon got used to the changes in music and fashion; to wearing loose and colorful clothes with dark wraparound shades, to cutting his hair differently and wearing more jewelry than he was used to and all the proper slang to use, not to mention a thousand other things. Learning how to fit in was a full-time job all by itself.

But he didn't mind, or not much. It kept his mind from dwelling too much on his circumstances, and that was all to the good.

Chapter Six

"Would you like to carry Chris today?" Annabelle asked him abruptly one morning, offering him the baby harness to put around his shoulders.

"Uh, sure, why not?" he agreed, accepting it. He had trouble getting the straps on at first until she showed him how to work it, but once that was done it was surprisingly comfortable. Chris was used to him by then and made no objection when Annabelle put him in the carrier. He simply put his head down against Mike's chest and promptly went back to sleep.

She took them to the promenade around the lake that day; a fairly predictable choice. It was a favorite hangout spot for couples with young children, which Mike supposed probably had something to do with why she was so fond of the place. Mike himself had always liked it well enough, but he found that walking next to Annabelle with a baby on his chest gave him all sorts of thoughts and feelings he wasn't used to. He felt unexpectedly domestic and family-oriented, all husband-and-fatherly, so to speak. He couldn't quite decide yet whether he liked the taste of it or not.

"So tell me, how'd you get involved with the tachometer in the first place?" Annabelle finally asked, breaking his reverie.

"Well. . . I always knew about it from hanging out with Joey's family, you know. But then I was working on my Ph.D. in astronomy, and that's when I got interested in tachyons. What they could do, how to manipulate them, all that good stuff. Pretty technical, actually; the kind of thing only a total geek would even remotely care about," he said, and she laughed a little.

"You don't seem like a geek to me," she said.

"Yeah, well, I grew up on a farm; that hides it a little. Get to know me for a while and you'll see," he said, and she laughed again.

"Maybe. So did you find out what you wanted to know?" she asked.

"No. The tachometer was broken to start with, but I thought maybe I could figure out how it worked and maybe even fix it. One of Joey's relatives was the one who had it; Matthieu Doucet. So I asked him to let me borrow it for a semester so I could study it and tinker with it. I guess I must have done a better job than I thought," Mike said.

"I'm sorry it worked out that way," she said.

"Oh, I'll survive. Takes more than that to knock out Mike McGrath," he said staunchly, and she laughed.

"I'm glad to hear it," she said.

They walked ahead quietly for a while after that, enjoying the sunshine and the breeze. It was still early enough that it wasn't too hot, and several other couples smiled and nodded when they passed.

"Do you like it here?" Annabelle asked him presently.

"I guess so. Still kind of homesick, though," he admitted, and she nodded.

"Yeah, so was I at first. It gets better after a while," she said.

"It's always the little things you miss the most, I think. Like sometimes I really wish you could see the stars from here, but there's so much light in the city that it washes them completely out," he said.

"You like to look at the stars?" she asked.

"Yeah. . . I guess you could say that," he admitted. It had been a long time since he'd done something that simple, actually, but her words reminded him of childhood days when he'd sometimes climb up to the top of Mount Nebo after supper, to pick out the constellations and remember all the stories of each one. Nebo wasn't really a mountain, of course; just a tall hill on his parents' place, but it had seemed enormous enough in those days, like Mount Everest itself to his childish eyes. He hadn't thought of it at all since he went away to college, and the reminder was both sweet and painful at the same time.

"I used to watch for falling stars sometimes when I was a kid," she said.

"You must have lived out in the country, then. You sure couldn't have seen one in town," he said.

"Yeah, in the booming metropolis of Sugar Hill, Texas. Right outside Mount Pleasant," she said.

"Yeah, I think I've been there a couple times. To Mount Pleasant, anyway," he agreed.

"Not since I lived there, I don't think," she said wryly.

"Why? When was that?" he asked.

"1864," she said, and his jaw dropped.

"But I thought you came here with Philip," he said.

"I did. But that was already my second jump through time, not my first," she said.

"But *how?* There was no tachometer back then," Mike asked.

"Honestly I was asleep for most of it, Mike. Philip and Joan could tell you a lot more than I could. I don't much like to think about it, myself. All that stuff was long ago and far away, and I'd rather focus on the here and now and try to make a life for myself with the cards I've been dealt," she said.

Her resolute determination made him feel a little bit ashamed of himself for spending so much time wallowing in self-pity lately, and he decided then and there to do better in the future.

"I like your attitude," he said.

"It's the only way I can be," she said, shrugging.

"So what are you going to school for?" he asked, changing the subject.

"Math. Turns out I'm what they call a *savant;* I can do math in my head without a calculator. I got a whole year's worth of credit by examination that way, believe it or not. So I'll graduate in only two more years and then my advisor promised me he'd get me a job on the math faculty if I wanted it. Sounds like a good opportunity to me," she explained.

"You can really do any math problem in your head?" he asked.

"Well. . . *almost* any," she amended.

"Can you do this one?" he asked, and proceeded to give her a tough problem in astronomical engineering. She thought for a minute.

"Eighteen point three two five. Is that right?" she asked.

"I have no idea, honestly. I just wanted to see if you could do it," he said, and when she laughed he joined her.

Thus began a friendship which cheered him up very much and sometimes even managed to make him completely forget that he was a hundred years and a thousand miles away from home and could never go back there. Indeed, as time went by he found himself liking Miss Annabelle Rusk very much, and even began to wonder if perhaps the accident might have had a small silver lining after all.

Two months after moving to Tampa, he was finally able to sell the Jeep to an antique car collector in Memphis for what seemed like an astronomical sum of money at the time. He was able to buy a secondhand car, and even more importantly, he was able to bribe an official in the Immigration Service to issue him a green card and a work permit, even though he lacked the necessary documents. It galled him to no end to have to pretend to be an illegal alien, but what other choice did he have? The bribe was a costly step, but a very necessary one if he expected to make any kind of future for himself.

It turned out that money wasn't worth quite as much in 2136 as he was used to, and what had seemed like a small fortune at first wasn't really quite as fabulous as he'd originally thought. After buying the car and paying for his immigration paperwork there wasn't all that much left, which made the need to find a job only that much more urgent.

"I might be able to say something to my faculty advisor, explain your situation a little bit. He might be able to get you a job at the University," Annabelle said.

"You really think so? Considering I can't even prove I have a degree?" he asked skeptically.

"I didn't say it'd be easy. Tell him you're a war refugee from when they bombed Witwatersrand two years ago; that's what it says on your immigration papers, after all. South Africa is a radioactive wasteland right now; *nobody* can prove they have any kind of degree from there," she said.

"He'll never believe I'm from South Africa, Annabelle. He'll know that's a lie the second I open my mouth," Mike said.

"Well. . . nobody can help it if you sound like a Texas farm boy. Clean up your accent a little bit and try to do the best you can. Fake it if you have to; I doubt he knows what a Boer is supposed to sound like, anyway. Or tell him your family moved there from Lufkin before you were born; I'm sure you can come up with *something,*" she said.

So Mike did his homework, determined to know everything it was possible to know about the University of Witwatersrand and his supposed doctoral studies in astronomy at that now-defunct institution, not to mention a hundred years worth of advancement in science generally. That was a pretty steep learning curve.

But he threw himself into it with a will, and in the end, things turned out to be almost disappointingly easy. The faculty committee seemed much more interested in how much he knew than in how he learned it, once they heard his cooked-up story and saw his immigration papers. And of course Mike *did* know his material, after all; there'd never been any question about *that.*

It was pure kindness on the part of the Board of Trustees, of course, but he ended up being granted an honorary doctorate from the University of South Florida on the basis of his demonstrated knowledge and his war refugee status. Then he was offered a job as a temporary adjunct instructor of astronomy when the fall term started in August. An honorary degree wouldn't be accepted at any other college, true, but still yet it was more than Mike had ever dared to hope for.

"You're amazing, you know it?" he told Annabelle after he got the news, sweeping her up in a hug. Her plan had worked wonders.

"Thanks. You're not so bad yourself, Doctor McGrath," she said, and hugged him back.

But in spite of his joy and relief, Mike soon found that teaching was a much more demanding job than he'd anticipated; one that often kept him busy till late hours. He almost always found time to eat supper with Annabelle in the cafeteria, though, and on Sundays after church they usually went to the beach for a few hours with Philip and Joan and Chris.

He hadn't forgotten about Joey's strange disappearance, or the possibility that the NADF might show up one day with a bullet that had his name on it, but those worries gradually faded as time passed and nothing of the sort occurred. Even though Philip warned him more than once not to get careless, Mike reasoned that he was probably the most unthreatening person on earth at the moment. He was just a mild-mannered astronomy professor who minded his own business and never meddled in politics at all. Surely the NADF wouldn't think *he* mattered, would they?

The new job meant he was finally able to move out of Philip and Joan's house, into a waterfront condo down by the Bay. True, it was a *cheap* condo, with no beach access, but it *did* have a marina. He bought a small sailboat to park there, and spent many a day out on the water from then on when he could take time away from his studies, sometimes with Annabelle and sometimes alone. It gradually became the accepted reality that they were unofficially dating, even though nobody explicitly said anything.

He found out many things about her as time went by; that she was named after the beautiful Annabel Lee in Edgar Allen Poe's famous poem, that she liked seafood, and she had a rather conservative view of the world in many ways. That part didn't really surprise him much, considering where she came from. The whole way she thought and looked at the world was so foreign to him that she was almost incomprehensible at times, but that only made her all the more intriguing, actually. In some ways she reminded him of an old woman in a young girl's body. She thought make-up was sinful and she wouldn't shave her legs or cut her hair, and as for wearing anything but an ankle-length dress, well, you might as well have suggested that she drink rat poison. She got up at the crack of dawn every morning to scrub the kitchen floor, and some of the words and expressions she used were so antique he almost laughed. She considered it vulgar for a girl to visit a man's house alone, which meant he always had to be the one to go pick her up if they wanted to go out.

He also quickly discovered that she wouldn't hesitate to deliver a stinging slap in the face to any man who dared curse in front of her; an unfortunate habit which embroiled Mike in several fights and earned him more than a few black eyes and loose teeth from having to defend her. He soon learned to avoid taking her places where that kind of thing might happen. In vain did he suggest that she might consider overlooking those kinds of things sometimes; there were standards to be upheld, and she dadgummed well meant to uphold them. She was no shrinking violet, that was for sure.

Mike found himself rather bemused by these things sometimes, especially when she said or did something that caught him completely off guard. But for the most part he was inclined to think her odd little habits and mannerisms were endearing. . . other than when he was nursing a black eye, of course.

In fact, he liked her so much that after a few months he even began to contemplate the idea of getting married. He was almost certain she'd say yes, if he asked. He had a house, and a car, and a job with good prospects, and they liked so many of the same things and got along together so well, after all. He knew he was letting his thoughts be colored to some extent by the rose-tinted glasses of love, but that was all right. Things really did turn out well sometimes; aside from Philip and Joan, his own parents had just celebrated their twenty-fourth wedding anniversary a few months before the accident, still happily married as always, so he knew it was possible to make things work.

But even though such pleasant daydreams made him smile occasionally, that didn't necessarily mean he was in any particular hurry to follow through with them. They were just nice to think about sometimes.

Thinking about his parents' anniversary made him realize with a twinge of remorse that that had been the last time he'd been home to see them, even though it was less than a two hour drive. They lived on a thousand-acre ranch named Goliad, raising cows and peaches and various other things from time to time, along with his Uncle Brandon and his grandma Josie and occasionally his two younger sisters when they weren't too busy with other things.

There'd been a time when his father had wanted Mike to take over Goliad someday, and continue the family ranching tradition. But raising cows and cotton had never been something that appealed to him; his mind and his heart had always been in the stars. So after a while, Cody McGrath had quietly stopped asking, and given his only son the freedom to do as he liked, to go away to college and follow his own dream. He'd never once tried to make Mike feel guilty for that, even though Mike knew all too well how much it cost the man. Goliad Ranch could only be passed down to a male McGrath willing to live on the property and work it; so said the terms of the land patent, and if none were available or willing, then the land reverted back to the State of Texas. Mike had only sisters, so when Cody McGrath died, then that would be that.

Mike supposed that was exactly what had happened at some point, though he was reluctant to actually check the records and find out. Cody might not have wished to inflict any blame on him, but there were times (like now) when he felt it anyway, as if he'd been disloyal to a sacred trust, or failed in something he'd always known he was meant to do.

But there was no use dwelling on all that. He had his private regrets, just as all people everywhere had them. But that was nothing to the purpose at the moment, and he could only look ahead and try to do the best he could from then on.

He shook his head to clear his wooly thoughts, mildly amazed at how fast his mind could go from daydreams about Annabelle to sad memories and then right back to contemplating the future again.

There were things he regretted as an astronomer, also, and the most jarring among them was what they'd done to the Moon. It was no longer the same silvery ball he'd always remembered, which the poets had written and sung about for ages. No, now it was blue with seas and shrouded with white clouds, just like the blue and green marble that Earth was said to look like from space. Most of the features Mike remembered had been obliterated, and even the site of the first landing was deep under water. The Lunar

Terraform Project was a fascinating study in science, but the arrogance of the whole thing appalled him. Especially since it had all been for nothing, apparently; the place had been completely abandoned right before the Union War in 2105. For perfectly sound and legitimate reasons, to be sure, but to be left with a permanently disfigured Moon for no good reason disgusted him.

And then he really did miss the stars, just as he'd told Annabelle. Although unlike the Moon that was really nobody's fault but his, for choosing to live in a large city. The lights of Tampa and its myriad suburbs simply drowned out even the brightest stars in the sky, leaving it a dull purplish-black. He had access to photographs and high-powered telescopes and all kinds of modern substitutes, of course, but somehow that wasn't quite the same as looking up at the starry host with his own naked eyes.

But those were minor things, and for the most part Mike couldn't complain too much about the life he found himself leading. In fact, he was even tempted at times to be thankful for the accident, and be glad that he'd landed in such a sweet spot.

Things were about to change.

Chapter Seven

Mike might not have been all that high on their list of priorities, but the NADF must have been quietly tracking him down for months. And so it was that as he parked his car after work one night in late October, he found himself suddenly surrounded by a squad of soldiers in slate-blue uniforms, all of them holding rifles pointed directly at his chest.

For a second he wondered how they could possibly have found him, and then decided it didn't matter. They had a million tell-tale clues, if they were determined enough. His Jeep tracks through the woods, the hole in the Containment Zone fence, perhaps even something with his name on it at the house in Arkadelphia or the title transfer when he sold his Jeep to the collector. There was no telling, really.

There was no point in thinking about escape, either. He meekly put his hands up high and offered no objection while they searched him for weapons. Then he found himself hustled away in handcuffs and leg irons; a humiliating spectacle for the neighbors to witness, no doubt.

They took him by van to a large white office building somewhere downtown, although it wasn't the jail or anything he recognized as a government facility. Just an unmarked, nondescript kind of place that seemed designed specifically for the purpose of attracting as little attention as possible.

The guards led him inside, and he was quickly taken up to a bare white room on the fortieth floor. It contained nothing but a wooden table with two chairs on opposite sides, and he was none-too-gently made to sit in one of these. It reminded him of an interrogation room, but for a long time there was no interrogation forthcoming. He simply had to sit there at the table alone. He knew this was a psychological ploy, to make him as nervous as possible before the interrogator came in to question him. Joey had talked about things like that now and then, and he'd seen it on TV lots of times. The only problem was, even though he knew exactly what they were doing, that still didn't keep it from working.

Eventually, a man in the same slate-blue uniform as the soldiers entered the room, flanked by two armed guards and carrying a tablet computer. He looked to be about thirty, but he had the dark gray eyes of a man much older, cold and hard as tempered steel. The name on his badge read *Luke Bartow, Lt. Col, NADF.*

The man sat down silently across the table from Mike, looking at files on the computer and sometimes frowning at whatever he saw. This was more manipulation, of course, and Mike tried not to let it affect him. Eventually the man looked up at him and cleared his throat.

"Your name is Micah McGrath, correct?" the man asked, his voice inflectionless and cool.

"Yes, sir," Mike agreed.

"Dr. McGrath, my name is Lieutenant Luke Bartow, with the North American Defense Forces. I'm afraid we have several serious matters to discuss. You do realize you're in violation of Union Code 38-6-229, and a dozen other laws relating to national security because of your recent trespassing in the William Clark Containment Zone, do you not?" the man asked mildly, polishing his gold-rimmed spectacles. Mike could only shrug.

"You further realize that, if we chose, we would be perfectly within our legal rights to execute you on the spot, or to incarcerate you for as long as we felt necessary?" he went on. Again Mike said nothing, though the words chilled him to the bone. Lieutenant Bartow seemed not to notice his silence.

"However, in your particular case, that isn't necessarily what we'd like to do. Is it true that you've recently been working on a device to read future events?" the man asked. Mike couldn't imagine how they might have found out about that, but there was no point in lying.

"Yes, sir," he said, and Lieutenant Bartow leaned closer across the table.

"Dr. McGrath, we believe your device is the reason for the original explosion which required the creation of the Containment Zone in the first place, and, more recently, for the reappearance of part of what was lost. We'd very much like to understand how that device works, and re-create it if possible," he said.

I bet you would, Mike thought to himself, but only nodded.

"You may be thinking of the unfortunate events of last April, when the remaining townsfolk were killed. That was a regrettable misunderstanding; the local commander had standing orders to shoot all trespassers on sight, and he was overzealous in carrying them out, I'm afraid. He has since been relieved of his duties," Lieutenant Bartow said.

"I see," Mike said, and the other man sighed.

"Let me be honest with you for a moment, Dr. McGrath. This is a dangerous world you've come to, a fact which I don't think you fully appreciate yet. There are new dangers all the time, some of which, if they ever came to pass, would make that little incident in Arkansas look like a Sunday School picnic. There are fanatical groups right this very *minute,* Dr. McGrath, who would lay waste the entire world if they got the chance. There are nuclear and biological threats of the most deadly kinds imaginable, and only swift and stern action by our Defense Forces has enabled us to survive as long as we have, with any level of civilization at all. Other parts of the world have not always been so lucky. I hope you appreciate the seriousness of what I'm saying," Lieutenant Bartow said.

Mike nodded. He did appreciate *that* much, all too well. He was himself supposed to be posing as a refugee from the radioactive desert of South Africa, and the nightly news was full of horror stories *almost* as bad as that. Some of it might be propaganda, of course, but Mike didn't doubt the basic truth of what Lieutenant Bartow had said. The world was indeed a dangerous place nowadays.

Nevertheless, he said nothing.

"That being the case, I hope you also understand what an invaluable tool for fighting these things your machine could be," Lieutenant Bartow went on.

"Yes, sir. I can see that," Mike agreed.

"Good; I'm glad we can agree on that much at least. Now, we really brought you here today because we're willing to offer you a deal, Dr. McGrath," Lieutenant Bartow said.

"What kind of a deal?" Mike asked, though he suspected he already knew.

"We want you to work on rebuilding your machine for us. We realize that the original has been lost, along with your notes and research. We know it will take some time to reconstitute that loss. What we're offering you is a state-of-the-art lab facility, with unlimited funds to continue your work. Anything you need will be provided. Moreover, we recognize the importance of your personal life, also. We're prepared to grant you immediate legal citizenship in the North American Union, not only for you but for your lady friend also. You may keep your job at the University if you wish, and your salary will be quite generous. If there's anything else you'd like, we might be able to make that happen, also. All we ask is that you work diligently on your research, give us regular status reports, and share it with no one else. I'll be your handler and your sole point of contact with the Defense Forces; you'll make your reports to me, along with any requests for money or materials or whatnot. You'll be doing something incredibly important for your country, and for the future of mankind, and making a good life for yourself in the meantime," Lieutenant Bartow said.

"I see. And if I don't agree?" Mike asked. It was a cheeky thing to say, but Lieutenant Bartow only smiled slightly, and it wasn't a very nice smile, either.

"I strongly advise you to agree, Dr. McGrath," he said, and the unspoken threat was crystal clear. The man didn't need to specify exactly what might happen, but Mike got the message plain as day. They surely had ways of enforcing their wishes, and if the carrot didn't work then the stick would have to do.

Mike much preferred the carrot.

"All right. I'll do it," he agreed.

* * * * * * *

Six weeks later, Mike cursed as he dropped the soldering laser on the floor for the third time in a single afternoon. It was a tool which hadn't existed in the past, and he was still trying to learn how to use it properly. He'd already burned his fingers more times than he could count.

He stuck his wounded thumb in his mouth and let it rest there while he picked up the laser with his other hand. There was no one else around to see him; he'd given strict orders that he wasn't to be disturbed for any reason unless he himself came out to ask for something.

By dint of hard work and a little luck, his staff (it still seemed unreal that he, Mike McGrath, should have such a luxury), had managed to acquire all the electronics components he needed to rebuild the tachometer, although in order to do so they'd had to rob several of them from obscure sources. Many of the parts were long obsolete and practically impossible to find anymore.

Well, they'd managed to acquire all the components he could *remember* needing, at least. Losing his research notes had been a serious blow, and even though he'd worked with Dr. Garza's books long enough to give him a general familiarity with how the thing was done, he certainly didn't remember *everything*. No one could have.

He wearily ran his fingers through his hair and put his face in his hands to rest and think for a few minutes. After a while, he remembered one more thing he'd forgotten. He pushed the intercom button.

"Yes, sir?" came the tinny voice of his secretary.

"Margaret, tell Amos to come in here, please," he said.

"Yes, sir, Dr. McGrath," she replied, and Mike took no further notice of the matter. Margaret was unfailingly efficient about such things.

Indeed, it was only a few minutes later when there came a knock on the lab door, and without waiting for an invitation Amos poked his head inside. He was Mike's general aide and lab assistant, nineteen years old, a brilliant student with a double major in chemistry and physics, and a bit too much of an eager beaver for his own good.

"You called, boss?" he asked.

"Yes, I need you to go to the library and find me some information, as soon as possible," Mike told him.

"Sure thing, boss. What do you need?" he asked, grabbing a pencil and a note pad from one of the lab tables.

"I need you to find me a place where I can get some khamrabaevite. It's a type of mineral that usually comes from carbonaceous chondrite asteroids. But I need to know exactly which asteroid it did come from, because the precise proportion of elements varies from rock to rock and it matters," he explained patiently. Amos scribbled busily on the paper for a few seconds, and then looked up.

"Is that all, boss?" he asked. Mike hated the way Amos called him 'boss'; it made him feel like a mafia kingpin. But he'd long since learned to put up with it.

"Yeah, that's all for now. If I think of anything else I'll let you know," he said, and waved a hand dismissively. Amos shut the door and left him alone again with his thoughts.

Ever since he'd agreed to Lieutenant Bartow's arrangement, Mike had found himself increasingly conflicted about what he was doing. Yes, everything the man had said about extremist groups was certainly true, and no doubt the tachometer would help fight them and save lives. He couldn't deny all that.

But on the other hand, he couldn't help noticing that fear of the Defense Forces ran wide and deep. There were certain things one simply didn't talk about, not even with best friends. There were certain topics only a fool would joke about, certain places and certain websites that everyone knew better than to visit even out of curiosity. People who ignored the unspoken rules had a way of dying in tragic accidents, or sometimes simply disappearing without explanation, never to be heard from again. And anyone who questioned such things was apt to follow them very quickly. Mike wasn't at all sure he wanted to help tighten the screws on people any more than they already were. The government might have good intentions (or it might not, for that matter), but everybody knew where good intentions led.

However bad the extremist cells might be, was a slow and steady descent into near slavery really all that much better? Mike struggled with that question almost daily, and honestly couldn't decide which was worse. Slogans and cheap lines were easy to repeat, but in real life the decision was far from simple. Sometimes he feared the world was doomed in one way or another no matter what anybody did or didn't do.

It would most likely take at least an hour or so for Amos to finish his assignment and bring the information back to the lab, so Mike took the opportunity to lay his head down on the lab bench and take a much-needed nap. He'd been surviving on very little sleep the past few weeks.

It seemed like only the blink of an eye before he woke to the sound of Amos knocking on the lab door. He glanced at the clock and saw that nearly two hours had passed, so he sat up and stretched, rubbing the sleep out of his eyes so he'd look slightly more respectable.

He barely had time to finish composing himself before Amos came in and put down a sheaf of papers on the lab bench in front of him.

"What did you find?" Mike asked, glancing at the papers without making any effort to pick them up.

"Well, I didn't find too many places to get something like that, boss," he began apologetically, as if he thought it was his own fault that nature hadn't seen fit to produce a khamrabaevite deposit right underneath the city park.

"I don't need but one, Amos, as long as it's the right kind. What did you find?" Mike asked.

"Most of the suppliers didn't specify in their catalogs where it came from, so I had to call a few of them and ask. Three of them can get us pieces of an asteroid in Uzbekistan, and then there's one company that works with a place in Mexico. The others I contacted couldn't tell me without doing some research first, so I don't know about them," Amos replied promptly.

"Is that all?" Mike asked skeptically.

"Yes, sir. That's all I could find," Amos replied.

Mike thought about this for a few minutes. It sounded somewhat promising; Dr. Garza had used part of an asteroid from Mexico when he built the original tachometer.

"Where *exactly* is the Mexican one?" Mike asked.

"Um. . . just a second," Amos said, riffling through papers.

"Looks like it comes from Chihuahua. It landed near a little town called Pueblito de Allende in February of 1969," Amos said.

"Excellent! How much of it can you get?" Mike asked. He couldn't believe his luck; that was the very same rock Dr. Garza had used. He wouldn't even have to do any comparative analysis to make sure it was suitable.

"They've got 4.8 kilos for sale, sir," Amos said.

"That's all?" Mike asked, disappointed. That was barely enough to be worth messing with.

"I'm afraid so, sir," Amos said.

"Well. . . go ahead and order what they've got, then. We *might* be able to extract enough khamrabaevite from that. I guess it's better than nothing, anyway," Mike said.

"Absolutely, sir," the boy replied, sounding crestfallen.

"All right then, good job," he said. It wouldn't hurt to be kind to Amos for once; the whole nasty situation wasn't *his* fault.

A few minutes after Amos left, Mike decided he'd had enough for one day. He closed and locked the lab, and left the University without saying a word to anybody. He was supposed to be teaching a class at two o'clock, but he knew well enough that the students wouldn't object to getting a day off when he didn't show up. He wasn't in the mood for dealing with any of that today.

He quietly drove home, putting his thumbprint up for a scan at the entrance gate absentmindedly and then parking in his assigned spot. Luke Bartow had been as good as his word, and Mike now made an obscenely large amount of money; enough to move into a gated subdivision in Clearwater Beach where the houses cost more per month than most people made in a year. His place had five bedrooms, no less, and everything from the rugs to the light fixtures practically screamed luxury. It wasn't that he needed so much space or cared about appearances, but he *did* want a house right on the beach, and that was the smallest one he'd been able to find.

He often wondered if he'd made a deal with the devil to get it.

He sighed and thumbed his way inside the empty house, troubled at heart and unsure what to do about it, or even if anything could be done at all. He fixed some noodles which he ate almost without tasting them, and then put the bowl in the dishwasher. The house seemed oppressively quiet and still when he finished, so he went to the computer and keyed Annabelle's number. It wasn't the time of day when she usually went walking, so she ought to be home with the baby if nothing else had come up. He hoped so; he needed some cheering up.

"Hello," she said, and he couldn't help smiling at the sound of her voice.

"Hello, sugar baby. You're not busy, are you?" he asked, and she laughed.

"I'm never too busy to talk to you, Mikey. But no, I'm just sitting at home with Chris, that's all. He's sleeping, so I was trying to clean things up a little bit while I had time," she said.

"Mind if I come over for a while?" he asked.

"Not at all, if you don't mind helping babysit," she said.

"You know I don't mind," he said.

"Then I'll see you in a little bit, okay?" she said.

"Sure thing. Love you, sugar baby," he said, and she laughed.

"Love you too, sugar daddy," she said, and that was all. It was a private joke between them to call each other those names, since they both loved caramel candy. It would have seemed obscure to the point of weirdness for most people since those brands hadn't existed in decades, but Mike supposed no one else ever had to hear their little pet names anyway.

He changed into jeans and a t-shirt, then put on his tennis shoes and his Florida Gators baseball cap before leaving the complex on foot.

One of the minor consolations of being suddenly rich was that he'd been able to give Philip and Joan enough money to buy a decent house for a change. Maybe not right on the beach, no; that was beyond even Mike's means, but three blocks from the Gulf wasn't so bad. He'd wanted them to find a place in Clearwater Beach so they'd all be close together, so Joan had picked a house on Papaya Street, and together they'd gone and paid cash for it.

He half-jogged, half-walked down the road for a mile or so, till he reached the house. Then he went up and knocked on the door.

It was warm outside for December, and Annabelle answered the door wearing a flowery dress which was daringly short for her; it was practically mid-calf.

"Wow, you're really taking a walk on the wild side today, aren't you?" he commented, staring at her legs. He could have sworn she reddened slightly.

"Well. . . it was hot today, and everybody keeps telling me it's really not immodest to wear things like this, so I decided maybe it'd be okay. Does it look bad?" she asked, sounding embarrassed.

"No, not at all. It looks beautiful on you, I promise," he said, giving her a hug and a kiss.

And it really did; Annabelle was a beautiful girl to begin with, and the outfit set off her figure and her long brown hair in a way that thoroughly bedazzled him and would have turned heads almost anywhere.

He often thought he was the luckiest man in the world.

Chapter Eight

They went to the beach that afternoon, taking off their shoes and walking barefoot in the foamy waves. It was overcast and the place was practically empty, but as far as Mike was concerned that was only so much the better. Chris was old enough by then to walk along beside them, holding one of Mike's fingers in his chubby little hand.

"You know, I'm glad I came here after all," he declared after a while.

"Are you? I thought you hated having to work for the government," she said, glancing at him curiously.

"Well. . . yeah, I could do without that part. But I'm still glad to be here. After all, what would I do without *you?*" he asked, and she smiled.

"I'm sure you'd find another young lady ten times as pretty, that's what," she said.

"I'm not sure that's even possible. Nah, I just would've had to become an old bachelor, that's all," he teased.

"You're still an old bachelor," she pointed out.

"Hey, now, I'm only twenty-three," he objected.

"Yup, one foot in the nursing home and the other on a banana peel," she agreed, and he laughed.

"Okay, you win. I'm still an old bachelor," he agreed, and for a little while they kept walking in companionable silence, listening to the sound of the waves and the occasional cry of the gulls. Mike was happy, and all his problems and moral dilemmas at work seemed faint and far away. A sudden upwelling of love washed over him, and he decided impetuously that now was as good a time as any.

"I don't really want to be an old bachelor anymore, though," he finally said, squeezing her hand.

"What do you mean?" she asked, slowing down. He stopped in his tracks and turned to face her, then dropped to one knee in the salty water.

"I mean that I love you, Miss Rusk, and I'd be most honored if you'd be my wife," he said, as formally as he knew how. For a moment she seemed speechless, with her lips slightly parted, and then she laughed.

"I was beginning to think you'd never ask," she finally said, and fell to her own knees to kiss him. When an errant wave sprayed them both with sea foam they couldn't have cared less.

"Any particular time you'd like?" he asked, when they broke the kiss and had a chance to breathe again.

"After Christmas, of course, but not *too* long after," she said.

"Hmm. . . what about the twelfth or the nineteenth of January?" he asked.

"Why especially those days?" she asked.

"Well, the twelfth is my birthday, and then my mom and dad's anniversary is on the nineteenth," he said, and she smiled.

"I like the thought, but those will both fall on Sunday this year, you know. Kind of an odd day for a wedding, don't you think?" she asked, and he wasn't surprised that she'd calculated the date so quickly.

"I don't think it'll matter. It might even make it easier to find something on short notice, if it's not the usual day," he pointed out.

"True. Let's make it the twelfth, then. I don't think I can stand to wait any longer," she said.

"I want you to have this, too," he said, slipping off the necklace that held his mother's silver sixpence and putting it in Annabelle's palm.

"What is it?" she asked.

"It was my mother's. My father gave it to her to wear in her shoe on their wedding day, and she asked me to give it to my own wife someday when I got married," Mike said.

"That's so sweet. I love it," she said, slipping the chain around her neck and kissing him again.

They scooped up Christopher and went home to change out of their wet clothes, and when Philip and Joan got home later that evening they shared the news with them.

"We all knew it was only a matter of time. Y'all make a beautiful couple," Joan said warmly, and then hugged them both.

"Congratulations; God bless you both," Philip said, and shook their hands.

Philip and Joan took them out to eat at a fancy seafood place in honor of the occasion, and Mike's first impulse was to offer to pay for everything himself. He had to remind himself that sometimes it's more blessed to allow others the pleasure of giving than it is to keep it always for ourselves.

"Where do you think you might go for your honeymoon?" Joan asked while they ate.

"We hadn't really talked about it yet," Annabelle admitted, taking a bite of her lobster.

"We can go anywhere in the world you want to, babe; the sky's the limit," Mike said expansively. He was in high spirits and felt generous, and wanted her to have something really special.

"Anywhere at all?" she asked, sounding bemused. He was about to say yes, when a sudden cloud crossed his mind. True, they might have the *money* to go anywhere she might like, but considering what he was working on, he wasn't totally sure they'd be given the *permission* to go just anywhere they pleased. They almost certainly wouldn't be allowed to leave the country. After all, that might threaten national security.

"Well. . . *almost* anywhere," he amended, and there was no need for anybody to ask what he meant by the sudden backtrack. They all knew.

"We can think about it and decide later. There are still several weeks left, and we don't even have to go right away if we don't want to," Annabelle said gracefully, and then the conversation moved on to other things.

Mike was careful not to let it show, but the incident only served to remind him that however much wealth and comfort he might have, the one thing he *didn't* have was freedom. He lived in a golden cage, and try as he might, he couldn't think of any way to get out of it.

* * * * * * *

The wedding was as grand as even a princess could have wished for, at one of the grandest cathedrals in town and with no expenses spared. Annabelle wore Lisa McGrath's silver sixpence in her shoe, and then afterwards took to wearing it as a necklace as Mike had once done. In a kinder and gentler time the wedding probably would have received a double-page spread in the society section of the *Tampa Tribune,* but as it was the Defense Department suppressed even the slightest mention of it. They didn't want one of their prize researchers attracting any attention to himself.

There was no more talk of honeymoons or exotic trips, either. The look on Luke Bartow's face the first time Mike mentioned *that* had been enough to convince him never to bring up the subject again. He did indeed live in a golden cage, and it did no good at all to rattle the bars. They ended up going to a resort in Tarpon Springs for two weeks, and Mike privately felt glad to be given even that much leeway.

Annabelle seemed not to notice the restrictions. She gladly moved into his lonely house and soon transformed it from a cold and quiet place into something warm and welcoming; a feat which truly amazed him. In spite of the prison he found himself living in, Annabelle was a comfort.

Toward the end of February, Joan announced that she was pregnant for the second time, and three days later Annabelle discovered likewise. The two sisters were enthusiastic about the prospect of having babies at the same time, but at first Mike was less than keen about the whole idea. It wasn't that he didn't want children, but it saddened him that one should be born into a jail cell. The baby was one more tool his handlers could use to manipulate and control him, and that was unfair to all of them.

He did his best not to think of that, though, or at least not to show it. On the surface he was excited and happy as could be, even while his heart sank.

But in the way of many others before him, Mike soon discovered that babies have a way of changing things, even before they arrive. He found himself more anxious about the future than he'd ever been, for one thing. Not so much financially; they had more money than they could have spent in ten lifetimes. And it wasn't even so much his situation with the Defense Forces, actually. He knew exactly what he had to deal with in that case, even if he didn't like it.

No, what really worried him was Joey. He still remembered with crystal clarity what he'd seen when his friend disappeared from the parking garage in Rockport. The possibility of something similar happening to Mike himself had been lurking in the back of his mind ever since, but now it truly haunted him. It hadn't even been quite so bad when it was only him and no one else involved, but things were very different now that he had a family to think about. If Mike suddenly disappeared, then what might happen to *them?* The uncertainty was almost unbearable.

His research offered him few clues as to what could have happened, and it wasn't till he confided his fears to Annabelle that he got any kind of break.

"Let me see your notes; maybe together we can figure something out," she suggested.

"Do you have any idea what Lieutenant Bartow would say if he knew I was sharing classified information, even with you?" Mike asked.

"Yeah, I've got a pretty good idea, actually. But if nobody tells him then it won't ever come to that, will it?" she countered.

"Meet me at the library tomorrow afternoon at two o'clock, then. I'll bring my lab journal and we'll see if you can spot anything I overlooked," he said. He didn't dare bring it home, let alone take Annabelle to the lab. Both those locations almost certainly had bugs in place, as compulsive as the NADF were about security. Mike wouldn't have been surprised to find out they kept logs of every keystroke he made on the computer. But they couldn't very well spy on him *everywhere*, could they?

He met her on the top floor of the library, in an empty study cubicle. The whole floor had been deserted when he arrived, so he had good reason to think they wouldn't be discovered there.

"Here it is," he said in a low voice, pulling the journal out from under his shirt. She didn't comment about the secrecy; she knew as well as he did what the stakes could be if they got caught. She opened the book and started reading.

"Here's your problem," she said, pointing to an equation on page thirty-four.

"Wow, that was fast," he said dryly, and she ignored the irony in his voice.

"This equation implies that the tachometer's bubble ring is unstable if you try to make it larger than a certain value, contingent on your power supply. It'll shrink back and pop like a rubber band if your settings don't match up, dragging everything right back where it came from. Doesn't matter so much if you're using mass conversion because then the size is almost limitless, but if you're using power from the electrical grid or conversion of enthalpy then it's severely limited. Do you happen to know what it was set on?" she asked.

"No, it wasn't even switched on. I was right in the middle of trying to replace a faulty capacitor when my screwdriver slipped and caused a static discharge. It could've been set on anything," he said, feeling foolish that he hadn't spotted the implications himself. But then again she was the math whiz, not him.

"Well, if you want my theory, it's this. I bet when you discharged the capacitor, it fried the tachometer's computer and switched it on with incompatible settings. It was probably set on either power grid or enthalpy mode and then tried to make the bubble too big, so it was unstable and started to decay almost immediately. So if that's true then Joey ought to be back in the past," Annabelle said.

"So why didn't I disappear too, then?" he pointed out, and she furrowed her brow, thinking.

"It's only a guess, but it's *possible* the bubble takes a while to completely decay, and in that case it wouldn't surprise me if the outer edges disappeared first. Joey would have been near the outer edge of the bubble when the accident first happened, wouldn't he?" she said.

"Yeah, our house was right at the edge, and as far as I know that's where he was," Mike agreed.

"And you were at the very center, so it might make sense that he disappeared sooner than you would," she said.

"So that means I'll still disappear at some point," Mike said. It was the very thing he'd feared most and hoped to refute.

"I don't know, baby," Annabelle said, reluctantly meeting his eyes.

Mike considered it. They were rapidly getting into uncharted waters with all this; theories were nice, but what they really needed were some hard facts. Lots of things sounded good at first blush and then turned out to be utterly laughable when the rest of the story came out. He hoped that's what happened *this* time, actually; he'd never in his entire life been so anxious to prove a theory wrong.

Nevertheless, he forced himself to be scientific about it.

"It sounds like a reasonable theory, but there's got to be some way to test it," Mike finally said.

"The only way I can think of to do that is to go look and see if the bubble ring is smaller now than it was before," she said.

"That's a pretty long trip, just to find out something like that. Surely there are records or studies that have been done on that place in the past hundred years, wouldn't you think?" he asked.

"I doubt it. Almost all the public records from before the Union War got destroyed, especially in places close to the border like Arkadelphia. The ones that are left are pretty spotty. Cyber-war was awfully popular back then; they loved to wipe out each other's databases. And then the NADF has kept a pretty tight lid on anything since then," she said.

She was right, of course; the Containment Zone might as well have been one of those blank spots on old maps where the mapmakers knew so little that they could only scribble *Here there be monsters.*

"Then I'll have to go in person. I can't stand not knowing," he said. And that was the simple truth; he'd go crazy thinking about it, if he had to constantly wonder if he might disappear at any moment. Annabelle only nodded, so maybe the question was bothering her as much as it was him.

"But how would you get there? You know they watch us all the time," she finally said.

"Yeah, but we might be able to use that against them, if we're smart," he said.

"Like how?" she asked.

"Well, you know the house is bugged, right?" he asked.

"Yeah, I figured as much," she agreed.

"So let's wait till there's a break when the University is closed so they won't expect me to be at work for a few days, and then I'll slip away. Play some of our home videos now and then so they'll hear my voice inside the house and maybe they won't suspect anything," he said.

"That's a big maybe, sugar daddy," she said.

"I know it's risky, but I think it'll work. They wouldn't think I'd run off without you, after all. Make sure you step outside to check the mail or stuff like that now and then and I'm pretty sure it'll work," he said, and she bit her lip as she considered all the various aspects.

"When do you want to try it?" she finally asked.

"Spring Break is coming up next week. That's as good a time as any," he said.

"But how will you get out of the house without them seeing you leave?" she pointed out.

"Pack me in a box and let Philip come pick me up like we're giving him some old clothes or something. Nobody will care what's inside a cardboard box you're sending to your sister's house," he said, and she laughed.

"Seriously?" she asked.

"Sure. Why not?" he asked.

"Well. . . I guess there's really no reason why it wouldn't work like that. Just seems silly, that's all," she said.

"Exactly. Which is why I hope nobody will ever think twice about it. I can come back the same way," he said.

"All right, then. Let's do it," she agreed.

"I'll still have to talk to Philip and Joan about it. None of this will work if they don't help," he said.

"They'll help," she said confidently.

He had to get back to the lab not long afterward, but that very evening he and Annabelle went over to Philip and Joan's house to discuss the issue.

"Sure, I'll take you," Philip agreed immediately, when he heard the situation.

"I was afraid you'd be a little harder to convince," Mike admitted. Christopher was playing with blocks on the carpet, and Mike picked him up while they talked. Chris had no objections; he simply sat on Mike's knee and kept playing with one block in each hand, knocking them together to see how much noise he could make. Philip watched him with a softness in his eyes that wasn't usually there.

"Well. . . I'd like to make sure Joey is all right, myself. I've been wondering about it ever since you first got here. I really do love the little booger, you know," he said, and Mike almost laughed. The idea of anybody calling Joey a little booger was too funny. If he'd been there, Mike would have rubbed his nose in it without mercy. But he wasn't, and never would be again, and that was enough to wipe out Mike's incipient mirth.

"All right, then. If you'll come over to the house at nine o'clock Saturday morning, I'll be packed up in the box. Do you think you can carry me out to the car?" he asked.

"Yeah, I think so. You're not *that* heavy, and it won't be very far, anyway," Philip agreed.

So that's what they did, and the whole thing went off so flawlessly that Mike had to marvel at how easy it had been. He waited inside the box till they got safely out of the city, and then Philip pulled over on a deserted road to let him out of the trunk. He clambered out, stretching his cramped limbs, and took his place in the passenger seat.

Then they were on their way.

Chapter Nine

Philip pushed hard and drove straight through, but even so it was nearly two o'clock in the morning by the time they reached Rockport. Mike had had his doubts about returning to a place where someone might possibly remember him, but then dismissed it. Rockport was the closest town to the Containment Zone, and they didn't have time to dally.

There was no way they could drive the car through the woods as Mike had done with his Jeep, so Philip bought two secondhand dirt bikes from an ad in the newspaper.

"You do know how to ride a bike, don't you?" Philip asked.

"Of course I do," Mike said.

"Okay, just asking. Better to be sure," Philip said.

They headed west on the highway, and then, when there came a time with no other cars or people in sight, Philip darted off the road and into the woods.

"Are you sure we're going the right way?" Mike asked when they stopped.

"Yeah, I got directions from the GPS grid a couple days ago," Philip said.

"You don't think anybody noticed, do you?" Mike asked. It seemed unlikely, but when dealing with the NADF one could never be too careful. They had a way of getting curious when people started looking up information like that.

"No, I used a public computer and downloaded the information for this whole quadrant. There was nothing for them to be suspicious about, I don't think. As for right now, I gave the computer a fix on our location as soon as we got to Rockport, and then I switched over to inertial sensors only so we wouldn't have to link up with the satellites and give away our position. I'm sure they could still find a way to track us if they knew we were here, but I don't think they do," Philip said.

"Good," Mike said, relieved.

They didn't talk much as they rode steadily southward through the woods, and after about two hours Philip figured they had to be approaching the fence.

"Should be any time now," he said, looking at their position on his GPS device.

And so it was. Not ten minutes later they came out onto a grass-grown access road very much like the one Mike remembered seeing on the south side of the Containment Zone. The fence was just like he remembered, too; twelve feet tall and topped with razor wire.

"How long do you figure it'll take to get down there to Arkadelphia?" Mike asked, staring at the fence.

"I figure about eight hours on foot," Philip said.

"We're not taking the bikes?" Mike asked, surprised.

"Not inside the Containment Zone. The satellites would spot the heat signatures from the engines immediately and then we'd be caught," Philip said.

"They didn't catch us when we drove the Jeep out that first night," Mike said.

"No, but the place was full of red hot bomb craters and swarms of NADF vehicles then. You had a chance to blend in, to some extent. That won't be the case this time," Philip said.

"Oh. Then won't they see the heat from our bodies, too?" Mike asked.

"Yeah, but we're not near as hot as a dirt bike engine, and we don't move near as fast, either. They'll just write us off as animals moving around in the woods," Philip said.

"Yeah, I guess so. Just didn't expect a fifteen mile hike today," Mike said.

"Oh, it'll do you good to get some exercise, boy. You sit on your tail in that lab too much, anyway," Philip said.

"No doubt," Mike agreed dryly.

"Well, come on then. We don't need to get caught here," Philip said, getting off his bike. They quickly hid the motorcycles under some heavy brush in a dry ravine, and Philip marked the spot on his GPS grid so they could find it again on the way back.

Then they attacked the fence with a pair of cutting dikes, and soon had a slit in the chain link big enough for a man to slip through. They did so, and then Philip used some thin pieces of baling wire to tie the sides of the gap back together.

"Good enough. I don't think anybody would notice that unless they looked really close," he said, scrutinizing his work carefully.

They talked now and then in low voices to help pass the time during the long walk, and about four o'clock that evening they finally reached what had once been the outskirts of Arkadelphia.

The tachometer had only taken the central core inside its bubble, of course; the rest of the town had been left behind. But there was precious little to see, nevertheless. A hundred years of wind and weather must have been awfully hard on whatever was left. Here and there was a bit of a stone wall or a weathered piece of brick-work or concrete, but that was all there was to even hint at the fact that there'd once been a city in that place. Mike didn't doubt that there were all kinds of things buried out there under the leaf litter, of course, if anybody cared to look. Metal, glass, maybe even some tough plastic. But that was of no interest to anyone except future archaeologists.

They were more or less following what had once been University Avenue, since even though the road itself had vanished, the grade was still there and the trees couldn't grow *quite* as big as elsewhere. But when they reached the top of a certain ridge, Mike stopped.

"This is where the ring should be," he said.

"Are you sure?" Philip asked.

"Yeah, I'm definitely sure. I saw it with my own two eyes. Pizza Hut ought to be right there beside the road, and that's where the cut-off was," he said, staring at the place. But there was no sign of the restaurant, or the wrecked Lexus he'd seen, or anything else except more woods. It seemed to confirm his worst fears.

"So does that mean Annabelle was right?" Philip asked.

"I'm not sure. Let's go on ahead a little bit and see what we see," Mike said.

There was nothing else to be done, so they trudged down into the valley and then up the next hill. Then Mike saw something at long last, and his heart sank.

"There it is," he said, pointing ahead through the trees.

They stepped across the ring just short of the university's baseball field, nearly half a mile south of where Mike remembered seeing it eleven months ago. Other than that it didn't look much different; the same razor-sharp division between the woods and the town, gently curving out of sight in both directions.

It was much easier going, after that. The weeds were thick in spots, but at least the streets were still paved and the buildings were still standing. Those that weren't bombed or gutted with fire, at least. There were an awful lot of those.

"It looks like a war zone," Philip commented as they rode along.

"I guess it was, there for a while," Mike said, remembering that first night when the NADF soldiers invaded. The memory didn't normally bother him too much, but here, among these quiet red-brick ruins, it was hard to keep the hairs on the back of his neck from standing up just a little.

"It's sad. I spent the summer here when I was seventeen, you know. It was a nice place back then," Philip said.

"Summer camp?" Mike guessed.

"Not exactly. We came up here with Matthieu Doucet to take scuba lessons and learn how to dive. It was the closest place we could find where there was some deep water," Philip said.

"Seems like I remember Zach telling us something about that one time," Mike agreed.

"You make it sound like it was such a long time ago, Mikey," Philip said, sounding amused.

"It *was* a long time ago. For me, at least; Joey and I were just kids when he told us all that stuff," Mike said.

"It was only three years ago for me," Philip said softly.

"I'm sorry, Cam. Didn't mean to pour salt in your wounds," Mike said.

"Eh, well. I knew what the price would be when I came here, and I'm not sorry for the choice I made. Just miss everybody sometimes, that's all. I wish Justin and Eileen could've been there when I got married, and when Chris was born, and all those things like that," Philip said.

"If it's any comfort to you, I know they watched all those things on the tachometer, back when it still worked. Zach told me so," Mike said.

"Did they? Well, that's good to know. I'm glad they got to be there in spirit, at least," Philip said.

They cut across the grounds of the aviation building and eventually came to the end of the university campus. Barely a block past that, they reached the southern edge of the bubble ring.

"There's barely *anything* left," Mike muttered.

"How fast do you think it's shrinking?" Philip asked.

"I'm sure we could measure exactly how far it's contracted in the past eleven months, but I don't think it would do us any good. The rate might be speeding up or slowing down as it progresses, and in that case a simple measurement wouldn't tell us anything. I can see just by looking that the whole thing will be gone in less than a year if it keeps on shrinking as fast as it has been," Mike said, and the thought brought a cold lump of fear and sorrow to his heart.

"So what do you think, then?" Philip finally asked.

"I think Annabelle was right about the bubble ring being unstable; the shrinkage we've seen is pretty good evidence of that. But we still don't know if that means it's reverting back to the past or not," Mike said, trying to suppress his misery by focusing on facts.

"What else could be happening?" Philip asked.

"I don't know. Everything could suddenly age a hundred years without ever going back to the past at all. It could just disintegrate into dust. It could be lots of different things," Mike said.

"I don't think that would explain what happened to Joey. He didn't suddenly turn into a skeleton, which is what you'd expect if he suddenly aged a hundred years," Philip said.

"No, but he did leave a little pile of dust behind. He might've disintegrated," Mike pointed out.

"I don't think so. There was nowhere near enough dust to account for all the mass in his body, even if you didn't count the water. People are 70 percent water, and if Joey weighed about 150 pounds then that's still almost 50 pounds of dust there should've been, if *that's* what happened. But it was no more than a handful or so. There's got to be a better explanation than that. I'm still in favor of the reversion to the past idea," Philip said.

"But then where did that little bit of dust come from? Why should there have been *any* dust, if he reverted back to the past?" Mike asked.

"That I don't know," Philip admitted.

They came to the ruins of the courthouse, like an ancient castle of red brick lost in the woods, and from there it wasn't too hard to figure out where Mike and Joey's house had once been. There was nothing there at all now, not even a clearing in the woods.

"This is where you and Joey lived?" Philip asked.

"Yeah, close enough. I'm pretty sure that gully down there used to be Third Street, so this is where the house would have been. I was hoping there might be something left; maybe even part of my computer or Dr. Garza's lab manuals," Mike said.

"There's no telling what happened to all that stuff, Mikey. The house might have been bombed to smithereens even before the ring contracted," Philip said.

"Yeah, I know. It wasn't much of a hope; just a little bit," Mike said.

There was nothing more to see, so Mike and Philip turned away from the empty lot and headed back toward the center of town.

"So if none of this proves reversion, how *would* you ever prove it?" Philip asked after a while.

"We just need to find some kind of evidence that Joey still existed sometime in the past, but *after* the point when I activated the tachometer. That would be enough proof for me," Mike said, after thinking about it for a minute.

"Yeah, but how can we do that when all the records have been destroyed?" Philip asked.

"Well, it's true the *public* records have been mostly destroyed, but surely there might still be some *private* ones left, like in old houses or such. Newspaper clippings, photos, anything like that. Let's say Joey really did make it back to the past in good shape. What would he have done next? I know he wouldn't have come back to Arkadelphia with it wrecked like this," Mike said.

"No, he probably would've gone home to Texarkana, if I had to guess," Philip said.

"Couldn't we go look down there at Justin and Eileen's house, then?" Mike asked.

"I don't think so, Mikey. That whole area was bombed pretty badly during the Union War; it's doubtful there's anything left to see. I know the house is gone, from the last time Joan and I came up here. Besides that, you're forgetting that everything past the Red River is in Brazoria now. The government would never let you leave the country like that," Philip said.

"They wouldn't have let me come here, either, if they knew anything about it," Mike pointed out.

"True enough, but I still think we should try to come up with something else first before we add illegal border crossing to our list of crimes," Philip said.

"Like what?" Mike asked.

"Maybe we're looking at things the wrong way. We keep talking about ways to find Joey, but surely if he did survive, he would've wanted to let us know it some way or other," Philip finally said.

"Yeah, probably, if there was any way he could have," Mike agreed.

"He could have written you a letter and left it somewhere he knew you'd find it a hundred years later," Philip said.

"But where would that be? He knew your address in Tampa, and he knew that's where I was going. He could've left a message there, if he really wanted to. How come he didn't?" Mike asked.

"Maybe he did. None of us ever thought to look for one," Philip said.

"Okay, so how would he have done it, then? I'm sure he would've known it might not be the same structure later on as it was way back then. So what would you do, if you wanted somebody to find a message in that case?" Mike asked.

"The only thing I can think of would be to bury it in the ground somewhere on the property, maybe in a metal box or something like that so it could be found with a detector when the time came. And then hope the people were smart enough to think to look for it," Philip finally said.

"So let's go look, then. It can't do any harm," Mike said, and Philip shrugged.

"Sure, I guess. Are we done here?" he asked.

"Yeah. We've already found out everything we needed to know," Mike said.

"We won't have time to hike back out to the fence before it gets dark this evening. We'll have to stay somewhere overnight and then hoof it tomorrow," Philip said.

"Well. . . there are beds and such, in the dorm rooms at the university," Mike said. He didn't much like the idea of spending even one night in the ruins of Arkadelphia, but if they had to then he'd have to just grin and bear it.

They quietly picked their way back through the woods until they reached the ring and stepped over, and then Philip hesitated.

"Which dormitory building do you think we should use?" he asked.

"Let's go to the one closest to where my lab used to be, if it's not bombed out. If we've got to be inside the ring then I'd like to be as far away from the edge as possible, just in case it decides to suddenly shrink again overnight. I'm not sure what would happen if it did, but I don't want to find out the hard way," Mike said, and Philip nodded.

"Sounds good to me. Lead the way," Philip said, and together they crossed the remains of the campus.

A bomb must have landed squarely on the library at some point, because the quad was littered with books lying everywhere amid chunks of brick and mortar. Pages fluttered here and there in the light breeze as Philip and Mike passed by.

"I used to spend a lot of time in there," Mike said sadly, glancing at the ruins of the library, and Philip only nodded.

They crossed a foot bridge over a deep ravine, passing by an enormous oak tree with one huge branch that was close enough to touch. Students had taken the opportunity to completely cover it with multicolored wads of used chewing gum, which had dried out hard as stone. Mike had added a few wads of his own now and then over the years, if the truth were told. It was called the Gum Tree, and seeing it brought back a wave of nostalgia and more than a little regret. He reached out to run his fingers along the lumpy surface as they walked by, but said nothing.

Gosser Hall was a four-storey residential building located just on the far side of the bridge, and it seemed to be more or less intact except for a few bullet holes and broken windows. But at least it hadn't been bombed or burned, and that was as good as they had any right to hope for.

"You don't think there'll be any dead people in there, do you?" Philip asked when they reached the front doors.

That was a nasty thought, especially since Mike had known several people who actually *lived* in that building. He didn't want to think too much about what it might feel like to stumble across the remains of one of his old classmates. He wished he'd thought of that possibility sooner.

"I hope not. We haven't seen any so far," he finally said.

"No, but we haven't been inside any buildings, either," Philip pointed out.

"It was late on a Friday evening when the accident happened. A lot of the kids went home every weekend, so the place should have been almost empty," Mike said.

He certainly hoped so, at least.

Unfortunately, they did in fact find quite a few skeletons inside the building, sprawled out in the hallways or the common rooms. Mike didn't recognize any of them, for which he thanked the Lord. Every door in the place was shot or kicked open, and there were several more dead folks inside the rooms. Whatever else one might say about the NADF, they were definitely thorough.

Mike tried not to look too closely, or even to think about it. It only fixed his own blame in the situation that much more firmly. He didn't want to know who those people were, or what kind of lives they might have had ahead of them if not for Micah McGrath and his tachometer.

"If I remember right, I think the fourth floor was closed for renovations. Maybe there won't be any skeletons up there," Mike said quietly.

That seemed to be the case; there were still ladders and painting supplies in the fourth floor hall when they made it up there. They soon found a double-bunked room as far from the stairs as possible whose windows were unbroken, and set their packs down in the middle of the floor. Neither of them said a word about what they'd just seen on the lower floors.

"I think this'll do," Philip said.

Nothing disturbed them during the night, but they were both eager to get up and leave as early as possible the next morning. Mike felt almost like he'd spent the night in a graveyard.

"Does it look any smaller than yesterday?" Philip asked when they reached the ring.

"I don't think so, but it's hard to say for sure. If it is then it's not by much," Mike said, scrutinizing the line. He wished he'd paid closer attention the day before to the exact location of the ring; even movement of an inch or so would have been good to know about. But there was no use worrying about it now.

The journey back out to the fence was uneventful, and as soon as they got there, they uncovered the bikes and rode back to Rockport to fetch the car.

They stopped somewhere in Alabama for the night; Mike was too preoccupied even to notice the name of the town. He wouldn't have admitted it to Philip, but after seeing the remains of Arkadelphia, Mike was privately convinced he didn't have much time left. A few months, maybe a year, and then he'd be gone just like Joey. He might possibly find himself back in the past where'd come from, but what did he care about that anymore?

He lay wakeful and sad that night, barely sleeping at all, and it wasn't till almost daylight that he finally closed his eyes.

Chapter Ten

It was mid-afternoon when they finally arrived back in Tampa, and Philip went immediately to a hardware store to buy a metal detector and a shovel.

"Now the next question is, how do we pull this off? I'm pretty sure whoever lives there now won't like it much if we show up and start digging holes in their yard with no explanation," Philip said.

"Maybe we could dress up like we're from the gas company or something like that," Mike said.

"Maybe, but let's go see if anybody lives there first. It's possible the place might be in between renters right now," Philip said. They cruised by the house without stopping, and sure enough, there was an old car sitting in the driveway.

"Scratch that idea, then," Mike said.

"Never mind. There's a costume shop over on Forty-Second Street. I'm sure we can find something in there to make us look official," Philip said.

They ended up finding a couple of NADF uniforms, and that seemed like the ideal choice. People didn't question the Defense Forces; not if they valued their lives.

"You know we're gonna strike terror into those poor souls, showing up on their doorstep dressed like this," Mike said.

"Yeah, but I can promise you they won't mess with us," Philip said.

Nor did they. The residents turned out to be an elderly couple, and Mike thought one or both of them might literally have a heart attack on the spot while he and Philip explained that they needed to search the yard with a metal detector. It was all Mike could do not to try to comfort them. But that would have been completely out of character, so he kept his face cool and uninterested the whole time.

"Where do you think we should start?" he asked Philip in a low voice when they got outside.

"There's no telling, really. We'll just have to go along slow and easy and make sure we cover the whole yard. It might take a while," Philip said.

They methodically searched the entire lot, being careful not to overlook even the flower beds or the front walkway. In short order they located eighty-six cents worth of loose change, three bottle caps, and a rusty set of fingernail clippers, along with several other unidentifiable bits of scrap metal. It was time-consuming work, but they were rewarded at last with a strong signal near the exact center of the back yard.

"There's something substantial down there, not just a dime or a quarter that fell out of somebody's pocket," Philip said.

Mike grabbed the shovel to start digging, and about a foot down he struck something solid.

"What did I hit?" Mike asked, and Philip knelt down to brush away the sandy soil.

"It looks like a block of concrete," he said, sounding puzzled.

"How could that be? Concrete wouldn't set off a metal detector," Mike said.

"No, there's got to be some metal down here somewhere. Keep digging," Philip said.

It turned out to be a cinder block; one which someone had filled up with concrete to make it solid. They pulled it out of the ground, but there didn't seem to be anything under it except dirt.

"Wait a minute. Look here," Philip said, brushing away the last of the sand. Mike leaned over to see what he was talking about, and saw that someone had carved his initials in the concrete while it was still wet, as people were apt to do sometimes. They were old and worn, but there was no mistaking what they were. J.J.W.

"Josiah James Wilder," Philip said, giving voice to Mike's own thought.

"Could be just a coincidence," Mike said, hardly daring to hope.

"Do you really believe that?" Philip asked.

"No," Mike finally admitted.

"There you go. Jo-jo was here at some point and left his initials in this block. I'll bet you anything you like," Philip said.

"Jo-jo?" Mike asked skeptically, and Philip laughed.

"Sorry. We used to call him that when he was a baby," he said.

"Seems like an awfully cryptic message," Mike said.

"Maybe it was the only thing he could think of that he knew would last long enough. But it might not be *all* he left. According to the detector there's something metallic inside this block," Philip said.

"So, what then? You're gonna bust up the concrete to find out?" Mike asked.

"The thought did cross my mind," Philip said.

"Go for it," Mike said, shrugging. Philip went to the car to fetch a hammer from the trunk, and then went to work on the block. It didn't take long before the whole thing was smashed to bits.

"Look what I found," Philip said in satisfaction, pushing aside rubble and powdered concrete. Underneath was a metal box about the size and shape of a wallet. It was made of red aluminum, and Mike recognized it immediately.

"That's Joey's wallet. He always liked the metal kind because he said they didn't rub the bar codes off his credit cards like the other kind did," he said, and was rewarded with a memory of teasing Joey that he'd end up with a permanent dent on his butt from sitting on that hard chunk of aluminum for too long. It seemed like ages ago.

"Come on, then. There's nothing else in there, so let's leave these poor people alone," Philip said, and Mike nodded. They quickly refilled the hole, and then drove across town to a supermarket parking lot.

"We really need to get these uniforms off as soon as we can. They attract a lot of attention," Mike said. The car itself had one-way glass, of course, but he knew they'd be the object of immediate scrutiny the instant they stepped outside. They quickly changed clothes in the car, putting the uniforms back inside their boxes to be returned to the costume store.

"Okay, let's see what's in that wallet," Philip said.

Mike had trouble getting it open and finally had to break the latch, but once he did it opened easily. Inside was a brass key and a single sheet of paper. It was only slightly yellowed with age, and this is what it said:

Hey buddy,

If you're reading this then I guess you figured out I'm back home. I didn't know any other way to get you a message, and I thought you'd probably figure out how to find this one sooner or later. We left another one buried at my mom and dad's house next to the front steps just in case you didn't find this one, but since you did I guess it's all good.

There are some things I need to tell you. When I disappeared from the parking garage I popped up in Rockport, exactly two days after you discharged the capacitor. Things were a mess. There's a huge crater right now where the middle of Arkadelphia used to be, and everything for about ten miles outside of that was frozen like the North Pole. Worse than that, even; trees and wooden houses shattered from the cold, and so did people and animals, even. They say the temperature must have dropped close to absolute zero there for a while. The Army has the whole place roped off and they're not giving out much information, but I do know that much.

Matthieu still had copies of Dr. Garza's original lab manuals, so we took them to several physicists to see if we could figure out what's going on. This is what we came up with; We think the bubble ring is shrinking slowly from the outside in, and reappearing back where it came from. We think that's what happened to me, and that it hurt so much because I had to leave behind all the molecules I picked up in the future from breathing and drinking water and all that. They got ripped out of my body when I went back to the past. We're not totally sure about that part, but I know I was sick as a dog for almost a week after I got back. We think I reverted back when the edge of the ring reached the place where I was sitting when you discharged the capacitor. I was really close to the edge, so it didn't take long to yank me back. You were at the very center so you're in a much different situation than I was.

We think the ring will stabilize at whatever maximum size is possible and then everything inside that point will never revert. That seems to be what six out of ten of the physicists believe. Three others think the reversion will keep slowing down but never quite stop, but by the time it gets really close to the center it'll take so long to finish that it might as well be permanent; several hundred years at the very least. And then the last one thinks we're all crazy. So take your pick, Mikey, but the general opinion seems to be that you're permanently stuck in 2136. I'm sorry to be so blunt about it, but I felt like you needed to know, if you don't already.

We also figured out a way to send you some things. Take the key and go to the Horizon Bank of Tampa, or whatever the place might be called by then. It fits safety deposit box 3299, and the rent is paid up for a hundred and fifty years. They thought we were nutty, but they accepted it. There are some things for Cam in there, too.

I talked to your mom and dad, so they know where you are and what happened. They said to send you their love, and then a couple of things in the box are from them.

I really don't know what else to say, bubba; seems like anything I come up with sounds lame. I hope we'll get to see each other again someday, but if not then I hope you'll think of me now and then and maybe laugh a little for old times' sake.

Your best friend,

Josiah

Mike put the letter down, his heart full. However apologetic Joey might have been for telling him he was stuck forever in the future, Mike treasured those words. It was the best news his friend could possibly have given him, and the second best news was that Joey himself was alive and well, back in his own time. Mike smiled to himself, and then put the letter and the key back inside the aluminum wallet before stuffing it in his front pocket.

"The power supply must have been set on enthalpy, if it sucked all the heat out of everything like that," he said, thinking aloud.

"I remember there was a setting on the tachometer for ENTH, but nobody knew what it meant," Philip said.

"Well, that's what it means. Latent heat of molecular motion. Not normally usable for anything; I wonder how Dr. Garza pulled that one off," Mike said, and Philip could only shrug.

"No idea. But I'm awfully glad to hear what they said about the bubble ring stabilizing at some point," Philip said.

"Yeah, me too. I'm pretty sure now that I won't disappear like Joey did, at least. Or if I do then it'll be so far in the future that it won't matter anymore," Mike said.

"Oh, I dunno, Mikey; you might startle some poor soul a thousand years from now, if they see your bones vanish into thin air," Philip said.

"Ha. If anybody's messing with my skeleton a thousand years from now then they deserve to get startled," Mike said, smiling a little in spite of himself.

"Good point," Philip agreed.

"I don't think it'll happen, though," Mike said.

"Why not?" Philip asked.

"Because of what Joey said about not being able to take molecules from this time back into the past. People don't keep the same molecules in their bodies all the time, you know; stuff is always getting replaced. Our bodies are kind of like a curve in a waterfall; we keep the same shape all the time but it's always different water. It takes about eleven years to completely replace every molecule in your body. So if I'm here longer than eleven years then I'll be made up completely of new molecules from this time and I wouldn't disappear no matter what. All the molecules that used to be part of me when I first got here might disappear, but they'd be so scattered throughout the world by then that nobody, including me, would notice even if they *did* vanish," Mike explained.

It was comforting in a way to remember that he'd be completely safe after eleven years, but in another way it was kind of scary, because it meant that in the meantime he'd be very *unsafe*. Suppose Joey were wrong and he reverted to the past after only five years, when his body would be made up of about half old and half new matter? He'd end up getting torn apart like a moth-eaten rug, without a prayer of survival. The thought was gruesome.

"So if we're only like the curve in a waterfall, and there's not a shred of matter that we could ever put a finger on and say that that's really *us*, then what *are* we?" Philip asked.

"That's an awfully deep question, Philip, and one which I don't have the slightest idea how to answer," Mike said dryly, and Philip laughed.

"Well, it can wait. Just curious, that's all," he said.

"No doubt. But I guess we better quit jawing and go see what's at the Horizon Bank before they close. Do you know where it is?" Mike asked.

"Yeah, I think so," Philip agreed.

Philip did know where the place was, and apparently it hadn't changed names in the past hundred years. No one seemed to blink an eye when they went inside and asked for Deposit Box 3299, but then Mike supposed there was no reason why they should. The bank might have thought it was strange a hundred years ago for someone to want to pay his fees so far in advance, but on this end there was no reason for them even to notice. The box rent was paid up and Philip had a valid key, and that was all they cared about.

A bored-looking bank employee fetched the box from the vault, and then escorted them to a small windowless room so they could examine the contents in privacy. It was about the size of a shoe box, and that could have left room for many different things.

"What do you think's in there?" Mike asked, as Philip fitted the key in the lock.

"No idea. I guess we'll find out soon enough," Philip murmured. Mike heard the lock snick open, and then Philip gingerly lifted the lid. The first thing they saw was a piece of white cloth, which turned out to be a t-shirt with matching holes in the front and back. Philip laughed.

"What is it?" Mike asked, mystified.

"I never thought I'd see *that* again," Philip said, turning the shirt over in his hands and still laughing a little.

"What's so special about a holey t-shirt?" Mike asked, and Philip sobered a bit.

"I got shot one time in Tennessee, wearing this. Bullet went right through here," he said, poking his finger through one of the holes.

"Oh. I guess I never heard *that* story before," Mike said.

"I'm surprised Zach never told you. Matter of fact, here's the very slug that did it," Philip went on, pulling a spent bullet on a string out of the box.

"It's a wonder it didn't kill you," Mike said, staring at the shirt. Those bullet holes were uncomfortably close to the chest.

"It was a true miracle it didn't," Philip said, and then put the shirt and the bullet necklace aside on the table before rummaging around some more.

"What else is in there?" Mike asked, trying to look over his shoulder.

"Well, there's this," Philip said absently, pulling out another necklace of a different kind. It had a metal chain, with a clear crystal the size of a peach pit for a setting. Mike recognized it as something Zach had worn occasionally.

There were several other things in the box, including a wooden music box that had belonged to Joey's mother Eileen. Philip gingerly turned the key and opened the lid, silently listening while it played part of Bach's *Jesu, Joy of Man's Desiring.*

"I'm surprised it still works after all this time," Mike finally said.

"Yeah, me too. I'll have it checked over at a music shop, though, just in case. Eileen always knew I liked it," Philip murmured.

There were pictures and knick-knacks of various kinds, including a heavy dagger made of truesilver, which Mike recognized as another one of Zach's possessions.

"Here's something for you for a change, Mike," Philip said, handing him a ring.

"That's my father's class ring," he said, turning it over in his hand. It was gold, with a dark red garnet. On one of the side panels was a cowboy holding the reins of a horse while he knelt in front of a cross, and on the other side was a Texas flag and a Confederate flag with the poles crossed, and below them the caption *Texas Rebel.* Mike wryly put it down after a minute; that was his father, all right. Country boy to the core.

There were other things he knew were for him, too. A solid glass ball about the size of an apple from Zion National Park, with a sprig of preserved wildflowers inside and a caption that read *In Beauty be it finished.* It had been collecting dust on his parents' trinket shelf for as long as he could remember. There was also a carved wooden bear cub his uncle Marcus had made for him at Christmas one year.

"Seems like mostly trinkets and keepsakes," he finally said, kind of disappointed. Nostalgia was nice, but not all that helpful in any practical way.

"What were you expecting?" Philip asked.

"I don't know; something a little more useful, maybe," Mike said.

"Don't look down on the past, Mikey. A man is only the sum of his memories," Philip said mildly.

"I guess so," Mike said. He didn't know if he entirely agreed with that statement, but he didn't want to argue about it either.

"Here's something a little more practical for you," Philip said. Down at the very bottom of the box were two hard-bound books of the kind you write in, and across the front was written *Lab Manual – Andrew Garza, Ph.D.*

"Cool!" Mike said, reaching for the manuals eagerly.

"Matthieu never let the last copy of anything leave the library," Philip said, but Mike was barely paying attention. He was too busy flipping through the pages of research notes, and before long he was so engrossed that he wouldn't have heard a fire alarm even if it had gone off in the very room where he was standing. Philip let him read for a little while, and then finally broke the silence.

"Well, I think I'll leave most of this stuff in here, just for safety's sake. There's no reason to take it home where it might get lost," he said at last, and Mike nodded absently.

Philip did take the music box and the dagger with him, for whatever reason. The music box to have it checked over, no doubt, but Mike neither knew nor cared why he took the knife. Mike himself took all the items he'd been given, and then everything else went back to its place in the vault.

He had answers now, or at least some of them. Joey was safely back home, Mike himself wasn't going anywhere, and the tachometer had serious limitations he'd never suspected before. All very good things to know.

But most importantly of all, he now had the keys to help fill in the gaps in his tachometer research, thanks to Dr. Garza's lab manuals. In spite of his uneasy relationship with the NADF, he couldn't help feeling just a twinge of excitement about that.

He couldn't wait to get started.

* * * * * * *

Life went on pretty normally for the next few months, and when they found out in June that the baby was a boy, Mike immediately wanted to name him Tycho, after Tycho Brahe the famous astronomer. Annabelle was skeptical to say the least.

"That's the weirdest, most geeky name I ever heard in my life," she objected, and he laughed.

"Well, so what? I've heard names a lot more unusual than that," he said.

"Yeah, I'm sure you have. Why do you like that awful name so much, anyway?" she asked.

"Hey, Tycho Brahe was a hero and one of the greatest scientists who ever lived. I want the kid to have somebody to look up to," he said, but she still looked unconvinced.

"Hmm. Is that your only reason?" she asked.

"No. . . there was a Saint Tycho, too, a long time ago in Cyprus. I want him to remember that, too," he said, on a somewhat more serious note.

"Anything else?" she asked.

"I'm sure I could think of some more reasons, if you really want me to," he said, and she finally laughed.

"Not gonna give up, are you?" she asked.

"Nope," he said.

"Okay, then, we'll name him Tycho. My poor, poor baby," she said, laughing again and shaking her head at the same time.

"Cool," he agreed in satisfaction.

"I do insist on one thing, though," she said.

"What's that?" he asked.

"He's got to have a normal middle name, at least, in case he decides later on he wants to use that instead. Not saying he will; I just want him to have the option, that's all," she stipulated.

"Well. . . all right," he agreed. He could grudgingly see her point, even if he didn't like it.

"What do you think about Nicholas?" she asked.

"Any special reason for it?" he asked, raising an eyebrow.

"Yeah, actually there is. That was my father's name. He was a rebel soldier who never came home, and I *also* want the kid to have something to look up to," she said, and he nodded.

"I agree. That's perfect," he said.

"So, Tycho Nicholas McGrath he will be," she said.

And so he was. He was born at the end of October, two weeks after his cousin Jesse James Carpenter, with dark hair and eyes like Annabelle's. They soon took to calling him Tyke for short, although Annabelle laughed at that, too.

"Tyke and Mike. How cute. He's really gonna hate us for that someday when he gets a little older, you know. Watch and see," she warned, though Mike could tell she wasn't really serious.

"Nah, it'll be all right," he said.

On so many different levels, he truly hoped he was right about that.

Chapter Eleven

Years passed, and when Tyke was three, Annabelle graduated from the University of South Florida with high honors. Then, just as her advisor had promised, she immediately moved into a faculty position in the math department.

"You know something? I think Jesse can do math in his head the way I can. Isn't that cool?" she asked Mike one day while they were sitting outside on the patio.

"Very cool. But how do you know?" he asked.

"I was over there talking to Joan today and playing with him a little bit and she was telling me about it, so I gave him a problem he could understand and sure enough, he told me the answer, just like that," she said, snapping her fingers.

"Well, hey, at least one kid out of the bunch inherited such a useful trait," he said.

"Yeah. I wish Tyke had it too, but I don't see any evidence of it yet," she said sadly.

"He's still young, babe. Give him a little time," he said diplomatically, giving her a hug. Tyke himself seemed oblivious to the conversation, playing with one of the black beetles that lived in the bark of the palm trees. He was a quiet and solemn kid who rarely spoke or even laughed, but he seemed to love nature at least.

"Maybe he'll be a biologist," Annabelle said wryly, watching him play with the bug.

"You never know," Mike agreed, shrugging.

Just then the phone rang, and Annabelle got up to go answer it. When she got back, she had a puzzled look on her face.

"Who was it?" Mike asked.

"Just Joan. She asked if we could come over for supper tonight about six," Annabelle said.

"Sure, I guess," Mike said.

"Yeah, that's what I told her," Annabelle said.

"Was something wrong? You don't usually have that kind of look on your face over a dinner party," Mike said.

"No. . . she just said she wanted to talk to me later, that's all," Annabelle said.

It was out of character for Joan to be so anxious to have a talk, and Mike couldn't help wondering what the big issue might be. But he didn't press Annabelle for more details; one never knew who might be eavesdropping, after all.

He didn't forget about it, though, and when they finally arrived at Philip and Joan's house that evening at five thirty, he was ready for answers.

The first thing he was confronted with when he walked in the front door of the Carpenters' house was a young couple whom he'd certainly never met before.

"Mike, Annabelle, I'd like to introduce you to Luther and Jenine Anderson. Luther is an intelligence officer with the NADF office in Asheville, North Carolina. He can be trusted," Philip added.

Once all the introductions and formalities were over it was time to eat, and while they ate they talked about various inconsequential things. Mike couldn't help noticing that Luther Anderson wore an Avenger's ring, and that seemed so out of place for a member of the Defense Forces that he had to look twice to make sure his eyes weren't deceiving him. He was so accustomed to thinking of them as ruthless and bloody-handed control freaks, it was hard to put aside prejudice and accept reality.

"Luther helps us a lot, finding out things that are going on in the world which wouldn't necessarily matter to the NADF, but which matter an awful lot to *us*. If he sees something like that, he passes along the information and then we can assign one of the group to go take care of it. We've been able to do a lot of good that way," Joan said, in between bites of steak.

"I can see how he might," Mike agreed.

"We've been trying to get him and Jenine to transfer down here to Florida so there's not as much risk of getting caught, but no luck yet," Philip said, and Luther Anderson smiled at the good-natured jab.

"Maybe one of these days, Philip. You know what I've always said about how I don't think it's a good idea for all of us to be bunched up together in one place, just in case anything goes wrong. That's my sober opinion as a strategist," Luther said.

"Yes, I know what you've said, and I respect the wisdom behind it. But considering the nature of the conversations we often need to have, it strikes me as safer on *your* behalf if we could meet privately in person instead of using phones and email which might be potentially traceable. You've done a wonderful job of keeping things hidden so far, but sooner or later everyone slips," Philip pointed out.

"True enough. We'll keep it in mind," Luther said, putting his hand on Jenine's, who nodded and murmured agreement.

"How's the baby doing?" Joan asked.

"Growing like a weed, of course. He's not really such a baby anymore, though," Jenine said.

"No, I guess not. He's the same age as Jesse, right?" Joan asked.

"That's right. Three months older, I think," Jenine said.

They continued with light conversation for the rest of the meal, until the table was cleared and all of them were sitting around the coffee table in the living room. Then Philip cleared his throat.

"We didn't want to discuss it at the table, but Luther came down here tonight partly because he's found some information about you and Annabelle," Philip said, looking at Mike with a very serious expression.

"What is it?" Annabelle asked.

"I think we'll let Luther explain all that; it's better to get your story firsthand when possible," Joan said.

"Okay, first things first. You *are* the same Micah McGrath who's the head researcher on the tachometer project, right?" Luther began.

"Yeah, that's me," Mike agreed.

"All right then. I'm not sure if you're aware of it, Mike, but the NADF is becoming impatient with your lack of progress on the tachometer. I recently intercepted an email from Colonel Burns, who directs the special projects division for the Southern Command, which includes the tachometer project. He was highly dissatisfied, to say the least," Luther said.

"I know the work hasn't been going as well as I'd like for quite a while now, but there are technical problems that are almost impossible to solve. I've had to-" Mike began defensively, but Luther waved him down.

"They don't care about all that, Mike. They want results, or else Colonel Burns is ready to cut off funding and use it for something more productive. In fact, he specifically said in his email that if there hasn't been a significant breakthrough by the end of this year, the project will be terminated as of December 31st," Luther said.

"I see," Mike said.

"But that's not the worst part. If the project *is* terminated, then Colonel Burns has specifically ordered that you and your family be liquidated immediately as security risks," Luther concluded.

"But. . ." Mike said, and honestly couldn't think of a single thing more to say.

"I'm afraid that's the brutal reality, Mike. But there's more," Luther said.

"More?" Mike asked, barely able to take in what the man was saying. Suddenly finding himself under a potential death sentence left him feeling ill and shaky.

"Yes. Colonel Burns has also ordered that if you *do* finish building a functional tachometer, or if it ever becomes clear that the program is useless or unworkable, then you're to be liquidated anyway," Luther said, and at that Mike found himself absolutely speechless.

"But why should that be, Luther?" Philip asked.

"Because he won't be any more use to them at that point. He'll suddenly switch from being an asset to being a potential security leak. You have to understand, this is nothing personal to Colonel Burns; he's charged with safeguarding the security of the Southern Command, by whatever means necessary. In his mind, it's better to sacrifice one man for the sake of protecting the interests of the nation. That logic isn't going to change," Luther said.

"So you're basically saying we're dead whether I give them the tachometer or not?" Mike asked, finding his voice.

"I'm sorry, Mike," Luther said.

"Then we'll have to get them out of here while there's still time," Joan said briskly, and for the first time Mike felt a glimmer of hope.

"Where would we go?" he finally asked.

"Well, there are several possibilities we could consider. It'll have to be somewhere outside the Union, of course. That goes without saying," Philip said.

"Why don't we send them to Damon's place in Brazoria?" Joan suggested, and Philip and Luther both nodded thoughtfully.

Mike tried to think of what he knew about the Republic of Brazoria. Long ago, there'd been a handful of areas around the fringes of the old United States and Canada who managed to make good on independence during the wars that birthed the North American Union, and Brazoria was one of them. It included everything between the Red River and the Rio Grande. Most of Texas, along with parts of Louisiana and New Mexico and even a small slice of Arkansas. They had a reputation for notoriously rocky relations with the administration of the Union, which meant they wouldn't be very likely to cooperate in the hunt for an escaped scientist. Better yet, it would feel almost like going home. Both Mike and Annabelle had grown up there, back in the old days.

It sounded promising.

"Who's Damon?" Mike asked.

"He's another Avenger. He lives in Natchitoches, in West Louisiana. He's Matthieu Doucet's great-grandson, if you remember him," Philip said.

"Oh, okay. Yeah, I remember Matthieu," Mike said.

"Damon's an interesting character, I'll say that much for him," Joan said.

"That he is. But what do y'all think about going to Brazoria?" Philip asked.

"It sounds good to me, if we can find a way to get there," Mike said, and Annabelle nodded in agreement.

"Leave that part up to me. I'll give Damon a call and see when he can come get you. He's a pilot, you know; he'll probably be glad for an excuse to come over here," Philip said.

"They'll never let us just walk out of here from the airport, Philip," Mike pointed out.

"Yeah, I know that. You'll probably have to meet him out on the Gulf somewhere; they still let you go sailing, don't they?" Philip asked.

"Yeah, so far, anyway," Mike agreed.

"Good. Tell you what; here's a set of coordinates. Go to that exact spot on the first cloudy Saturday after today, and I'll tell Damon to meet you there a little bit after nightfall," Philip said, writing down a set of numbers and handing them to Mike.

"Why cloudy?" Mike asked.

"Just in case, that's all," Philip said cryptically, but Mike didn't have a chance to ask him what *that* was supposed to mean.

"I'd be very careful and keep a really low profile for a while after I got there if I were you. Natchitoches is right on the border, and I know Lieutenant James in the Vicksburg office wouldn't be above doing a quick raid across the river if he thought he could get it done fast and get away with it. Don't underestimate your opponent," Luther warned.

"We'll keep that in mind," Mike agreed.

As it happened, the next two Saturdays were frustratingly clear, and Mike walked on pins and needles the whole time, expecting something to blow the plan at any moment. They never discussed it again, but he began packing stacks of cash into an old backpack until it was crammed so full it wouldn't hold another single bill, and Annabelle did the same. The rest of the money they moved to Philip and Joan's house, although they had to be careful about that; whenever they took a bag of it over there, they made sure to cover the top layer with baby clothes or food or some other innocuous item like that, and they didn't dare do it too often, either.

The majority of their funds were still in the bank, and they didn't dare touch those lest it make someone suspicious that a plot was afoot. If worse came to worst, it would simply have to be sacrificed.

But at long last there came a Saturday morning that dawned gray and cloudy, but no rain was expected. That was an important point, since people might have wondered why they were going sailing in a downpour.

They drove down to the marina and walked to the boat, trying to look nonchalant while carrying such enormous quantities of cash on their backs. No one at the marina paid them any attention, and that was all to the good.

Mike sailed leisurely northward along the coast for a while, as if they didn't have any particular destination in mind, and then headed out for deeper water. There were only a few boats out that day; a given, with the weather conditions as they were. He sailed the boat smoothly to the coordinates Philip had given him, checking with the onboard GPS system to make certain they were exactly where they needed to be. It was still several hours till dark, but he'd brought poles and tackle so they could pretend to fish for marlin in the unlikely event that anybody showed up.

Then they waited.

"Do you think he'll come?" Mike asked worriedly after a few hours had gone by.

"I'm sure he will. It's a long way, Mike. Give him some time," Annabelle said.

About eight o'clock that evening, a small seaplane appeared from the west and came in for a landing maybe a quarter mile away. Then it taxied up as close to the boat as possible.

"You're Micah McGrath?" the man inside asked, opening his door. He was older than Mike had expected, with thin gray hair and a face that looked like it had seen a lot of rough years. He had to have been pushing seventy, at least. His voice was tense, and Mike wondered why.

"Yeah, that's me," he confirmed.

"Come on, then. Get aboard, and hurry," the man said, opening the rear door. They quickly scrambled aboard, carrying nothing with them but the backpacks. Annabelle buckled herself in next to Tyke in the back seat, and Mike took shotgun next to the pilot. As soon as they were strapped in, he turned around and took off in a hurry.

"Why such a rush?" Mike asked.

"They know I'm here, that's why. I don't think they know what for, exactly; they probably think I'm trying to smuggle something. Which I am, of course; just not exactly what they think," he said, with a hint of humor in his voice.

"What makes you think they know you're here?" Annabelle asked.

"They've been following me all the way from Morgan City, way back in the distance where they wouldn't think I'd notice. But watch and see if they don't get real curious when they see me coming back this soon. They might even try to make us land and search the plane," he said.

"I didn't think they could do that in international waters," Mike said, shocked.

"They do whatever they want to, sonny boy, if they think they can get away with it," the man said darkly, and Mike had no answer for that.

"By the way, my name's Damon. Damon Doucet," he said, and offered his hand. Mike shook it, and then Annabelle, and Mike took note of the Avenger's ring on his left middle finger. Damon was by far the oldest Avenger Mike had ever seen or heard of, but he supposed that was really none of his business to judge. The man could fly, and he was willing to risk his own neck pretty substantially for their sakes, and that was enough.

Damon flew the plane down close to the surface of the Gulf, to better avoid radar he said. But that only worked for a short while, because before long another small plane appeared from the north.

"Uh-oh. I was afraid of that. Here we go," Damon muttered, and Mike tried to swallow the sudden lump of fear that came up in his throat. Sure enough, he saw the unmistakable insignia of the North American Defense Forces on the tail of the plane, and before long a voice came on the radio politely asking them to land. Damon ignored it, and soon the voice came back with a harder edge this time, telling him if he didn't land immediately then he'd be shot down.

"Young pup over there flying tonight. Don't know much. That's good," Damon muttered.

He suddenly banked hard to the left and went into a steep climb at the same time, shoving Mike and Annabelle up against the doors from the sudden shift in momentum and making Tycho squeal. Damon himself seemed to take it in stride, tapping a code on the computer screen and pressing a flashing red button with one hand while he steered the plane with the other. The sharp staccato rhythm of automatic gunfire reverberated in the cabin, and the other pilot must have been taken by surprise at the sharp turn of events. It took him at least two or three seconds to return fire, and even then his aim was wild.

But he didn't give up, and the other plane definitely had a stronger engine than the one they were in. He was gaining on them, and his aim was getting better, too. One bullet smashed the window right in front of Mikes head, sending stinging flecks of glass against his face. Damon cursed in French and did some more fancy maneuvering, but didn't seem scared at all.

They were way up amongst the clouds by then, and for a second Mike dared to hope they might be able to elude their pursuer that way, but Damon didn't relax. It was still daylight when he popped out above the clouds, and they found themselves flying over what looked like a tranquil meadow of fluffy cotton balls. But the other plane was hot on their heels, and as soon as it appeared out of the clouds the gunfight resumed immediately.

For several minutes they played cat and mouse amongst the mountainous thunderheads, and then Damon pulled the stick back so hard that for a few seconds they were actually flying upside down and coffee cups and pens and various assorted trash rained down off the floor onto the ceiling all around them, while they were held in place only by their safety belts. For a moment they were right above and behind the other plane, and Damon laughed.

"Eat this!" he yelled, and pressed another flashing button on the console. Seconds later the entire tail end of the other plane exploded in a white ball of fire. It immediately entered a nosedive, and Damon was quick to follow closely behind it.

"What are you doing!" Mike yelled, when the trash had fallen back to the floor again and his stomach had stopped doing loop-de-loops.

"Got to follow him. They're watching us on radar! Want to make them think we both crashed!" Damon yelled, and that made sense, in a crazy kind of way. He pulled out of the dive in the nick of time before they hit the ocean, and then scuttled away from the scene hugging the waves as close as he could. He seemed exhilarated.

"Man, what a fight!" he exclaimed, as if it were the most exciting thing he'd done in years.

"You get in dogfights like that very often?" Mike asked, brushing dirt off his chest and out of his hair. Tyke was screaming, and Annabelle was trying to comfort him while brushing the trash out of her own hair.

"No, only once in a while. But they all know I'm the best!" he said proudly.

"I hope that young man got out okay; he was just doing his job," Annabelle said softly, and Damon nodded.

"*Ouai*, missie, I'm sure he did. I only aimed for the tailfin; he had plenty of time to eject. Now he'll even have a tale to share with his grandchildren, how he tangled with Damon Doucet and lived to tell about it!" Damon said, and Annabelle laughed.

"You sure are an interesting character, Mr. Doucet," Mike said.

"You don't know the half of it, sonny boy. Now, they'll be out looking for us soon. No doubt they already know that other pilot was in a gunfight and shot down, though hopefully they don't yet know we survived. But that young whippersnapper will likely tell them so, as soon as they find him. We can't be any more obvious than we have to be," Damon said, and proceeded to switch off all the lights on the plane, both inside and out. There was a pale ghostly light from the moon beyond the clouds, and the greenish phosphorescence of the waves uncomfortably close below them, but that was the only light there was.

"Can you see well enough to fly?" Mike asked uneasily.

"Well enough, yes. The sea is calm tonight, and there's nothing to hit. It's a tiny risk, yes, but not so much as getting caught by the Defense Forces again," Damon said.

"You're the pilot," Mike said noncommittally.

"That I am. Don't worry, folks. I've done this longer than y'all have been alive. We'll make it home safe and sound," Damon promised.

Mike wondered privately if the old man had any idea who they were and what their real ages might be; he suspected not. But then again, age is measured in experience, not in years, so maybe he was right after all.

Fortunately the NADF didn't seem to realize they'd survived, or if they did then they never found them. Around three o'clock in the morning they made landfall at Vermillion Bay, and Mike felt a wave of relief wash over him.

They were finally in Brazoria.

Chapter Twelve

Just before the sun rose, Damon landed the plane on a private airstrip near Natchitoches, West Louisiana, and they wearily stumbled to a waiting car for the drive into town.

"You really *don't* live far from the border, do you?" Mike said uneasily, noting on the map that the Red River flowed just east of town. It was uncomfortably close to Union territory on the far bank, and Luther's warning about cross-border raids came vividly to mind.

"Yes, but don't worry. No one lives in the bottoms on the far shore, and there's not even a bridge or a border crossing here. It's not as close as it seems, in some ways," Damon said.

"This is Matthieu's place," Mike said when they pulled up to the curb in front of a fine old house made of red brick. He'd only been there twice, but he still recognized the place.

"*Ouai*, that was my great-grandfather. But we'll talk more about that tomorrow. Right now we all need rest," Damon said.

They sleepwalked through the door and practically collapsed into the bed he showed them, having to put off curiosity till later.

They slept most of the day, and Mike woke up near evening with a headache, feeling grungy and uncomfortable. Annabelle and Tyke were still asleep, so he carefully got up and went to the bathroom to clean up a little and take a hot shower. After that he felt much better, and even ventured downstairs in search of something to eat.

The old house didn't seem to have changed much in a hundred years; a little dustier and less tidy, perhaps, but still quiet and full of books, even though Damon didn't strike him as the type who liked to read very much. But when he walked past the door to the dining room, he caught sight of a pretty girl with long braids sitting at a mahogany table with a paperback.

"Um. . . I hate to bother you, but is there anything to eat?" he asked, and the girl looked up with a smile. She couldn't have been more than fifteen or sixteen.

"Sure. Papa had to go out for a while, but he told me y'all might be waking up soon and to give you whatever you asked for. My name's Katrina, by the way," she said, getting up to offer her hand.

"You mean like the-" he began, and she laughed.

"Yeah, like the storm. But anyway, are you very hungry or just a little bit? I can cook something if you'll tell me what you like," she offered.

"You don't have to go to that much trouble, really, whatever you've got is fine," he said.

"Well. . . let's go see what we can find, then," she said, and moved past him down the hall till she reached the kitchen. She went immediately to the refrigerator, surveying the contents critically and chewing on her lip.

"Would fried chicken be all right?" she asked uncertainly.

"That would be wonderful," he agreed, and she proceeded to take a package of chicken drumsticks out of the refrigerator along with a container of milk and a box of breading. Then he sat at the table while she breaded the chicken and started it cooking. After a while she covered the frying pan with a lid and came to sit across from him at the table.

"The secret to good chicken is to cook it slow," she confided, and he smiled a little.

"So are you still in high school?" he asked, for the sake of something to say.

"Yeah, for two more years anyway. Then I'm out of this dinky little town," she said.

"Going off to college?" he asked.

"Yeah. Not sure where, yet, but we'll see. Someplace that has a good biology or chemistry program; I love all the sciences," she said.

"Really? I'm an astronomer myself, and my wife is a math professor," he said, and the girl wrinkled her nose.

"Well, except for *those* kinds of science. No offense," she said apologetically, and Mike laughed.

"Oh, well. Can't win them all," he said. He wasn't offended, just amused.

Katrina got up to check on the drumsticks and turn them over, and then came back to sit down again.

"It'll be done before long. Anyway, Papa says you're from Florida, right?" she asked.

"Well, sort of. That's where we live, but we're both from Texas, actually," he said.

"Really? Where?" she asked.

"She's from Mount Pleasant and I'm from Ore City," he said, thinking to himself that Katrina Doucet had more curiosity than a cat on steroids.

He was spared any more quizzing when Annabelle appeared in the doorway with Tyke, who was still yawning.

"Aw, he's so cute! Does he like chicken?" Katrina asked, reaching out to poke Tyke's belly with her finger. He stared at her solemnly at first, and then a faint smile appeared on his lips, and finally a laugh.

"To answer your question, yeah, he likes chicken. He'll eat pretty much anything that doesn't run too fast or bite back too hard," Annabelle said wryly. He could tell that she'd had a shower, too, but there were still circles under her eyes from the long night.

"How are you feeling, sugar baby?" he asked, giving her a kiss and then kissing Tyke too. She sighed.

"Well, I'd be a liar if I said I'd never had a better day, but I'll get over it. I'm just glad we're finally safe now," she said, and he nodded.

"Amen to that," he said with feeling.

Katrina was busily serving the chicken while they talked, and for a little while they ate with a mixture of silence and desultory conversation

"Did your father say when he'd be home?" Mike asked after a while, and Katrina shook her head.

"He didn't know for sure, just sometime this evening. I think he expected y'all to stay here for at least a few days, though," she said.

"Oh. Well, I guess we'll talk to him when he gets here, then, if not tonight then tomorrow," Mike said. He had a lot of questions to ask Damon and a lot of plans to make, but he felt tolerably safe at the moment and all those things didn't seem quite so urgent as they would have back in Tampa.

And that was a good feeling, indeed.

Damon still hadn't shown up by the time he and Annabelle got ready for bed, so they didn't wait on him.

"Do you think they'll come looking for us?" Annabelle asked quietly.

"I hope not," he murmured, although in his heart of hearts he suspected it was highly likely. His work was too valuable for them to let him escape *that* easily.

"I hope they never make any connection between us and Damon, and they think we drowned at sea when the boat sank," she said.

"Maybe they will," he agreed.

"Where do you think we should go from here? We can't stay with Damon and Katrina forever, you know," she said.

"I've been thinking about that," he said.

"And?" she asked.

"Well, I know one place we maybe could go," he said.

"Where's that?" she asked.

"It's possible I could get my family's ranch back, if the state hasn't already sold it to somebody else a hundred years ago," he said.

"Do you think that's such a good idea? That's a place where you've got known connections; they might be able to track us down over there," Annabelle said.

"I don't think so. Everybody keeps talking about how all the records from before the Union War got wiped out, and that's really the only way I know of that they could connect me to the place," Mike said.

"Well. . . true. It's still pretty close to the border, though. You know what Luther said about that," Annabelle said.

"It's nowhere near as close to the border as Natchitoches," he pointed out.

"Yeah, that's true too. I guess it might be worth going to see," Annabelle finally agreed.

"I'll call the tax assessor tomorrow and see how it's listed; that'll tell us a little bit, anyway," he said, and with that plan in mind he went to sleep.

The next morning, Damon met them at breakfast.

"Now, y'all can stay here as long as you need to. I know you'd rather be a little farther away from the border if possible, but I know it might take a little while to find somewhere to go," he began, waving his fork in the air as he ate his bacon and eggs.

"I'm sure we'll find somewhere soon. We don't want to impose," Mike said.

"No, it's no trouble at all. Just me and Kat here in this big old house. Plenty of room for visitors," Damon said.

"If you don't mind me asking, what happened to your wife?" Annabelle asked.

"Don't rightly know, to tell you the truth. She was a lot younger than me, ended up finding her a trophy buck and running off to Dallas with him. Haven't seen her since Kat was a baby," he said.

"I'm sorry," Annabelle said, and Damon shrugged.

"Some things were never meant to be, that's all. Old coot like me should have known better than to get married in the first place, much less to a little slip of a thing like her. I was forty-nine and she was twenty-one, if that tells you anything. We were doomed from the get-go," Damon said.

"How did you meet her?" Annabelle asked innocently, and Damon hesitated.

"She was an exotic dancer at a club in New Orleans," he finally admitted, and Annabelle's face turned a shade of crimson rarely seen outside a box of crayons.

"Oh!" she said, and Mike would have laughed if it had been anyone else. But as it was, the kindest thing he could do was to pretend not to notice her embarrassment.

"Well, at least you have a beautiful daughter out of the deal," he said, and Damon seemed glad to change the subject, too.

"*Ouai,* at least there's that much. She *is* beautiful, isn't she?" he agreed, taking another bite of eggs.

"She certainly is," Mike said.

"Tough, too, and she can fly almost as well as I can. It'll soon be time for her to start going on these midnight dogfights over the Gulf and such; I'm getting too old for that kind of thing. But enough talk about that. The first thing we need to do is get you some transportation. Philip said you'd be bringing some cash; do you have enough to buy a car?" Damon asked.

"Yeah, no problem," Mike agreed.

And so it was that Damon took them to a car dealership on the west side of town, and Mike paid cash for a used but still sturdy Dodge Esperanza, the most nondescript-looking vehicle they could find on the entire lot. The last thing they wanted was to attract attention with something flashy.

As soon as that was done, they bought some new clothes and a few other necessities they hadn't had time or space to bring with them from Florida, and then things were much more comfortable.

But as Annabelle had pointed out, they couldn't move in with Damon and Katrina permanently, no matter how well they got along. Nor would they have wanted to even if they could have. In spite of what Damon had said about no bridges, Natchitoches was much too close to the border for comfort.

Mike found his thoughts turning to Goliad again, but when he called the county assessor he received a surprise.

"Now that's weird," he said, as soon as he got off the phone.

"What's weird?" Annabelle asked.

"The place is still listed in my father's name, and somebody's been paying the taxes every year so I guess they haven't had any reason to think twice about it," Mike said.

"I wonder who it could have been," Annabelle said.

"I have no idea. But I sure would like to find out," he said.

So they made the two hour drive, and when they arrived at the old place it was in sad shape. The fields and pastures Mike remembered were gone, grown up in dense woods. The white rail fence had disappeared, and even the driveway was impassable, though he could tell where it had once been.

"I barely recognize the place," he muttered under his breath.

"Well, let's get out and see. We drove all this way, we might as well look," Annabelle said. So they parked at the edge of the road and headed up the old driveway on foot, pushing branches out of the way. There were wild yellow roses growing profusely everywhere, and the thorns were wickedly sharp.

Before long they came to a huge pecan tree, and Mike stopped.

"This tree should have been in the center of the circle drive. The house ought to be right in front of us," he said, although they still couldn't see it.

They struggled through thickets for a little while farther, till they finally stumbled against a set of flagstone steps leading up to the porch. The porch was like a green cave heavily overgrown with vines and dead leaves and creepers, and it was easy to see that the house itself had also begun to suffer the ravages of time. The screen was hanging loosely off its hinges, and the wood of the front door had warped over the years from sun and rain until it no longer quite fit the jamb. Mike had to kick it hard to get it open.

It was dim inside, and they had to wait a few minutes for their eyes to adjust before moving on. A few really determined vines had managed to make their way into the living room, but for the most part the place was clear of vegetation, thankfully. There was nothing worse to contend with indoors than a thick layer of dust on everything, and the musty smell of a place that hasn't been opened up in a long time. But there was still furniture in place, and all the other things that should have been there, almost as if the people had walked away one afternoon and then never come back.

"I wonder who lived here last," Annabelle said.

"My parents, I guess. Maybe Uncle Brandon or one of my sisters," Mike said absently. There was a portrait in a frame above the fireplace, and he quietly walked over to blow the dust away. It was of a young couple standing in a field of bluebonnets in front of a lake, next to a white wood rail fence. He was wearing a white straw hat with a black t-shirt, and her long auburn hair lay prettily against her dark blue sleeveless blouse.

"That's my mom and dad, a long time ago," he said, staring at the portrait. He could dimly remember when the two of them had still looked like that, when he was very small. Annabelle came up behind him and put her arms around his middle, almost as if she could feel his mood.

"Don't be sad, sugar daddy. Nothing is meant to last forever," she said, laying her head on the back of his neck.

"No, I don't guess it is," he said softly.

They wandered all around Goliad for several hours that day, what little there was left to see of it. The lake was still there, and some of the trees in the peach orchard, and the road up to the cemetery on top of Mount Nebo. The cemetery itself was weedy and unkempt, but it was probably the least overgrown part of the whole place when they reached it. The black wrought-iron fence was still in place, and if Mike closed his eyes just a bit he could almost imagine that no time at all had passed.

For a little while, he indulged his melancholy and visited the graves of the people he remembered or at least knew something about. Reuben and Hannah, who first settled the place. Blake and Josie, his grandparents. Uncle Marcus and aunt Jenny. He found his parents almost at the end, and hard as that was, he was comforted to see that both of them had lived well into their nineties. The inscription on their stone read

May the words of my mouth
and the imaginings of my heart
be acceptable in Thy sight,
O God, my strength and my Redeemer.

Cody McGrath had been a songwriter and Lisa a lyric poet, so perhaps those words were appropriate for the two of them. Mike got a little teary-eyed, seeing all that, and Annabelle could only squeeze his hand and murmur a few soft words of comfort.

"Come on, let's go," he finally said, wiping his eyes dry with the sleeve of his shirt, and they left the cemetery.

"I think we could make this place livable again, if you really wanted to. It'd take some work, sure, but mostly just cutting down all this overgrowth. It didn't look like the roof leaks yet, or anything major like that," Annabelle said. She was trying to be optimistic and constructive, bless her heart, but he wasn't in a mood to hear it.

"Maybe," he shrugged.

"Don't you want to? I think it could be a really pretty place, with a little work," she said.

"It always used to be," he admitted.

"Well, there you go," she said.

"Would you really want to live here, though? Way out in the sticks like this? No shopping malls, no good restaurants, no movie theaters or anything to do?" he asked skeptically, and she laughed.

"Remember who you're talking to, boy. I grew up farther out in the boonies than you ever did. I don't mind at all. The real question is whether you're ready to give up being a high powered intellectual and settle down to raise cows," she said, and as usual, she was devastatingly accurate. He could almost see his father smiling.

"You're absolutely right. I'm *not* ready for that and I never will be. Daddy might have been a redneck farmer but I'm most definitely *not,*" he said.

"Then don't do it. We'll find something else," she said, and he sighed.

"Have I really got any other choice, Annabelle?" he asked.

"Human beings always have a choice. Do this if you want to, and don't if you don't. I've already told you I'm okay with it, but I don't want you to feel like you have to," she said.

"Give me a while to think about it," he said, resigned.

Chapter Thirteen

He thought about it quite a lot that day, during the long drive back to Natchitoches. And even though working the land wasn't something he'd ever foreseen himself doing in life, he grudgingly supposed he could take care of the peach orchard, at least. The land patent only said that he had to work the place; it didn't specify exactly what that meant or how much. He didn't need to have a full-blown ranch and farming operation going on like his parents had had. He could devote a little time to raising fruit and then spend the rest of his time doing something else.

Although, when he got to thinking about it, he couldn't figure out what that something else might be to save his life. He'd been an astronomer and a scientific researcher for so many years, it was hard to imagine himself doing anything else. Maybe he could switch from astronomy to agronomy, he thought wryly.

It wasn't funny.

"I guess I'll do it," he finally said, just as they were coming into the city limits of Natchitoches.

"Do what? Move out there to Goliad?" Annabelle asked.

"Yeah," he agreed.

"I thought you would," she said.

And so it was that they moved into the old home place, as soon as Mike was able to get the power turned on and the well working. Everything else could wait.

For a while, they both had to work like demons to get the place cleaned up and even semi-habitable, and it seemed that the more they fixed and cleaned, the more things they discovered that still needed to be done. Mike tackled the driveway first, clearing out a wide enough lane to at least get the car through and park it under the old pecan tree, and then he cleared paths through the woods so they could reach all the important spots. He didn't even attempt to start on the yard or anything else yet, for he soon found there were leaky pipes to be fixed and doors to be re-hung and windows re-glazed, and on and on and unendingly on. Annabelle swept and scrubbed and cleaned till her hands were raw, and still there was more.

"I found something today," Annabelle told him at supper one night, about a week after they first moved in.

"Oh? What's that?" he asked absently, his mind lost in other things.

"An envelope with your name on the front. It was in a drawer upstairs in one of the bedrooms, all by itself," she said, pulling it out of her dress pocket and laying it on the table next to his plate. It didn't seem like anything unusual, other than a white envelope, but on the front was indeed written *Micah McGrath* in a flowing script that he recognized immediately as his mother's handwriting.

He picked it up to turn it over, but there was nothing on the back.

"I'll read it after supper," he said, unexpectedly disconcerted by the incident. It was like getting a letter from the dead.

"What do you think it could be?" Annabelle asked.

"No idea. That's my mother's handwriting so I guess it's from her, but I can't imagine why she'd write me something and then leave it in a drawer somewhere. Was it in her room?" he asked.

"I'm not sure whose was whose. It was the last one on the left at the end of the upstairs hall," she said.

"Yeah, that was my parents' room," he said.

"Well, it was in the top drawer of the nightstand on the right side of the bed," she said.

"That was the side she always slept on. But it still seems like if she wanted me to find something like that then she would've picked a more obvious place. It's a thousand wonders you ever found it, or even that we were here to find it in the first place," he said, and Annabelle shrugged slightly.

"Maybe she didn't really mean for you to find it," she said.

"Why would she write me a letter if she didn't really expect me to find it?" he asked, mystified.

"Oh, sugar daddy, you're funny. Women are like that sometimes. We like to talk, and if we can't talk to the person we want to talk to then writing them a letter is the next best thing sometimes, even if we know they'll never read it. Maybe she just missed you, that's all," she said.

He considered it, and tried to imagine a set of circumstances when he might feel like doing such an illogical thing. He supposed it was possible he might find himself in a situation like that someday, though he couldn't actually imagine what it might be.

He finished his pork chop and wiped his mouth with the napkin before heading for the living room. Reading at the table was one of those things his mother had always disliked, he recalled.

He found a spot on the old couch and sat down, switching on a lamp so he could see better. Then he opened the envelope, with more than a little trepidation. It was definitely from his mother; he saw that immediately. The handwriting on the paper was the same as on the envelope, and this is what he read:

Dear Mikey,

Letters like this are hard to write, because there are so many things you want to say and so little time to say it all. I hope you're safe and well, and remembering to say your prayers at night and think on good things. Everyone sends their love, and especially your dad and your sisters and me, and Uncle Brandon.

We know where you are, son. Joey came by to let us know. I'm not sure if you'll ever read this or not, but I figured you'd probably make it home at some point. If you haven't already found it, there's a cinder block buried in Cameron and Joan's back yard in Tampa, with a key to a safety deposit box. There's an identical one buried at Joey's house beside the front steps, just in case you can't get to the first one. It's not much, I'm afraid; just some things we wanted you to have.

Your daddy set up a trust at the bank to keep the taxes paid on this place, just in case you found yourself in a tough spot and needed a place to come home to. We didn't want you to be lost in a strange time, alone and with nothing.

I wish I could give you some comfort, Mikey; I can only imagine how it must be. The only thing I know to tell you is to cherish the time that you have, and be glad for the days you've been given. They don't last forever, and they'll pass by faster than you think.

But God is good, in this as in all things. I trust and believe that that's true, son, and so should you. No one escapes this world without trials of some kind, you and I both included. All I can say is, when your time of testing comes, trust in His love and do whatever it may be that He asks of you, even if you can't see the reason why.

One of these days when you have a wife and children of your own, make sure you give them a kiss for me and let them know I would have loved to meet them.

Love you always, baby boy,

Mom

"I love you too, Mama," he said, half to himself. After a few seconds he got up and returned to the kitchen, where Annabelle was clearing the table. He kissed Tyke on the cheek for his mother.

"There, that's from your Grandma Lisa," he murmured.

"Who's she?" Tyke asked.

"My mother," he said.

"Oh," Tyke said, not terribly interested. But then, Mike supposed he shouldn't expect a three year old to be all that interested in someone he never met before. Mike took him out of the high chair and put him down on the floor to play, and then came up behind Annabelle to put his arms around her midsection and rest his chin on her shoulder.

"Did you read the letter?" she asked.

"Yeah, it didn't really say much. She basically just said that she loved me and wished she could have met you and Tyke," he said.

"That's all?" she asked.

"Yeah, that's pretty much all. She told me about the safety deposit box in case I hadn't found it yet, and then she said something about making sure to cherish the time we've been given, and trusting God in hard times, or something like that," he said.

"Oh. Well, that's always good advice," she said.

"No doubt," he agreed.

That was all they said about it, but whatever his mother might have meant by her choice of words, he supposed they were probably wise ones. And since they were also something in the nature of a loved one's last wishes, he decided to make a conscious effort to put them into practice.

It wasn't always easy to be thankful for a day of hard and sweaty manual labor, cutting brush and saplings and fixing things. But gradually the heavy workload eased up as the place became livable, even if it was nowhere near the level of luxury they'd been used to in Tampa.

Indeed, as the summer wore away and he tried consciously to be glad for the days he'd been given, he gradually found that his heart tended to look more kindly on their circumstances than it had to begin with. Goliad was quiet, yes, and backwoodsy and perhaps even dull, but it had its compensations. Dark nights when he could lie on the rock atop Mount Nebo and watch the stars with Annabelle and Tyke, just as he'd done when he was a kid himself. Swimming in the bayou. Fresh peaches from the orchard. They weren't spectacular things, no, but he found himself enjoying these small pleasures more than he thought he would.

He took to wearing his father's ring sometimes, and the glass ball and the wooden bear cub from the deposit box he placed on opposite ends of the fireplace mantel so he could see them now and then.

Occasionally they went to Natchitoches to spend a day or two with Damon and Katrina, at least whenever Damon was home. He seemed to be gone quite a lot on secret missions both near and far, and came home looking worn and weary. He rarely talked about what he did on these expeditions, except to say that they were worth it.

"Your dad looks tired," Mike said to Katrina one day, when Damon had come in more exhausted than usual and gone straight to bed.

"Yeah. . . he's really too old to keep doing the work he does. I wish he'd go ahead and retire. I'll be turning sixteen in November so he keeps telling me to wait till then, but I'm not sure that he won't come up with some reason to put it off even after that. He loves it too much; he's been an Avenger for almost fifty years now. Longer than anybody," Katrina said.

"Shouldn't he be the leader, then?" Mike asked. He vaguely remembered something about the oldest Avenger also being the leader of the group, but he wasn't sure.

"He used to be, till Philip got here," Katrina said.

"But Philip's only twenty-five years old," Mike said.

"Well, yes and no. He's twenty-five in physical years, but he's more like a hundred and fifty in calendar years. That makes *him* the oldest, strictly speaking. Papa was ready to let somebody else do it, anyway. He never did enjoy having to assign cases and coordinate efforts and anoint new members and all that stuff the leader has to do. Not his cup of tea," Katrina said.

"What *does* he like to do, then?" Mike asked, and Katrina looked at him sidelong.

"Well. . . I'm not supposed to talk about current missions because that could be dangerous, but you're welcome to read about some of the older ones if you like. There are case narratives for every mission going all the way back to 1872, and spotty ones for about a hundred years before that. Papa makes me read them because he says it'll teach me things I need to know when I start doing it myself. If he ever decides I'm old enough, that is," she added.

"Sure. Where do I find them?" Mike asked.

"Um, everywhere, really. There's a catalog system in the computer; if you give it a keyword then it'll pull up a list of books and case histories that deal with that topic, and tell you where the book is supposed to be. Just like in a library," she said.

"All right. I'll read a few," Mike said, not giving it much more thought at the time. But later that evening when Damon was still asleep and Katrina had gone walking downtown with Annabelle, he found himself alone at the house and bored.

There were computers in every room, of course, so he went to the nearest one to see if there were anything he cared to read about. The user interface was self-explanatory; it simply asked for a subject keyword, as Katrina had said. He thought about it for a second, and then idly typed *time travel* in the box, just to see what it would say. He didn't really expect to find anything.

To his surprise, the computer pulled up two references containing that subject, which piqued his curiosity considerably.

"Now that's strange," he said aloud to no one in particular. When he followed the links, he found that one of them led him to a thick bound volume entitled *Case Notes of Zachary Trewick,* and the other was the *Lab Manual of Dr. Andrew Garza.*

Both of them were located on the second floor, according to the reference, so he quickly went to fetch them. He already had a copy of the lab manual, of course, but at the moment he was much more interested in the case notes anyway. He started flipping through them as he went down the stairs, and before long he was so engrossed that he forgot to keep walking. He just stood on the stairs and kept reading.

They told everything from Zach's point of view, naturally, and Mike knew from personal experience that the old boy wasn't averse to throwing in his own opinions about things from time to time. That part only made things more entertaining, though.

Then he came across a section which made him purse his lips and furrow his brow with concern, and this is what it said:

Justin told me once that it's perfectly all right to pray about things which took place in the past, as long as you don't know what the outcome was. Such as, you could pray that your mother survived a plane crash that happened two hours ago, as long as you don't actually know whether she did or not. Once you know, that's your answer. But the same thing holds true for things that happened hundreds or even thousands of years ago, or things that will happen hundreds of years from now. God is outside of time completely, and therefore so are your prayers to Him. In that way, it's quite possible for you to be the partial cause of something that happened long before you were even born.

Nothing at any point in time is outside your reach because nothing is outside His.

But for that very reason, looking through the tachometer at the future is like looking at God's will revealed. You can't change it because your own free choices are already built into what you see in the first place. Whatever you choose, that's the result it will lead to.

Up till then, Mike had always assumed that if he saw something happen in the future, then he could take steps to prevent it or alter the outcome. But if that wasn't so, then the tachometer was almost useless for the kinds of purposes the NADF had in mind. They wouldn't be able to prevent attacks or change future events at all.

It was scary, in hindsight. They never would've put him to work as a researcher in the first place if they'd known *that* little tidbit. He would have been a dead duck as soon as they first arrested him three years ago, or possibly rotting away in a prison cell if Lieutenant Bartow had been feeling particularly generous that day.

In fact, Mike was glad *he* hadn't known about that particular secret till now; the constant fear that it might be discovered at any time, with fatal results, would have driven him crazy over the past several years.

Then he reminded himself firmly that that was all a thing of the past, never to be worried about again. So he told himself, and as months slipped away with no sign of pursuit, he more or less came to believe it.

Indeed, by the time early fall arrived in September, he was relaxed enough that he could even whistle while he worked at times, something he'd never done in all his years at the University. In fact, he was whistling an old tune mindlessly to himself when Lieutenant Bartow stepped unexpectedly into the barn where he was fixing the lawnmower.

Mike looked up and dropped his screwdriver in shock, but before he could think or react, the man sat down. For some reason, that simple action made it impossible for Mike to run, although if he'd considered the matter he couldn't have said why.

"You've led us on a merry chase, Dr. McGrath, I'll certainly grant you that," Lieutenant Bartow said conversationally, crossing his legs and leaning back in the chair. Mike had no idea what to say.

"Surely you didn't think we wouldn't find you sooner or later, did you? I'm frankly disappointed in you, Dr. McGrath. I expected more intelligence," he went on, and then paused as if he expected Mike to answer. When nothing was forthcoming, he went on.

"In any case, we'll expect you to be back at work Monday morning. We've already notified the University," Lieutenant Bartow said, and at that Mike found some emotion.

"You can't do that," he said.

"I think you'll find that we can, Dr. McGrath. Naturally, our relationship will have to be adjusted in light of this unfortunate series of events," Lieutenant Bartow said.

"What do you mean?" Mike asked.

"You've become a flight risk, Dr. McGrath. Therefore, until you convince me it's in the best interests of the country to do otherwise, we'll be keeping your wife and child at a secure location. They're already en route even as we speak. Now don't mistake me; they'll be perfectly fine. This is just to ensure that you don't develop another sudden urge to disappear again, and to encourage you to work a little more expeditiously than you have in the past. If you're a very good boy, you might even get to visit them every weekend. Can I be any more fair than that?" Lieutenant Bartow asked reasonably.

There were a lot of things Mike wanted to say at that point, but his mouth was too dry for words. They knew all the tricks, all the pressure points, all the ways to force a man to dance to the right tune if he wouldn't do it willingly. He was trapped, and they both knew it.

His shoulders sagged in defeat, as he mentally prepared himself to be taken back into slavery.

Chapter Fourteen

On the surface, nothing much had changed when he got back to Tampa. He quietly went to work every morning and came home every evening to his empty house in Clearwater Beach. No one asked where he'd been for the past few months, and from that fact alone he knew that the Defense Forces had been twisting arms at the University to make sure he kept his job. Anyone else would have been asked to resign over such an unexplained absence, but it wasn't healthy to question the NADF.

And Mike played along, pretending the incident never happened. In fact, as time went by the whole summer really did begin to seem unreal; like a dream he'd once had or a story he'd read in a book. They'd even gone out to pick up the abandoned boat and returned it to the same old slip at the marina. If Mike tried really hard he could almost imagine that Annabelle and Tyke were just gone to visit friends for a few days.

But they weren't, of course. They were prisoners, and he was reminded of that fact every single weekend when he was allowed to visit them.

They were being kept on Edgmont Key, a small sandy island at the mouth of Tampa Bay. No one mistreated them, to be sure, but there was no chance of escaping the place either. It was much too far to swim, especially with a three year old, and even if they'd dared the waves or been able to arrange some kind of rescue attempt, he and Annabelle both had implanted, heat-sensitive tracking chips under the skin on the napes of their necks. The Defense Forces had no intention of letting them slip away for a second time.

The island itself was home to a naval station and lighthouse down at the southern tip, complete with a guard tower and a platoon of marines on call at all times. But the rest of the place was deserted, and Lieutenant Bartow had arranged for Annabelle to be given a cottage by herself up toward the north, out of sight of the base. It had its own self-contained power supply and water system, just like some of the fancier cabins that rich folks maintained in remote locations. And indeed, at times it was easy to imagine they were on some far-flung South Seas island a thousand miles from civilization. The whole set-up gave a powerful illusion of solitude and privacy, but Mike never doubted the place was bugged and telemetered so thoroughly that the NADF knew every move they made and every word that was spoken.

But no one meddled with them other than that, and if they liked they were free to walk the beach or have picnics on the dunes, or go fishing, or whatever else they pleased, as long as they didn't try to leave the island. There was an old abandoned fort with brick streets and larger than usual palm trees which Annabelle particularly liked to visit sometimes, and the jailers even let Tyke have a puppy for his birthday in October; a chocolate Labrador retriever. It was a semblance of freedom, at least, even though they both knew it had strict limits. They were reminded of it every time they wandered a little too far south and caught a glimpse of the guard tower.

Mike was reminded of it every time he went home, too, for he soon found himself under surveillance of a different kind. Lieutenant Bartow calmly moved in right next door with his family, the better to keep an eye on him, no doubt. Mike knew perfectly well that they could have watched him in more subtle ways, had they wanted to. But no, they wanted him to *know* they were watching, and Luke's presence never let him forget it for a second. The fact that Lieutenant Bartow had a pretty young wife (eight months pregnant, no less), and a daughter the same age as Tycho were just another way of rubbing his nose in things; a not-so-subtle reminder of what the stakes were in all this.

He wasn't surprised by any of it; not really. As he'd often thought before, when it came to manipulation they never missed a trick.

To add insult to injury, the man even had the gall to invite him over for supper at least once a week, and then Mike had to pretend to be having a good time all evening in front of Marie Bartow, who apparently knew nothing about what her husband's real interest in the situation was. After one of those weekly ordeals, Mike wanted to choke the man.

But it didn't stop even there. Lieutenant Bartow even deputized Marie to get friendly with Joan, who was also pregnant at the time. No doubt as a way to let Mike know he was on top of *that* relationship, too. No doubt Joan knew perfectly well what the game was, but she didn't dare snub the woman any more than Mike would have.

The only mildly satisfying thing about the whole affair was that it gave him an excuse to start calling Lieutenant Bartow by his first name, Luke, which he knew irritated the man. It was cheap vengeance, but better than nothing.

And all the while, he lived with the sure and certain knowledge that December 31st was creeping closer by the day, with inescapable death just beyond it.

He didn't let it show on the surface, but nonetheless in his heart of hearts Mike soon found himself sinking into a black pit of hopeless depression. There was no way out, and whichever way he turned he met only a brick wall. He worked slowly and carelessly on the tachometer, not really caring if he made any progress or not beyond the bare minimum necessary to keep the NADF at bay. He rarely shaved anymore except on Fridays before he went to see Annabelle, and whenever possible he took refuge in sleep from the misery of living.

Then one day a new thought crossed his mind, one so blindingly simple and stunningly elegant that he could have kicked himself for not thinking of it sooner. What if they used the *tachometer* to escape? After all, he and Annabelle had both traveled to the future once already. This time wasn't where either one of them belonged, so why should they hesitate to leave it? They could permanently ditch the NADF, escape Colonel Burns's death warrant, and never have to worry about political intrigue again.

It was *perfect*.

True, they'd have to give up some things. They'd have to leave Philip and Joan behind, and that would be hard. And then if he were to be brutally honest with himself, Mike had grown to like that fine house on the beach, and the new car every year, and all the other nice things that money could buy. That would all have to be cast aside, too.

But he was quite willing to trade all those things in exchange for life and freedom. All he'd have to do to make it work would be to finish the tachometer, find a place in the future that suited them, and then somehow smuggle the machine down to Edgmont Key. Then Lieutenant Bartow and his cronies could kiss them goodbye.

Mike seized on the new plan with enthusiasm, all his depression and hopelessness blown away like a vapor in the wind. He went to work on the tachometer with redoubled effort, spending almost every waking moment in the lab and barely taking time even to eat or sleep, so determined was he to finish the thing.

He must have made progress, because there came a day in late November when it actually *worked*. He sat there staring at it when he was done, feeling a kind of exhausted joy.

But Mike was nothing if not methodical. The very first thing he did was to run several final tests and system checks to make sure everything operated properly; the last thing they needed was a repeat performance of the accident that started this whole adventure.

As soon as he was sure everything was in order, he immediately got to work looking for a good time in the future for them to escape to. He knew he wouldn't be able to keep the tachometer a secret for long, so he needed to put the rest of his plan into motion at once.

He set the controls for twenty years ahead, for no particular reason other than the fact that it was a round number. Then he activated the tachometer, to see what the future might hold.

Tampa Bay was deserted. Completely.

Mike scrolled through the empty streets in puzzlement, but wherever he looked he saw not a single human being, nor even a cat or a bird for that matter. Tampa might as well have been a city of ghosts.

He looked elsewhere, curious in spite of himself, and found the same conditions everywhere. London, Tokyo, New York, Karachi; all of them were utterly forsaken by every living thing except the weeds growing up through cracks in the pavement.

He soon found that it wasn't just the cities, either; the small towns and villages were exactly the same. Wherever he looked on the whole Earth, there wasn't a single living soul to be seen.

Disturbed, he backed up the controls by one year and checked again. Nothing had changed.

By dint of careful looking, he soon narrowed down the time when whatever-it-was would happen. The last week in January of 2154; a little more than twelve years away.

In twelve more years was the end of the world.

Well, maybe it was a bit hasty to go *that* far; he couldn't check *everywhere* for survivors, and some of them might easily have slipped through the cracks, so to speak. He could only hope so. But even if it wasn't necessarily the end, then it was still a catastrophe of unbelievable proportions.

Nevertheless, in spite of all his efforts he couldn't figure out exactly what it was that happened, except that it was very sudden. The lack of sound on the tachometer hindered him, and so did the graininess of the image. All he could tell was that swift and total destruction had overtaken the human race, and no one had been able to stop it. When he looked more closely at the victims, all he saw were people and animals lying down and going to sleep, never to wake up. The only thing that gave him even the vaguest hint of what might be happening were the quarantine barriers he glimpsed in a few spots. That suggested some kind of disease, though the symptoms he'd seen didn't look like any disease he'd ever heard of.

He wondered uneasily if he should tell Lieutenant Bartow. Much as he hated the man and resented his presence, the NADF *did* have some power. If there were really a major calamity about to hit the world, then it was possible they might be able to do something about it. Not to prevent it from happening, no, but they might possibly find a way to save at least a few.

Telling them anything at all would be a major risk, of course. It might even imperil Mike's own escape plan, but if the catastrophe were really *that* bad then he might have to chance it for the sake of humanity. Maybe if he thought about it for a while, he could figure out a way.

He knew it probably wasn't wise, but he couldn't resist the temptation to look at his own family. He noticed immediately that his house in Clearwater Beach was occupied by someone else in 2154, and incidentally that Lieutenant Bartow had moved, also. Not all that surprising, maybe, but it left him out of luck as far as seeing anything related to his own family. The tachometer was useless unless you already knew exactly when and where to look.

He idly scrolled down the street to Philip and Joan's house, and soon found that they at least still lived in the same place. But then, that wasn't so very surprising either. The house on Papaya Street was bigger and nicer than anything they'd ever be able to manage on their own, at least not without getting into crippling debt to afford it. They had every reason to stay put.

They looked a little older, of course, and the boys were teenagers by then. The baby girl Joan should be having any day now was twelve years old, and seemingly there was another boy who must have been born a few years after her. But most interestingly of all, he saw Tyke.

There was no doubt in Mike's mind that's who it was; he still had the same solemn look on his face he'd had ever since the day he was born. Mike soon discovered that he and Jesse were both attending the advanced math and science academy downtown, and for a second he allowed himself a small flush of pride at that.

Then things changed. It was still hard to tell exactly what was going on, but from the urgent discussions Tyke went around having with various people, Mike surmised that his son must have discovered something. Close as it was to when the plague struck, he could only imagine it had something to do with that.

And so it must have. He was able to skip ahead bit by bit, until he saw Tyke board a space plane at the MacDill Aerospace Research Center just south of downtown, along with several other people. Philip and Joan were there along with their children, of course, and there were a few others Mike recognized as well. Katrina Doucet. Amos McClendon, his eager-beaver lab tech. Luther and Jenine Anderson and their three children. Then his eyes narrowed as he recognized Marie Bartow. Luke wasn't with her, although their two children were. That was puzzling, but Mike had no way of figuring out what might have happened to the good Lieutenant or why he wasn't part of the group. He forced himself to stuff his knee-jerk resentment at seeing the Bartows there; he had nothing against Marie, and certainly not against the kids.

The really disquieting thing about the whole situation was that Mike himself and Annabelle were nowhere to be seen. In fact, he hadn't seen either one of them ever since he started looking at the future.

He hesitated to guess what that might mean; several unpleasant possibilities came to mind without even trying. But he didn't know, and he much preferred not to speculate.

He couldn't tell where Tyke and the others were going. The plane moved too fast for the tachometer to scroll after it, and since he didn't know where to look he wasn't able to skip ahead and pick it up later. All he could do was pray they succeeded in whatever desperate plan they'd come up with to save themselves. God bless them and good luck to them.

Mike sighed and switched off the tachometer, unable to decide whether he should be troubled or comforted by what he'd seen. It had ramifications he hadn't fully thought through just yet.

For one thing, it bothered him that Tyke was still the same age as Jesse and still living in this time period, since obviously that could only mean that Mike's plan for using the tachometer to escape to the future hadn't worked for some reason.

For another thing, it downright alarmed him that he and Annabelle were apparently nowhere to be found. Were they dead? Captives? He couldn't imagine any other reasons why they wouldn't be there or why Tyke wasn't with them.

For a third thing. . .

There came a knock on the door, breaking his train of thought, and Amos came in without waiting for an invitation. Mike wondered if he ever did.

"Here's your lunch, boss," Amos said, setting down a tray from the cafeteria. It was his last year at the University, and Mike was supposed to be writing him a letter of recommendation for graduate school. He supposed he needed to get around to doing that before he left, if he could ever collect his wandering thoughts long enough.

"Thanks, Amos; I appreciate that," Mike said, though he really wasn't all that hungry. But before Amos could say anything else, the door burst open and hit the wall so hard it shattered the glass.

"Hey, what-" Mike said, and then the words died on his lips as he beheld none other than Katrina Doucet. Amos was staring at her in shock, and Mike wasn't far off.

"Come on, let's go. Now!" she cried urgently, and turned to leave.

"But-" Mike began, and she cut him off.

"Mike, we've *got* to go. There's a bomb about to explode any minute!" she cried.

That was enough to get him moving, and Amos too for that matter. Mike had the presence of mind to grab the tachometer as he left the room, but there wasn't time to gather up his papers and research notes. He expected Katrina to run for the exit doors, but instead she immediately took them up the fire stairs as fast as she could go.

"Where are we going?" Mike yelled from behind her.

"Up to the roof!" she called back, and even though that didn't make any sense at all, he followed her anyway. The building was only three stories tall, and it was a good thing, too. Mike was out of breath by the time he ran all the way up that many flights of stairs.

As soon as they reached the flat roof, Mike saw the reason why she'd brought them there. Someone had landed a big black helicopter up there, crushing several unidentifiable vents and antennas in the process. The engine and rotors were still running.

"I don't think you're supposed to land anything up here," Amos said uncertainly, coming to a stop in the doorway.

"If you don't come on you won't be alive to worry about it," Katrina hissed, grabbing him by the forearm and yanking him toward the copter. There was barely room for him and Mike to squeeze into the back seat, and Katrina didn't wait for them to get buckled. She took off with a roar of the engines as soon as she could get her door shut, nearly clipping the top of a tree in the process.

"You're crazy!" Amos yelled, and Katrina ignored him. She pushed the helicopter to the utmost speed she could squeeze out of it, and Mike buckled himself in while he still had the chance.

"What's going on?" he demanded, when their flight evened out just a bit.

"A group of anarchists planted a bomb somewhere on the university campus. I didn't even find out about it till about fifteen minutes ago. I already called the university police, but I didn't know if they'd have time to do anything or not. So I decided to come get you myself," she said.

"Where'd you get the helicopter?" Mike asked, puzzled.

"It's my dad's. We were at the airport when we heard about the bomb, so I grabbed the copter to come get you before it was too late," she said.

Just then there was a flash of light from behind them, and a second later an unbelievably loud explosion and a blast of hot air that sent the helicopter spinning wildly out of control.

"Get ready to crash!" Katrina yelled while she fought the controls.

No sooner were the words out of her mouth than they hit the ground with bone-crushing force, and then Mike knew no more.

Chapter Fifteen

His eyes were sticky when he tried to open them, and when he rubbed them with his left hand it came away bloody. He hurt in a million places, and for a few minutes he couldn't remember where he was or how he got there. He groaned, but if anyone heard him there was no response.

He wiped semi-dried blood from his eyes and tried to look around. All the glass in the helicopter was shattered, and the door nearest him was completely twisted off. He was lying half on his back and half on his side, still buckled in to his seat but almost touching the ground. No, that wasn't right; it was *mud*. They seemed to have crashed in a patch of swampland and partially sunk in.

He thought immediately of alligators and pythons. Some of the kids in his astronomy classes had enjoyed telling horror stories about snakes and gators attacking helpless passengers of airline crashes and boat wrecks in the Everglades, snickering while they dwelt lovingly on all the gruesome details. It was the kind of thing only a teenager would consider funny, of course, and Mike hadn't believed a word of it at the time. But still, he sure didn't want to find out the hard way that all those lurid stories were true after all.

Or even *partly* true, for that matter.

He quickly checked himself for injuries and found no obvious ones, other than cuts and bruises. There was a nasty slice on his forehead right at the hairline, which was probably where the blood in his eyes had come from. It hurt like the devil.

He glanced over at Amos, who was still knocked out but didn't seem to have any worse injuries than Mike himself did. Then he leaned forward to check on Katrina. Or tried to, at least; his seat belt had locked in place and wouldn't let him move even an inch. He fumbled for the catch with his bloody fingers and finally managed to release it, but he'd forgotten about his change in position. He fell out of his seat into the swamp, getting himself soaking wet and coated with stinking black mud from head to toe before he was able to struggle back to his feet.

Katrina's eyes were open when he managed to climb up to a place where he could see her, and that was a relief.

"Are you okay?" he asked hoarsely.

"Yeah, I think so. Can't get out, though; my legs are trapped under what's left of the control panel," she said.

"It's a wonder it didn't crush you," he said, staring at the wreckage of the copter's nose.

"Well, you know what they say. Any landing you walk away from is a good one," she said, with a weak smile.

"I didn't know you knew how to fly," he said, and then remembered that yes, he *did* know; Damon had mentioned it back in Natchitoches. There'd been a lot of water under the bridge since then.

"Yeah. Papa's had me flying almost since I learned how to walk. Lucky for you he did," she said, and Mike couldn't have agreed more. But there was something that puzzled him.

"What are you doing in Tampa, anyway?" he asked, raising one brow and then shutting his eyes when the movement sent a bolt of pain through his cut.

"We had to come see Philip. Last week was my birthday, so Papa decided it was finally time to retire and let me have this," she said, holding up her left hand. On her middle finger was the same silver

Avenger's ring that Damon had been wearing when Mike first saw him.

Mike stared at it for a second, and realized he'd barely spoken a word to Philip or Joan in *weeks;* not since coming back from Brazoria, in fact. Just a very occasional brief call, during which he couldn't have said anything substantive even if he'd wanted to. He'd told them Tyke and Annabelle were away on vacation and he was very busy with work, and that had been pretty much the extent of their conversations. At first he'd been so lost in misery that he hadn't wanted to speak to anybody, and then later on he'd been feverishly busy with the tachometer, of course.

Still, he felt a twinge of guilt for ignoring them so long.

"Well, congratulations, Katrina," he said.

"Thanks. We would've invited you to the anointing ceremony, but Philip said the NADF were keeping a pretty close watch on you and he didn't dare ask," she said.

Well, that was good to hear, in a way. At least Philip and Joan understood he was on a tight leash and it wasn't safe to have too much contact with him. No doubt the bombing would provide enough distraction that the NADF wouldn't have the time or the resources to spy on him quite as thoroughly as they had before, but he knew that would only be a temporary reprieve at best. Before long the screws would be tightened down again, as soon as things returned to some semblance of normalcy.

"Anyway, Papa was about to come get you himself when we heard about the bomb, but then Philip said to let *me* go, that it'd be a good first mission for me," Katrina said proudly.

"I think he gave you a humdinger of a first mission, girl," Mike said, staring at the wrecked helicopter again.

"Well, we thought there'd be a little more time, you know. And we didn't know the bomb would be that big," she pointed out.

"I guess. I wonder who planted it," he said.

"It was a group called the Western Brotherhood. They're anarchists. Those are people who think we'd be better off with no government at all, just everybody doing their own thing," she said.

"Yeah, I know what an anarchist is," Mike said.

"Well, they found out the University has been doing research work for the Defense Forces, and they wanted to teach other schools a lesson not to make the same mistake," she said, and Mike felt a twinge of guilt at *that,* too.

"But how did *you* find out?" Mike asked.

"Luther hooked us up several years ago with an informant who tips us off sometimes when they plan things like this. Not that he disagrees with what they're doing, you know. He just wants to give us the chance to save a few people from getting killed now and then. Soothes his conscience, I guess. If we could find a way to stop them completely we would, but in the meantime we can only do what we can do. Things aren't always perfect," she said.

"That's the truth," he muttered.

"Do you think you can walk all right?" she asked.

"Yeah, I think so," he said, after considering it for a minute.

"You may have to go get help. I doubt anybody will come looking for us out here, considering what just happened at the University. They've got bigger fish to fry right now," she said.

"That's true," he agreed.

"See if you can find Papa and Philip. They'll know what to do," she said, and he nodded. Any other time Joan would have come along, too, but of course at the moment she was nine months pregnant and big as a house, not to mention utterly exhausted.

"I'll be back as soon as I can," he said, and then hobbled off as fast as he could toward the west. South would have taken him directly back toward the University, and that seemed unwise. Thick black smoke was still rising from the remains of the campus, blotting out most of the Tampa skyline, and he wondered exactly how powerful of a bomb the Western Brotherhood had managed to plant. It must have been massive, to cause that much damage.

The sheer magnitude of the disaster made it almost impossible to comprehend. There had to be incredible destruction back in the city, untold hundreds or even thousands of lives lost. It was hard to believe even an anarchist could be so cruel as to blow up an entire university full of innocent students who mostly cared no more for politics than they did for the price of tea in Shanghai. Kids who liked to joke about plane crashes and alligator attacks, and sometimes sleep in class when they thought Mike didn't notice.

But the earth was full of blood and deceit in these last days, just as it had been long ago in the time of the prophet Micah. Mike had always had a particular liking for his namesake, of course, and now he found himself pondering something else the man had said. It was one of the most famous lines in scripture, a promise that in spite of all the murder and treachery in the hearts of men, there'd come a day when all those things would be done away with, when peace should come to a blood-stained world and things like the university bombing would never happen again.

> *For they shall beat their swords into plowshares,*
> *and their spears into pruning hooks;*
> *nation shall not lift up sword against nation,*
> *neither shall they learn war any more.*

Mike wished it could have come true already.

He thought about those and other things while he plodded steadily onward. It was hard to believe there could be such a big patch of swampland so close to the city, even in Florida. Slogging through heavy mud slowed him down, but even worse than that it exhausted him at a time when he didn't have much energy to spare in the first place. If he didn't find help soon then he might end up having to spend a whole night out there in the swamp with the gators, a prospect he didn't relish at all.

It took almost three hours before he stumbled across a deserted access road, but after that the going was much easier. He didn't know exactly where he was, but it couldn't have been *too* far from civilization. The helicopter hadn't had time to get *very* far. But there was nothing to be done except to plod along slow and steady, one foot in front of the other, till sooner or later he came out of the wilderness somewhere.

Eventually the road carried him into the suburban town of Lake Magdalene, and even there he found occasional signs of damage; broken windows and such. But for the most part things seemed to be semi-normal in that neck of the woods, and soon he was able to borrow a phone from a passing stranger.

"Philip, can you come get us?" he asked.

"Where are you? They've got the whole area around the University blocked off," Philip said.

"No, I'm in Lake Magdalene, at the corner of Main and 34th Street," Mike said.

"Is Katrina with you?" Philip asked.

"No, the helicopter crashed in the swamp. She's okay but she's stuck in the wreckage. We've got to go get her out," Mike said.

"All right. No problem. Just stay where you are and wait on us. We'll be there as soon as we can," Philip said.

Mike sat down on a street bench in utter exhaustion. His aches and pains had subsided for a while when he'd been walking, but now that he wasn't moving anymore they'd returned with a vengeance.

Philip and Damon arrived nearly two hours later, and by then evening was gathering.

"Sorry it took us so long, but the city is in chaos. It's hard to drive anywhere," Philip apologized.

"It's okay, I figured that much," Mike said.

"Where is she?" Damon asked, and Mike told him which way to go.

"We've got one of my lab techs with us, too. Amos McClendon. He was with me when Katrina showed up screaming about a bomb. I'm not sure if he's hurt or not, but he was still knocked out when I left earlier," Mike said.

"That's all right. We'll fix him up, too," Philip said.

They were able to reach the crash site faster by circling around to the north on another access road Mike hadn't known existed, and from there it was only a half mile walk back to the copter. Amos was awake when they arrived, which was a relief.

"How are you feeling, Amos?" Mike asked as soon as he got close enough.

"Aw, I've been worse," he shrugged, as if he were talking about a cat scratch or a chest cold. Mike suspected some of that was due to the need to put up a show of toughness in front of a girl, but he let it pass. If Amos was in good enough shape to care about flirting then he was probably in good enough shape not to have to worry about him anymore.

In the meantime, Damon and Philip had brought some kind of contraption to extract Katrina from the wreckage. It resembled the old Jaws of Life equipment that Mike had seen on movies and whatnot in the past, though it wasn't quite the same. In less than an hour they had her out.

Damon carried his daughter back to the car, while Mike and Philip had to help Amos, who it turned out had a broken bone in his right foot.

"Where's Joan?" Mike asked during the walk.

"She's at home with the kids, but Marie came over to sit with her just in case she has to go ahead to the hospital," Philip said absently.

"How nice of her," Mike said dryly, not liking this unwelcome reminder of how deeply Lieutenant Luke Bartow's snoopy tentacles reached into every aspect of his life. But he didn't say so.

They reached the car and slowly drove back to Clearwater Beach. Most of the roads through Tampa proper were on lockdown, so Philip had to steer them far out of the way through Tarpon Springs and Dunedin before they finally made it home.

"You're welcome to stay with us tonight if you want to, Amos; I don't think you'll make it home with the traffic all snarled up like it is," Philip said.

"I appreciate that, Mr. Carpenter," Amos murmured. He lived on campus at the University most of the time, but his parents were in Temple Terrace, uncomfortably close to the blast site.

Indeed, when they got inside the house and were finally able to see live footage from the bomb scene, the damage was horrific, even worse than Mike's bloodiest nightmares. Hundreds of blocks of northern Tampa were either leveled or heavily damaged, and windows had been shattered for miles. The University itself was utterly obliterated. There was nothing left on campus except a blast crater, and the death toll would almost certainly be in the tens of thousands, if it could ever be known at all. It was theorized that the perpetrators had used a small nuclear device of the "clean" type;

that is, one which wouldn't leave behind any contaminating radiation.

Praise God for small mercies, Mike thought to himself. If the bomb had been a dirty type, then thousands upon thousands more might have died.

"Where did a group like *that* get hold of a nuclear bomb?" Mike muttered to himself, staring at the screen.

"Nuclear technology is two hundred years old, Mikey. It's not hard to come by anymore. This isn't the first time it's been used in a bomb, nor even the worst time. I know they've been used in Spain and in China, not to mention during the Boer War in South Africa. They ended up with nearly ten million dead from *that* little episode. This won't be a drop in the bucket compared to that," Philip said sadly.

"This is the first time it's happened in North America, though," Mike said.

"Well, yes. . . but I don't know why that should come as a surprise to anybody. We're not immune to tragedy just because we speak English," Philip said.

"No, I don't guess we are," Mike said.

"I don't think the world can go on much longer like this. Mark my words; sooner or later some really big catastrophe will come, probably of our own doing, and then that'll be the end," Philip said.

"You really think so?" Mike asked, startled. His mind went instantly to the empty world he'd seen through the tachometer, and he couldn't decide whether Philip was psychic or simply wise.

"Well. . . the end of this current situation, at least. But one way or another the world will die for lack of love, and if there's anything to be saved from the ruins then it'll only be love that saves us," Philip said.

"I don't know, Philip," Mike said without rancor. He was used to Philip's habit of digging for deep truths, but sometimes the little nuggets he came up with required a lot of thoughtful chewing before you got much nourishment out of them.

"You need to come see us one day as soon as you can, Mikey. Time is short," Philip said in a low voice, and Mike nodded.

He knew well enough what Philip meant. They needed to come up with another escape plan while there was still time, but they couldn't do it with Amos in the house. Not that anybody believed the boy was a secret spy for the NADF or anything like that, but then again on the other hand you never really knew. It would have been highly foolish to take an unnecessary risk.

They were showing fresh footage of the bombing victims on TV, and Mike unwillingly watched a whole new parade of horrors march across the screen.

He thought once again of his students in the astronomy department, and all the others like them. It had been the busiest time of day on campus, with untold thousands of students in class or eating lunch. It wasn't hard to imagine the tears and the wailing of grief from a million hearts that he knew must surely have been going on at that very moment, from all the families who'd lost children that day.

Would love have saved them, as Philip seemed to think? Well, perhaps; even a little bit of love in the hearts of the Western Brotherhood might have kept them from doing what they did. But there'd been nothing left in their souls except poisonous hatred, and they were far from the only ones in that condition. So perhaps the world *would* die for lack of love, whatever specific form that might end up taking, and in twelve more years it would breathe its last gasp.

He thought of Tyke, and then finally sat down and wept at the blood and the horror of it all.

Oh, my son, what kind of world have I brought you into? he thought to himself.

And for that there was no answer at all.

Chapter Sixteen

It turned out that Damon and Katrina and Amos had to stay several days with the Carpenters, since all of Hillsborough County was put under martial law while a massive manhunt was conducted for the perpetrators of the University bombing.

To no avail. Not a single member of the Western Brotherhood was ever brought to justice for the attack.

But in time the lockdown was eased, and the airports reopened, and Amos went home to his parents and Damon and Katrina went home to Natchitoches. Then Philip and Joan's daughter was born the very next morning at the same hospital in Saint Petersburg where Joan worked, preventing all efforts to get together and talk about escape plans at least for a few more days.

They named her Veronica, a name which meant *truth*. Hunter Bartow was born two hours later in the very next room, and Mike wondered for a moment if Luke were so determined to twit him at every opportunity that he'd use even his own son's name as a vehicle to remind Mike that he could never escape or he'd be hunted down. Then he told himself not to be an idiot. If Luke had him *that* paranoid then he obviously needed to see a therapist, because he was plainly losing what few marbles he still had left.

But on a more practical note, Mike's lab and everything it contained had been completely destroyed, and he wasn't at all sure what that would mean as far as his future was concerned. Would Colonel Burns decide to cut off the tachometer program six weeks early since there was so little chance of accomplishing anything? Or would Mike simply be shifted to other facilities and told to keep working? That seemed much more likely, actually; Colonel Burns probably had too much on his plate at the moment to waste time reviewing old low-priority orders.

So Mike judged he was fairly safe for a few more weeks, as long as the NADF never found out he'd saved a working tachometer at the last minute. Whatever happened, he certainly didn't intend to tell them *that*.

But he still had to consider the scary future he'd glimpsed before the bomb exploded, of a dead and empty world with no human life to be seen. He might not be able to prevent it from happening, true, but he finally decided that at the very least he should do everything in his power to save as many as he could. Compassion demanded that much.

Unfortunately, that involved having a chat with Lieutenant Bartow. Yes, the man was treacherous and manipulative to the core, but he also had the power to make things happen. Under the circumstances, Mike wasn't above doing a little manipulation on his own account. Therefore he determinedly went next door the next morning and rang the bell. After a few minutes Marie came to the door, looking tousle-headed and tired, holding Hunter in one arm and with Leah clinging to her leg.

"Oh, hey Mike. You're out early this morning," she said, trying not to yawn.

"Yeah, I'm sorry to disturb you but I really need to talk to Luke for a minute," he said.

"Well, he's still asleep right at the minute; he's had some long nights here lately what with the bombing and everything. But it's time for him to get up anyway. Please come in," she said, dislodging Leah from her leg and moving aside. Mike followed them down the hall to the kitchen.

"Can I get you some coffee? I've got a fresh pot brewed; I was just fixing to have some myself," she offered.

"I'd love some," he agreed. She handed him Hunter without a word so she'd have access to both hands, and then quickly made two cups of coffee.

It had been a while since Mike held a baby, and he looked down to find Hunter gazing up at him with his slanted, slate-blue newborn's eyes. He had a fine dusting of sugar-white hair on his head, which was still slightly misshapen from being born.

"Welcome to this sad old world, kid. Make it better someday if you can," Mike told him in a low voice.

Then Marie was handing him his coffee, and he passed the baby back to her. His cup had a picture of a noble-looking young man in the Defense Forces, saluting a flag and standing at attention. The Bartows had lots of items like that.

"I'll wake him up in just a minute. Got to get some energy going first," Marie said with a little laugh.

"Sure, no problem. It's not *that* urgent," he agreed, taking a sip of his own coffee. He could use some extra energy himself, for the encounter that lay ahead.

Marie chatted on about the baby and some nice items she'd found at a garage sale two weeks ago and other inconsequential things of that nature. She didn't involve herself in her husband's business, and didn't even seem curious about it. But then again, maybe she realized as everyone else did that knowledge could be a dangerous thing. She seemed to have recovered remarkably well for having just had a baby so recently, but then he'd always heard some women had an easier time than others.

Luke must have woken up on his own, because just then he came padding into the kitchen in nothing but his boxer shorts. He had dark circles under his eyes, evidence of several long nights with little sleep. Mike had never seen him in such a condition before, either so exhausted or so scantily clad, but if he were annoyed to find Mike sitting in his kitchen so early in the morning he didn't show it. He simply poured himself a cup of coffee and drank the whole thing black, without even any sugar. Then he rubbed his eyes.

"Good morning, sweetie. I was just about to come wake you," Marie said.

"It's all right. Excuse me just a minute while I get dressed," he said, and then disappeared back down the hall. He returned in fairly short order, dressed as always in his somber NADF uniform. Mike wondered sometimes if the man actually owned any other clothes.

"I'm sorry to disturb you so early, but I didn't know when else to catch you at home, Luke," Mike said as soon as he got back to the kitchen.

"Well, I'm afraid there's been a lot to do the past few days, as I'm sure you understand. Was there something on your mind?" Lieutenant Bartow asked.

"Yeah, there is. I need to talk to you," Mike said.

"Come on, then. I still have an hour or so before I have to go in," Lieutenant Bartow said. Mike followed him to the last door on the right at the end of the hall, and went inside to find a home office. Lieutenant Bartow shut the door behind them and sat down at his desk.

"Can anybody hear us in here?" Mike asked uneasily.

"Marie, you mean? Certainly not. She knows better, for one thing, and besides that this room is completely soundproofed. Now, what was on your mind, Dr. McGrath? I don't have unlimited amounts of time this morning," Lieutenant Bartow said.

"Just before the bomb exploded, I finally got the tachometer working," Mike said, getting right to the point, and interest flickered in Lieutenant Bartow's cold gray eyes for the first time. It was a calculated risk, but Mike had already decided nothing less would do.

"I see. And I take it you saw something?" Lieutenant Bartow asked.

"Yeah, I did," Mike agreed, and then hesitated as if he were reluctant to go on. It was dangerous, trying to play a player like that, but Mike could only cross his fingers and pray. As he hoped, Lieutenant Bartow picked up on his hesitation.

"Dr. McGrath, I know you may have doubted me in the past, but do you finally understand why we have to do the things we do?

You see what happened at the University, and that was only one of the ones that slipped through the cracks. You have no idea how many other plots we put a stop to before they can be carried out. If you know something, please tell me. Lives might be at stake," he urged.

Now came the *really* dangerous part. He knew Lieutenant Bartow had specific orders to liquidate the entire McGrath family immediately if it ever became obvious that the tachometer program were useless or unworkable, and Mike was just about to hand him that very information on a silver platter. It was practically like signing his own death warrant.

He was counting on the fact that Lieutenant Bartow and indeed the entire Tampa NADF office were still snowed under by the aftermath of the bombing, and that liquidating a potential security risk such as himself probably wasn't a terribly urgent priority for them at the moment. They'd probably take at least a few days to get around to it under the circumstances, and with a little luck that would be enough time to slip the noose.

Unless Lieutenant Bartow shot him on the spot, of course. Mike was ninety-nine percent sure he wouldn't; that would be awfully messy and inconvenient, after all. But then again you never knew.

"Well, that's the thing, sir. Anything you see with the tachometer, you can't change. No matter what you do, that's how it'll turn out. The actions you take to prevent it might even be the very ones that end up causing it to happen," Mike said, his heart in his throat.

"So then the tachometer is useless?" Lieutenant Bartow finally said. He hadn't reached for his pistol, so maybe he didn't intend to carry out the execution immediately.

"No sir, I don't think so. You can always take action about the things you didn't see; the things you don't know yet. But once you see it, you're stuck with it. So, you couldn't have prevented the bombing once you saw it, but you maybe could have saved a few extra people, if you didn't actually see what happened to them," he said, and Lieutenant Bartow thought about this for a while.

"I don't know that that suits the purposes of the Defense Forces very well," he finally said, and Mike felt a chill at the cold-bloodedness of the statement. Then it was almost instantly replaced by a surge of anger.

"It may not. But does it suit your purposes as a human being?" he asked hotly.

"What I think and how I feel are irrelevant," Lieutenant Bartow said.

"Not even about your own family?" Mike asked.

"No, not even about them. We can argue metaphysics all day, Dr. McGrath, and neither of us will change our minds. You obviously came here to tell me what you saw, so please get on with it. You have twenty minutes," Lieutenant Bartow said, tapping his watch. Mike looked at the man with disgust, but there was no point in backing out now.

"I saw the end of the world," he said.

"Really?" Lieutenant Bartow said, placing his fingertips together like a tent and leaning a little bit forward.

"Yes. Twelve years from now there won't be a single human being left alive in Tampa Bay, or Florida, or the Union, or even the whole world for all I know. I saw the cities standing there empty, nothing but weeds and dust. *All* the cities, everywhere on earth. And there's nothing you or anybody else can do to stop it," Mike said.

"What happens?" Lieutenant Bartow asked, getting out a notepad and a pen.

"I couldn't tell for sure. It looked like some kind of disease," Mike said.

"Biological warfare?" Lieutenant Bartow asked.

"I don't think so, because there was no country in the world that was safe from it. Seems like that would be a stupid way of waging biological warfare, if it comes back and wipes out your own people too," Mike said.

"It might not have been a country. There are certain groups who think humanity is a plague on the earth and deserves to be destroyed. Most of them are pacifists, thankfully, but I wouldn't rule out the emergence of a militant one somewhere in the world. India is a particular hotbed for that kind of fanaticism, because of the belief that so many of them have in reincarnation. Destroying all of humanity wouldn't matter much, if you thought everybody would come back to life as a tree or a dragonfly and live in eternal harmony with a rejuvenated earth," Lieutenant Bartow said, and the scorn in his voice was almost palpable.

"Sounds like you know a lot about things like that," Mike said.

"I'm a counter-terrorism specialist. It's my job to know things like that," Lieutenant Bartow said tiredly.

"Well, whoever they are and whatever their reason may be, it looks like they're going to succeed," Mike said, and Lieutenant Bartow shrugged as if the thought didn't trouble him at all.

"It was only a matter of time. And you saw no survivors at all?" he asked.

"There were none that I saw, and I looked ahead for almost a hundred years. Everything was still empty. But I guess they could have zigged while I zagged, so to speak. The world is a big place. But what I do know is, there was no civilization; no countries or governments or anything like that. None of that survived. Under those circumstances, don't you think it's worth trying to save just a few?" Mike asked, and Lieutenant Bartow frowned, rubbing the stubble on his chin and thinking.

"It isn't my place to say what ought to be done about the situation, Dr. McGrath, nor yours. I'll pass along this information to the proper individuals, and then we'll see what gets decided. In the meantime, continue with your work. You've been assigned temporary lab facilities at the University of Tampa, until something more permanent can be arranged," he finally said, and Mike realized with a sick heart that that was all he'd get out of the man.

"Thank you for your time, sir; I'm sorry to have bothered you," Mike said, getting up from his chair. He said nothing about Tycho's part in the future, nor about Marie or anything else he'd seen. It wouldn't have done any good, anyway.

He left the Bartows' house wishing he'd never said anything in the first place. Lieutenant Bartow would make his report, it would get buried in paperwork on some bored bureaucrat's desk in Atlanta, and then that would be that. It was virtually certain that nothing would ever be done about it. Mike had put himself and his family at serious risk of death, and all for nothing.

Well, so be it. In spite of the danger, Mike didn't think he could have lived with himself if he hadn't at least tried.

But in the meantime, he had far more pressing issues to think about than what might happen twelve years down the road. Because sometime within the next few days an NADF soldier would almost surely put a bullet in all three of them, and Mike didn't need a tachometer to see *that* coming.

He had no illusions about how foolhardy and hopeless another escape attempt would be, especially if they couldn't use the tachometer. But the barest glimmer of hope was still better than none at all.

He had to try. Somehow.

He left the house, unable to face the thought of sitting there alone all day. Philip and Joan wouldn't be home till six o'clock or so, but he had no one else he dared speak to till then.

All around him was the bustle of an ordinary morning; kids going to school, business people talking on phones, even a few early beachcombers headed out to fish or collect shells. He watched all these things from behind his sunglasses, and for a little while he envied those people for their normal lives.

Then he was reminded of something Joey had liked to say, about how there's no such thing as a normal life and every person in the world has his own burdens and issues, most of which you'd never guess. He wondered how many of those people on the street who seemed to have it all together were really broken to pieces inside. He could believe that quite a few of them might be. After all, anyone who saw *him* walking down the street wouldn't have had the faintest clue what he was going through. They'd just see a young man in dark shades and rope sandals, like any of a million others, and never realize he was living under a death sentence.

He spent the day wandering aimlessly, staring at clocks and beachwear and electronics in the shop windows, with his thumbs hooked in his belt loops and his mind far away. He could've bought anything he really wanted, of course, but trinkets and baubles held no appeal for him anymore. He stopped at a kiosk to have a pistachio ice cream cone and a deep-fried cheese enchilada for lunch; yeah, it was horrible nutrition, but who cared anymore?

Then he slowly made his way to Papaya Street as the first long shadows of evening fell.

It was a normal evening in the Carpenter house when Philip let him in. Chris and Jesse ran up to him when he walked in the door, and he smiled tiredly and picked one of them up in each arm.

"Uncle Mikey, you know what I did at school today?" Chris asked. He'd lost his top two front teeth since the last time Mike had seen him, which made him look something like a young vampire.

"Lay it on me, bubba," Mike said.

"I climbed all the way up to the top of a tree on the playground and they had to call the fire department out there just to get me down!" he said proudly.

"You didn't get scared, way up high like that?" Mike asked.

"Nope, it was fun," Chris said.

"You've been a real daredevil today then, haven't you?" Mike asked, and Chris nodded.

"Well, y'all run along, boys. I need to talk to your daddy for a while," Mike said, so they both squirmed down and ran off, dear old Uncle Mikey already forgotten in favor of more interesting things.

"So what's up, Mike?" Philip asked.

"Where's Joan? I'd really like to talk to her too," Mike said.

"Just a second; I think she's upstairs. Have a seat and I'll be back down in a minute," Philip said, so Mike did. Before long Philip came back down with Joan, who looked tired.

"Sorry, Mike. I was just getting Veronica to sleep finally. What can we do for you?" she asked, sitting down next to Philip on the couch across from Mike.

"I think maybe I did something stupid today," he admitted, not trying to sugarcoat it.

"Is it something the boys need to hear about?" Joan asked.

"No, it'd probably be better if they didn't," Mike said, and Joan nodded.

"Hold on a second, then. Let me get them out of the way," she said, and proceeded to herd them next door to the neighbor's house.

"Andrea said she'd keep them tonight; I told her we had an emergency come up," Joan said briskly, as soon as she got back. The house seemed unnaturally quiet with no kids running around.

"All right, Mikey. It's safe to talk now, whatever it is," Philip said, when Mike still hesitated.

He tried to think where to start.

Chapter Seventeen

"Okay, then. First of all, ever since we got back from Brazoria two months ago, the NADF has been holding Annabelle and Tyke prisoner down on Edgmont Key, to make sure I behave myself," Mike said.

"Yeah, we figured that much. We knew you couldn't talk about it, but things like that are not hard to guess. That's why we never asked too many questions," Joan said.

"I hoped you'd guess; I hated having to lie about it," Mike said.

"It's okay. We all understand what the circumstances are," Joan said.

"Right. Well, anyway, I remembered what Luther Anderson said about how Colonel Burns wanted to terminate the tachometer program at the end of December, so I knew I had to think of some way to escape again before the time was up. For a long time I couldn't think of *what*, though. They've been keeping such a close eye on me, it seemed like anything I came up with was impossible," Mike said.

"Yeah, that's the problem we've had, too. We've been trying to think what could be done ever since you got back here. But it wasn't safe to try anything again too soon, and then we haven't seen you much lately to talk about it, either," Joan said.

"Yeah, I know; I'm sorry about that. But anyway, after a while I got to thinking if I finished the tachometer, then maybe we could use that to escape into the future where they couldn't touch us. So I worked really hard on it, and I finally got it working the same day as the bombing," Mike said.

"So then we just need to find a way to smuggle you out to the island and then everything will be fine," Philip said, sounding relieved.

"Well, I *wish* it could be that easy. But I saw some things in the future that I don't understand, except to say that we can't use the tachometer to escape, after all. So now I don't know what to do. But whatever it is, it'll have to be soon. Like within the next few days," Mike said.

"We've still got several weeks before the end of December," Joan pointed out.

"Yeah, we do. But that's what I wanted to tell you about. I went to Lieutenant Bartow's house this morning and told him the tachometer couldn't be used to change the future," Mike said.

"What possessed you to do such a thing as *that?*" Philip demanded.

"Because there's something really bad on the way, something that will make the university bombing and even the Boer War look like a cakewalk. In fact, I think it'll kill practically everybody on Earth. I thought maybe the NADF might at least have the power to save a few people, if they knew about it ahead of time," Mike said, and went on to tell them about the plague he'd seen with the tachometer.

"It doesn't surprise me; I've been expecting something like that for a long time," Philip said sadly.

"You did the right thing, though, Mikey. We don't blame you for trying," Joan said, clasping Philip's hand.

"No, but it *does* mean we won't have near as much time to work with for any kind of escape plan," Philip said.

"How much time *do* you think we have?" Mike asked.

"If I had to guess, I'd say Lieutenant Bartow probably has in mind to get rid of you sometime this weekend, while you're all three down there together on the island. That way it'll be quick and easy, with no witnesses. I don't think he'll wait another week," Philip said.

"I think he's probably got it planned for Sunday evening," Joan said quietly.

"What makes you think that?" Philip asked.

"Well, Marie talks about her husband all the time, you know. I feel like I know him better than my own brother sometimes. He's a slave to protocol and he's completely ruthless when it comes to serving the greater good as he understands it. But he's not quite so far fallen that he takes pleasure in cruelty. He still has a faint tinge of conscience. A man like that would give you and Annabelle one last weekend together, as long as it didn't interfere with his orders or cause him any problems. Then he could kill you on Sunday evening and still feel good about himself," Joan said.

"It sounds like you've known him all your life," Mike said, impressed. He was certain she was right in her analysis; that was exactly the way Luke Bartow would think and behave. Mike wasn't entirely surprised, though; Annabelle had that same piercing insight at times, sharper than a razor's edge.

"It's not hard to read between the lines, if you pay attention," Joan said.

"Well, at least that gives us a *little* breathing space, then," Philip said.

"Not much, if there are any arrangements that have to be made," Joan said.

"Which is exactly why we've got to finish hashing this out tonight. Did they put a chip in you, Mikey? That's what they usually do when they want to be able to track somebody," Philip asked.

"Yeah, me and Annabelle both. Right here on the backs of our necks," Mike said, turning his head to expose the small scar where the chip had been embedded.

"All right, then. The first thing we'll have to do is to cut those out," Philip said.

"I know that much. But what then?" Mike asked.

"We'll have to find somewhere for y'all to go. You really should've stayed with Damon for a while when you got to Brazoria, Mike; Luther said the only way they ever found you last time was because you went to a place they knew you had connections to. You've been too loose with your tongue these past few years; you've told too many people where you're from and how you grew up and all kinds of things like that. All the NADF had to do was go snooping around asking questions. You can't be that careless next time or you'll end up dead," Philip said sternly.

"I know," Mike said, chastened.

"Brazoria is out; Luther says they've already been alerted to keep an eye out for you, that you're a known terrorist with links to the University bombing. You're liable to be shot on sight if they find you in their territory. Same thing with Cuba and most of the Mexican city-states," Joan said.

"I was afraid of something like that," Mike said.

"There's always Campeche, I suppose. *They* wouldn't care two cents how big of a criminal or a terrorist you might be. I know it's an awful place to live, but it's better than nothing," Philip said.

Mike privately had his doubts about that. Campeche was usually lumped in as one of the Mexican city-states, but in reality it was an artificial country, a city built on steel pilings driven into the shallow seabed of the Campeche Bank, out in international waters nearly a hundred miles north of the Yucatan Peninsula. It was barely more than an overcrowded slum in the middle of the Gulf, a refuge for outlaws and criminals of every stripe and kind. There were quite a few such artificial city-states here and there in the world, built atop seamounts or underwater ridges or wherever the ocean was shallow enough. Campeche was the only one in the Gulf; the Union and even Brazoria had never allowed any such places to gain a foothold near their own shores. But Mexico had been too weak and divided to do likewise, and now Campeche was too large and strong to be gotten rid of.

Nevertheless, it was a hellish place in every sense of the word, and only a fool would ever set foot there.

Unless, of course, you were rich. The upper crust in Campeche had all the luxuries that people anywhere else were accustomed to. Mike had no shortage of money, but still, it was just the *thought* of it.

"I wish there was somewhere else than that," he finally said reluctantly.

"So do I. But it's the only place I can think of where you *might* not get caught, unless you decided to go hide out in the Everglades and turn into a swampbilly," Philip said.

"No, I think even Campeche is better than that," Mike said quickly.

"Then we'll see what we can do about getting you there. The first problem will be getting y'all off that island without getting caught," Philip said.

"How can we do that?" Mike asked.

"It won't be easy. I'm certain they scan the sea all around the island and they'd notice any kind of boat with a motor; the heat signature alone would give it away even if the radar didn't," Philip said.

"Damon said it breaks up radar signals if the water is rough," Mike said.

"It does. But that won't help the heat problem; not unless we used a little row-boat and had everybody wear thermal suits to hold in your body heat," Philip said.

"I think we'd roast, trying to row a boat two miles across the Bay in choppy water with a thermal suit on. Even at night," Mike said.

"I don't doubt it'd be uncomfortable, Mike. You might sweat off ten pounds by the time you made it to shore. But I don't think you'd die," Joan said.

"But how would we get a boat in the first place, though?" Mike asked.

"We'll get to that part in a minute. First of all, how well do they search you when you go over there?" Philip asked.

"It depends. They always go through my bags pretty thoroughly, if that's what you mean," Mike said.

"What about body searches?" Philip asked.

"Well. . . they *usually* just pat me down and let it go at that. But they've also strip-searched me now and then, just to make sure I know it could happen, I guess. You never really know," Mike said.

"Are you willing to risk a strip search tomorrow evening?" Philip asked.

"To smuggle what? An inflatable boat?" Mike asked wryly.

"No, just a pack of razor blades. So you can cut out your tracking chips,"

"Yeah, I'll stick them in my underwear. Even when they do a strip search they don't usually look in there," Mike said.

"All right, then. Here's what we'll do. I'll slip over there Saturday night in a rowboat and pick you up on the eastern shore of the island. I'll be waiting in the first mangrove thicket as you head southward. Have your chips out already by then, and I'll bring the thermal suits with me. We're supposed to be getting some blustery weather that night, so that'll help. Be there at ten o'clock," Philip said.

"Why couldn't you just bring the razor blades then, too?" Mike asked.

"Because it'll be dark and we can't risk a flashlight to let us see anything, that's why. We don't need any last minute delays," Philip said.

"Okay, so what then?" Mike asked.

"We'll cross over to old Fort Desoto and meet up with Joan. She'll drive us to the marina in Treasure Island. I'll have Damon buy you a boat with a strong motor and park it there. Then head out for Campeche as fast as you can go. You won't have long before the guards figure out something's up and start looking for you," Philip said.

"No, not long at all, after our tracking chips don't show any movement and don't register any body heat," Mike pointed out.

"I think I've got a solution for that, anyway. It won't last forever, but it'll buy us a little time," Philip said.

"I'd love to hear it," Mike said.

"You said Annabelle had a dog, didn't you? So have him swallow the chips after you cut them out. He'll move around and show movement, and it'll be close enough to body temperature inside his guts that it won't set off the alarm," Philip said.

"Well. . . I guess that *might* work," Mike admitted.

"I still wouldn't dally, if I were you. There are a thousand things that could happen which might make them suspicious enough to come check on you, and once they do then the game is up," Joan said, and Mike nodded.

"All right, then. That's what we'll do. Saturday night at ten o'clock, right?" Mike asked.

"Right," Philip agreed.

"I don't know how to thank you both," Mike said.

"Thank us by getting away and living happily ever after," Joan said, and Mike laughed and hugged her for that.

"Okay, but I need to tell you something else while I still can, now that you mention all that stuff about living happily ever after. When the plague comes, I saw a few people escaping on a space plane, including you and the kids and several others. Don't know where you were going, though," Mike said.

"That's good to know, but you probably shouldn't tell us much more than that; not even exactly when it happens. *Twelve years from now* is close enough. It feels too much like wearing a straitjacket, when you know too much and can't change anything," Joan said.

"I do wonder where we managed to come up with a space plane, though. As far as I know, nobody's had one of those since the Union War. One of the many technical skills lost and then never recovered, I'm afraid," Philip said.

"Yeah, I did wonder about that myself. The space program has been allowed to decay to such an extent that we can barely maintain the satellites and the stations anymore. It's really shameful from a scientific standpoint," Mike said.

"Well, be that as it may, I don't foresee the government making any big push to get back into space within the next few years. But nevertheless, *somebody* must end up developing a workable space plane before the plague strikes, if you're sure that's what you saw," Philip said.

"I'm absolutely certain that's what I saw," Mike said.

"Any idea who might be working on something like that?" Joan asked.

"How would I know?" Mike asked.

"Well, you're an astronomer. I assume you'd keep up with whatever's going on in space science," Joan pointed out. That was true to some extent, and Mike thought carefully.

"There are always people interested in reviving the space program, especially in Florida. I know there's one lady right here in Tampa who keeps pestering everybody she can think of to fund her project to develop a new long-distance space vehicle. She's kind of an idealistic flake, but she's the only one I can think of offhand," he said.

"What's her name?" Philip asked, grabbing a pen and a piece of paper.

"Um. . . Weiss. Peggy Weiss. She's an astrophysical engineering professor at the University of Tampa. Why do you ask?" Mike asked.

"We might have to see about funding her work, if you think twelve years is enough time for her to accomplish anything worthwhile," Joan explained.

"Yeah, she ought to have enough time to get something done, if she had the money. But how would you manage *that?*" Mike asked. He knew full well that Philip and Joan didn't have the kind of cash to fund research programs; even *he* didn't. Talking about it was laughable.

"Damon inherited a pretty large fortune, actually. He's got the money to fund something like that, if I asked him to," Philip said.

"He'd do that, just because you asked? Wouldn't he want to leave it to Katrina?" Mike asked.

"He'd do it if he understood the reason why. If he knows this modern world is coming to an end in only a few more years, then he'll also know money won't be worth anything after that, anyway. Why keep it if it's no good?" Philip said.

"That's true," Mike admitted.

"All right, we'll see about getting that arranged, and doing whatever else we can do to be ready when the time comes. It'll take some thought and some deliberate choices about a lot of different things between now and then. But in the meantime, I think we'll keep all this on a strictly need-to-know basis. We'll have to tell Damon, of course, but aside from him it'll be top-secret information. Don't you think, babe?" Philip asked, turning to Joan.

"I definitely agree. The fewer people who know, the better. Besides Damon, not even the other Avengers need to know," she said firmly, nodding her head.

"Okay, one last thing. Do you know anybody who's good with computers?" Mike asked.

"Like what do you mean?" Joan asked.

"I mean a good hacker," Mike said, and neither of them even blinked.

"I believe we could get hold of one," Joan said easily.

"Good. I need somebody to hack into the Defense Forces computer downtown and erase all my research notes since I started working at the University," Mike said.

"That might be a dangerous assignment, Mike. What's the purpose behind it?" Philip asked.

That was a hard question, since Mike had trouble explaining it even to himself. But he knew he didn't want the NADF getting their hands on a tachometer of their own. True, it might not suit their purposes of manipulating the future, but it still might turn out to be an excellent escape hatch for some of the leaders of the administration and the Defense Forces when the plague arrived. That was the very thing Mike did *not* want. If the plague had to happen at all, then it was far better that mankind should start off with a clean slate, free of the mistakes and the heavy hand of the past. It was best that the current crop of leaders be completely wiped out, since it was their policies in large part which had led to the current sorry state of affairs in the first place.

"I don't want them to know how to build a tachometer. They always made me enter everything I worked on into the database, so it wouldn't take much for them to reconstruct what I did," Mike said, and then went on to explain his reasoning.

"I think you're right, Mike," Philip said, and then turned to his wife.

"Let's go ahead and get Jennifer over here tonight so she can get started on that project immediately. Once Mike disappears they're liable to increase the security level on those files even higher than it already is," Philip said. Joan nodded, pulling out her phone to text someone.

"Can she come over tonight?" Philip asked after a while.

"Yeah, she'll be here in just a little bit," Joan said.

Jennifer Rayburn arrived in about thirty minutes, and immediately set up her computer on the coffee table. Mike noticed that she also wore an Avenger's ring, unsurprisingly.

"So what are we doing tonight?" she asked after a few minutes. Joan hadn't discussed anything like that by text, naturally.

"We're erasing some files from the NADF mainframe," Philip said, and Jennifer smiled slightly.

"Well, hey, we all love a good challenge, don't we?" she murmured, cracking her knuckles. Then she got started. She must have been a computer genius, because her hands flew across the keypad faster than Mike's eyes could keep up with them, while she kept her gaze focused intently on the holographic screen.

"All right, we've got fourteen minutes before they realize we're not supposed to be in here. What needs to be erased?" Jennifer finally said.

"Anything having to do with Micah McGrath, or tachometers, or time travel, or Arkadelphia, or the Clark Containment Zone," Mike said, and Jennifer immediately got back to work, typing feverishly.

"All right, it's done," Jennifer said, shutting off the computer. There were still almost two minutes to spare.

"Thanks, Jen; you're a lifesaver," Joan said, giving her a hug.

"No problem. I better go ditch this hot little notebook before they track it down, though. I'll see y'all in a few days," Jennifer said, and then hurriedly left; presumably to get rid of the computer she'd used.

"She was an Avenger, too?" Mike asked after she left.

"Yeah, we wouldn't trust that kind of job to anybody who wasn't. Jen's our technology expert; I bet she could make a computer dance ballet and sing the blues if you asked her to," Philip said proudly.

Mike reflected that he'd now met five of the six Avengers in this time. Philip and Joan, Damon (well, Katrina now), Luther, and Jennifer. He wondered who the last one might be, but it didn't seem the time to indulge his idle curiosity.

He left the Carpenters' house soon afterward, going home to pack up what few things he cared to take with him. He doubted they'd have time to stop by the house on the way to the marina Saturday night.

He didn't have much, actually. Pictures, money, his mother's letter from Goliad, his father's ring, a few other odds and ends. The plan seemed like a good one, even though he knew of a thousand things that could go wrong.

He could only hope that nothing did.

Chapter Eighteen

The next evening he rode the Defense Forces cruiser from the naval station in Saint Petersburg out to Edgmont Key, just as he'd done every weekend for the past two months. His heart was in his throat the moment he stepped off the dock, but the guard only rummaged through his bags for contraband and patted him down in a desultory kind of way before waving him on. They never noticed the pack of single-edged razor blades stuffed inside his underwear, and it was all he could do not to sigh with relief when they let him through. They put him outside the northern wall of the compound, just like always, and then he had to walk the mile and a half or so to where the cottage stood.

Then for a night and a day he walked the sands, and lived quietly, and said nothing at all to Annabelle about the upcoming escape attempt. But when Saturday evening came, he knew he couldn't put it off any longer.

"Come on, sugar baby; let's take a walk," he said lightly, offering his hand and doing his best to smile.

"It's awfully late for a walk on the beach," she said.

"I know, but we won't go far. Bring Tyke's life jacket though, just in case we decide to swim a little," he said. He didn't dare say anything incriminating while they were still inside the cottage, of course.

So they walked along the bayward side of the island, throwing sticks for the dog and talking about nothing in particular. It was indeed a blustery evening, just as Philip had predicted, with gusty wind and occasional spits of rain. Mike was glad to see it.

He could make out the point of Fort Desoto and the line of the Sunshine Skyway Bridge across the choppy waters of the bay, maybe two miles off. Otherwise there was nothing to be seen but sea and sky.

Soon they were far down the beach, with Tyke running ahead to play with crabs or collect shells or whatever it was that caught his eye for a few minutes. The beach was one of the safest spots for them to have a private conversation, without needing to worry that a transcript of everything they said would immediately end up on Lieutenant Bartow's desk. There were directional microphones which could have picked up what they were saying even then, of course, but Mike hoped no one was determined enough to listen to baby-talk.

"We're leaving tonight," he whispered in her ear, as if telling her a sweet line. She never missed a beat.

"I thought it was something like that. What's the plan?" she whispered back, giggling as if he'd said something funny. Annabelle was no fool; she knew all the tricks just as well as he did.

"Philip is coming to pick us up at ten o'clock with a row boat and a set of thermal suits. We'll cross over to the fort, and then Joan will take us to the marina in Treasure Island. Damon is supposed to buy us a little ship to get away in. Then we'll see what we see," Mike said, and she didn't ask how all this was possible or why he hadn't told her sooner. She simply nodded.

"We'll have to cut the chips out or they'll track us," she said immediately, and he nodded.

"Already got that covered," he said, pulling the razor blades from his pocket.

"What about the body heat alarm?" she asked.

"Let Spot swallow them. He'll keep them nice and warm for us," Mike said.

"We can't take him, then?" she asked.

"No. He'd give us away with his body heat; they don't make thermal suits to fit dogs. I know Tyke will be sad, but we'll find him another dog when we get to Campeche," Mike said.

"We're going to *Campeche?*" Annabelle asked, and he couldn't mistake the distaste in her voice.

"Yeah, for a little while at least. Maybe not forever, but it was all we could think of on short notice," Mike said, and Annabelle sighed.

"I'm sure we'll learn to adjust," she finally said.

"I hope so," Mike agreed.

"Well, we might as well get this done. It'll be dark soon and we don't dare do it back at the cottage," she said, taking the razor blades from his hand.

"Yeah, you're right," he agreed, getting down on his knees so she could reach his neck.

"I'm afraid this might hurt pretty bad," she said apologetically.

"I'm sure it will. But it can't be helped. Try to do it fast instead of slow; then at least it won't last as long," he said, and braced himself. Then she slashed the back of his neck open with the blade, and it *did* hurt, like white-hot fire, and he felt warm blood running down his back. But he gritted his teeth and didn't say anything. Seconds later she showed him a tiny chip barely half a centimeter across, lying in her bloody hands. As soon as he saw it, she closed her fist to keep it warm.

"I'm glad you found that so quick," he muttered, putting pressure on his cut with both hands.

"I'm not sure I would have, if the scar hadn't been there to tell me where to look," she admitted.

"All right, then. Your turn," he said, and she nodded and turned around. He pushed aside her long brown hair to expose the tiny scar where her own chip was buried, and then hesitated. It was hard to make himself hurt her, even though he knew it was dire necessity.

"Come on, I'm ready. It just makes it worse if you wait," she said, and he forced himself to do it. Bright red blood soaked the back of her dress, and he heard her hiss with pain. But he quickly found the hard little cube which was her tracking chip, and then held it in his fist as she was holding the other one.

"Come here, Spot!" she called, and the puppy quickly galloped over to snuffle her feet in excitement.

"Here you go, boy," she said, opening her hand so he could lick the blood. In the process, she made sure he swallowed the tracking chip. Then Mike did the same.

"Well, there's that much done, at least," he said.

"Yeah, I just hope they don't pay too much attention and start to wonder why we're moving around so close to the ground all the time," Annabelle said wryly.

"I doubt they'll look at all, unless they get an alarm because the chip got too cold or left the island," Mike said.

"Hopefully," she agreed.

Neither of them wanted to go back to the cottage, so they sat down and waited on the sandy beach for Philip to get there, talking quietly and watching the lights of Saint Petersburg in the distance.

"I wonder if they have lights in Campeche," she murmured after a while, and he laughed a little.

"Not like this, but yeah, I'm sure they have electricity, sugar baby. It's not like they're still living in the Stone Age, you know," he said.

"I know. I've just heard so many awful things about that place," she said.

"Yeah, so have I," he admitted.

"Will it be safe, do you think?" she asked.

"I've heard the rich people hire armed guards for protection. I guess we might have to do the same thing," he said, not liking the idea much.

"I'd almost rather stay on the ship and cruise the ocean forever, just you and me and Tyke," she said.

"Maybe someday we will, sugar baby; nobody said we had to stay in Campeche forever. Just till the heat slacks off a little," he said.

"All right, then, sugar daddy. I'll take you up on that offer someday," she said.

About ten o'clock they heard the soft sound of oars splashing in the water, and a few minutes later Philip's boat slid ashore.

"Come on, let's hurry up and get out of here while we still can," Philip said, handing Annabelle a thermal suit for each of them. They quickly put them on, and Mike noticed the heat almost immediately. It felt like wearing a heavy winter coat on a hot summer day, and sweat was soon running down his back and stinging the cut on his neck. He could only imagine how Philip must feel after rowing all the way across the Bay. He was probably parboiled.

Together they launched out into the fitful sea, headed for the distant lights of Fort Desoto. Mike rowed while Annabelle quietly buckled Tyke into his life preserver and Philip took a well-earned rest. There was no immediate outcry from the guards, and they were encouraged as the bulk of the island gradually slipped farther and farther behind them.

"I don't see how you did it, Philip," Mike said after a while. He was sweating so much even his palms felt greasy on the oars, and the rough seas made it even harder than usual.

"Not so loud, Mikey; sound carries a long way over water," Philip said.

"Sorry," Mike said, in a much lower voice. Then he turned his attention back to rowing; he couldn't really spare the breath for conversation anyway.

It took them about an hour to reach the point of Fort Desoto, which was actually a park maintained by the county. It was deserted at that hour, of course, and the first thing they all did when they stepped out on shore was to strip off the thermal suits. Mike's clothes were soaked, and he felt like he'd suddenly stepped into the Arctic Circle.

Joan was parked under a grove of palm trees a little bit farther down the shore, and they quickly made their way to the car, tossing the thermal suits in the trunk. She'd brought towels and dry clothes, not to mention pizza and Cokes, too; a small detail for which Mike wanted to kiss her. They hadn't had anything to eat since noon.

It took only a few minutes to get dried and changed, and then they sat in the car eating while Joan left the park and drove northward on the coast highway. Had they followed it all the way to the end it would have taken them right back to Clearwater Beach, but of course they had no intention of going anywhere near that far.

Fifteen minutes later Joan pulled in to the marina at Treasure Island and killed the engine. Mike grabbed their few possessions while Philip and Joan disposed of the wet clothes and the thermal suits in a trash receptacle. They didn't want any evidence of the escape, just in case anybody came around asking inconvenient questions.

"Here she is," Joan said, leading them to a thirty-six foot Bluewater Cruiser named the *Lusitania;* as beautiful a ship as ever sailed the seven seas, and well able to travel anywhere in the world they might choose to go. Annabelle nudged Mike, and he knew what she was thinking.

"Someday, babe," he murmured.

"Please thank Damon for us, when you see him next time," Annabelle said.

"He knows. But we will, anyway," Joan said.

"All right, then. Y'all better get gone," Philip said. Joan and Annabelle cried and hugged, and while they were doing that Philip spoke in a low voice.

"Don't try to contact us for a while; I'm sure the NADF will suspect we might've had something to do with this, even though they won't be certain enough to arrest us or anything. They probably *will* be watching us for a little while, though. Get in touch with Damon if you need anything. Here's his address and phone number," Philip said, handing Mike a slip of paper.

"Okay," Mike agreed, slipping the paper in his pocket.

"The cash is stowed under the sink in the galley along with the tachometer; they don't accept anything else in Campeche. There's a little bit of gold, too, just in case," Philip said.

"I don't know how to thank you," Mike said.

"You know we're glad to do it. Just one more thing, though," Philip said.

"What's that?" Mike asked.

"When it comes time to start thinking about the plague, make sure you *do* get in touch with us at least a few months ahead of time so we can make all the last-minute plans; make sure everything is ready to go," Philip said.

That once again reminded Mike unpleasantly of the fact that he hadn't seen himself and Annabelle on the plane with the others.

"Philip, there's something else you really need to-" he began, but Philip cut him off.

"No, Mike. Don't tell me. Whatever it is, I'll find out soon enough," he said firmly, and with that Mike had to be content. He consoled himself with the thought that he didn't have much to tell, anyway; he only knew what he'd seen, not how it came about or why, or even what it meant.

"All right, then," Mike said.

The girls were done saying their goodbyes by then, and there was no more time to waste. Mike and Annabelle went aboard the cruiser with Tyke, while Philip and Joan stood on the dock waving.

The ship was set up like a small but luxurious apartment below decks; with a little luck they wouldn't even need to find another place to live in Campeche. That suited Mike just fine.

He started the powerful motor and cast off, maneuvering the boat out of the marina and into the Gulf. Then he pointed the nose of the ship west by southwest, and left Tampa Bay behind as fast as the *Lusitania* could take them.

The city lights gradually dimmed and faded behind them, till they were left with a dark sky full of clouds and intermittent rain showers, with no sound but the hum of the engines and the wash of the restless waves against the keel. Annabelle came to stand beside him at the wheel, and he put one arm around her.

"Where's Tyke?" he asked.

"Asleep on the couch. He won't wake up till morning," she said.

"Good; he's had a long day," Mike nodded.

"So have we, sugar daddy," she said wryly.

"True 'nuff. But we can't stop till we get to Campeche, you know," he reminded her.

"Yeah, I know. No rest for the weary," she sighed.

"I promise you when we get there, we'll sleep all day long and then I'll take you out to the nicest restaurant in town," he said, and just as he hoped, she laughed.

"Not sure how nice that'll be, but I guess it's the thought that counts," she said.

They stood there in companionable silence, and for a while it seemed as if they might actually make it.

Then things changed.

"What's that?" Annabelle asked suddenly, pointing at a pair of lights approaching rapidly from the southeast.

"Uh. . . I don't know; it looks like one of the boats the Defense Forces always use when they bring me out to the island," Mike said.

There was nothing to be done except keep moving ahead, but it quickly became obvious the other ship was much faster than the *Lusitania.*

"They're not slowing down, Mike," Annabelle said when the other ship had gotten very close indeed. If anything, it was gaining speed.

"They're fixing to ram us," Mike said. Lieutenant Bartow must have discovered they were missing somehow, and then decided to get rid of them once and for all. Just like Joan had said, he was completely pitiless when it came to serving the greater good.

So that's how it would be, then. A tragic accident at the mouth of the Bay, deeply regrettable. No doubt the NADF would send their sincerest and most heartfelt condolences to Joan on the death of her sister.

But there was still one last way out.

"Go grab Tyke and the tachometer, and the life preservers if you can find them. Quick!" Mike said urgently, and Annabelle hurried off. She returned in only a few minutes, and Mike quickly punched in the numbers with shaking hands while she put on Tyke's vest and then her own. Fifteen years or so should do it; just enough for the plague to be over with.

He was just about to push the button when a thought came from nowhere.

Leave him behind.

In the heat of the moment, Mike was so startled that at first he didn't even comprehend what such a thing could mean. Then he remembered.

Tyke was supposed to grow up here, in this place and time. Mike had seen him as a teenager at Philip and Joan's house, and Zach's words came to mind like a ghost from the past, about how to look through the tachometer was to glimpse the will of God revealed.

They didn't dare try to take him fifteen years ahead; not when they knew already what was meant to be. But on the other hand, they didn't dare skip ahead only a few months or a year, either. The *Lusitania* would be long gone by then, along with all their money and their only way of getting to Campeche, or anywhere else for that matter. They'd either drown in the Gulf or be captured and killed almost as soon as they made it back to shore. Yes, they had a promise of sorts that Tyke would survive no matter what, but they had no such promise when it came to themselves. Quite the opposite if anything, for what else could it mean that he and Annabelle didn't exist in 2154? There was no escape for *them;* at least not that way.

There came to him unbidden a memory of his father, watching him from the porch as he drove away from Goliad. Cody McGrath would probably have said that sometimes we have to make sacrifices for the people we love, even ones that break our hearts and cost us dearly. Uncle Brandon would have told him that few things are dearer to the Lord's heart than a child who obeys even when it seems that obedience will lead only to heartbreak. His mother would have said that love and possession are polar opposites.

He knew all these things from the tenor of a thousand talks, and up till now he would always have said he believed them. But when it came to the point of decision and his own back was up against the wall, he found that things were quite different.

For a second Mike's heart rebelled, and he almost pushed the button anyway. In spite of what God's will might be, in spite of what Daddy and Uncle Brandon might have said, in spite of all the hard and bitter truths in the world.

He could almost hear his mother's voice.

God is good, in this as in all things. When your time of testing comes, trust in His love and do whatever it may be that He asks of you, even if you can't see the reason why.

Mike looked at Annabelle in desperate agony, and saw the same look reflected in her eyes. Her mind was as quick and lithe as a cat; she already knew everything he knew, and there was no need for either of them to say a single word. They both glanced in unison at Tycho.

"Put him out," Annabelle whispered.

There was no time left to think, and though it broke his heart, Mike made his choice. They both kissed him one last time, and then Mike picked up his son by the scruff of the neck and threw him across the stormy ocean with all his strength. The last sound he heard was a four-year-old's cry of terror and the heavy splash when he hit the water. And even though he knew in his heart that the kid would be safe, why oh why did it have to feel so much like killing him?

He quickly switched on the tachometer, letting the silvery bubble form around them. Then he sat down next to his weeping wife and held her in his arms, and heard her praying. Then he shut his eyes, and pushed the button while he still had the courage.

Seconds later, the *Lusitania* was crushed to pieces.

Epilogue
Sunday, November 25, 2141

"Are there any survivors?" Luke Bartow asked, when the boat was able to come around for a pass through the wreckage.

"No sir, I don't think so. We're still searching for the bodies," the sailor answered.

"Let me know when you find them," Luke said.

"Yes, sir," the sailor said smartly, and Luke paid him no more mind. It was an unpleasant business, even though he knew it was better in the long run. Normally he never doubted the necessity of such things, but there were times, like now, when it made him feel very old.

He nursed his coffee and told himself somebody had to do it. The world might end in twelve years or it might not, but it had to get on in the meantime, and that meant having to do things he didn't like sometimes. Simple as that.

About an hour later, the sailor returned.

"Sir, we found the boy. You asked to be notified," he said formally.

"Dead?" Luke asked, without much interest.

"No sir, he's still alive. We found him floating in a life preserver," the sailor said, and Luke privately cursed. Complications, always complications.

"Bring him here, then," Luke said.

"Yes, sir," the sailor said, and five minutes later he returned carrying a dark-eyed four year old still dripping sea water.

Luke stared at him, and the boy stared back, solemn and quiet. He had a fleeting thought of taking off the kid's life preserver and throwing him back in the Gulf; he'd drown soon enough, and nobody ever the wiser.

Except Luke himself would know, of course, and even he found it hard to stomach *that* idea. But what other choice did he have?

"Now what am I going to do with *you?*" he finally muttered, and the boy said nothing.

Luke scratched the stubble on his chin and considered the matter. The kid was too young to know or remember anything, and Colonel Burns *did* allow him a certain amount of leeway. He could probably afford to let the boy live, under the circumstances. If asked, he could always say the decision was purely practical; rescuing a little child from stormy seas after his parents' tragic death in a boating accident made for an excellent public relations story. Besides which, they could always kill him later if it turned out to be necessary.

Satisfied, Luke nodded his head.

One thing which didn't satisfy him at *all* was their failure to find any trace of the boy's parents. He hated loose ends like that. But after two hours of searching the dark ocean with no luck, he finally had to give up and admit defeat. Strong storms were moving in from the west, and he couldn't in good conscience risk his own men without need.

He finally decided the boy's parents had no chance of swimming thirty miles back to shore in stormy seas, anyway, even if they'd somehow survived the wreck and managed to evade being found. And if by some miracle they *did* turn up still alive, then he'd deal with that later, too. Lieutenant Luke Bartow was a very patient man.

There was nothing dry for a child to wear on the ship, but that couldn't be helped. When they landed at the naval station in Saint Petersburg, Luke put the kid in his own car before driving back to Clearwater Beach. It left a wet spot on the seat, which annoyed him, but that couldn't be helped either.

He dropped the kid off at Philip and Joan Carpenter's house on Papaya Street before going home, and then thought no more about the issue.

* * * * * * *

It wasn't quite five a.m. when Cameron heard a loud knock on the front door and sat up in bed sleepily. It was still awfully hard for him to get used to thinking of himself as Philip, and there were times when he didn't feel like trying.

"Who could *that* be, I wonder?" he muttered to himself, getting up to put on a robe. Joan was still asleep, and he hurried downstairs in his bare feet to see who it was before the noise could wake her. Rain had been falling off and on for hours, but it seemed to have more or less stopped for a while at the moment, leaving the house quiet as death.

He saw nothing through the fish-eye, and was tempted to think it might have been one of the neighborhood kids playing a silly prank in the middle of the night. He almost dismissed it and went back to bed without opening the door at all, but then thought better of it.

He fumbled with the latches and chains, then turned the knob and stepped outside.

And there, standing alone on the dark steps in the drizzling rain, was his nephew Tycho. The kid was soaking wet and smelled of salt, and around his neck was (of all things) a dog collar and a leash, which someone had tied to the step rail. For a split second, Cameron stared at him in astonishment.

"Where did *you* come from, champ?" he finally asked, scanning the yard and then squatting down in front of the boy when he saw no one. Tyke looked at him solemnly with his big brown eyes, but said nothing. Then Cameron spotted a note tied to the collar, and thought to himself that it reminded him of the way people used to drop off orphans on a stranger's doorstep. The paper was wet, and the ink had run pretty badly in places, but there was no mistaking what it said.

Ask no questions.

Cameron stood up swiftly and looked around again, but still saw nothing unusual. He felt a twinge of fear in his gut, and untied the collar as quickly as his shaking fingers would work. Then he scooped up his soaking nephew and carried him swiftly inside, out of sight of prying eyes, leaving nothing behind on the steps but a nylon leash and a puddle of salty water.

* * * * * * *

Sunday, June 18, 2157

Mike and Annabelle splashed down suddenly into the Gulf, and came up coughing and sputtering to a world that had changed in the blink of an eye. The sea was warm as summer, the dark sky strewn with a million stars. The faint orangey glow of Saint Petersburg in the distance had winked out like a candle in a draft, and the waves had subsided to almost nothing.

But all those things were to be expected; it was mid-June of 2157, if the tachometer had delivered them to the right place. Fifteen years after Lieutenant Bartow had rammed the *Lusitania,* and two and a half years after the plague had destroyed the world.

"Can we swim all the way back to shore, do you think?" Annabelle asked. She didn't seem fearful, but then she'd always been brave of heart.

"I think so, with the water calm like this. We've got the life preservers; we can rest whenever we need to. Long as we keep heading in the same direction we'll have to hit the coast sooner or later, probably a little bit south of where we left," Mike said, with a lot more confidence than he really felt.

So they headed east, steering by the stars at first and then by the sun. It was a brutal distance to have to swim, but nearly twenty hours later they finally emerged exhausted on the beach at sunset.

"Where are we, do you think?" Annabelle asked.

"I don't know; looks like an island to me," Mike said doubtfully.

Almost unbelievably, it turned out to be Edgmont Key, the very spot they'd just escaped from. Wind and waves had resculpted the beaches and dunes considerably over the past fifteen years, but Annabelle recognized the place as soon as they came across one of the brick streets of old Fort Dade. Mike couldn't decide whether to laugh or cry.

"That sure was a long trip, to end up right back where we started from," he said wryly.

"That's the truth, but I'm glad to be here, anyway. As a matter of fact, this might be a good place for us to stay for a little while, at least till we figure out what the situation is elsewhere," she pointed out.

"Eminent good sense as always, my love," he agreed. They clasped hands and walked slowly back to the cottage at the northern tip of the island, each thinking their own thoughts.

"It looks just the same as always," Annabelle said when they got there, shaking her head just a little.

"It's not *quite* the same, though. We're not prisoners anymore," he pointed out, and she smiled.

The porch was covered in sand and scattered bits of gulfweed from passing storms over the years, but the lights still worked and the water still ran, and the place seemed to have survived the elements more or less intact. There were even still a few boxes of food in the cupboards. For a second Mike could almost imagine it was just a normal night, like any of a hundred others he'd spent in that place.

But it wasn't, of course.

"Do you think he's okay?" Annabelle asked softly. Neither of them had mentioned Tyke yet, but of course the subject couldn't be avoided forever.

"I'm sure he is. I know I saw them leave on that space plane," Mike said staunchly, though he had his own fears, too.

"He'd be nineteen years old by now; I'm not sure he'd even remember us," she said.

There was no good answer for that, but he tried his best.

"We'll find out soon," he promised, squeezing her hand a little tighter.

Then Mike quietly shut the door against the fall of night, and there was nothing more to hear but the soft wash of waves on the desolate shore.

The End

Free Sample of

Tycho

Book Two of the Tyke McGrath Series

Chapter One
Tuesday, January 22, 2154

I was at school the day the world fell apart, in Dr. Weiss's advanced genetics class, as a matter of fact.

Back in those days I'd never heard of the Orion Strain, the Moon was nothing but a light in the sky, and the worst problem I ever had to deal with was forgetting to turn in my chemistry homework. Mrs. McClendon used to be a real beast about late assignments.

I know the world can never go back to the way it was before, but sometimes I can't help wishing, you know.

I remember I was supposed to be comparing two different strains of mouse DNA that afternoon; deadly dull stuff, to be honest. So maybe it was just boredom that led me to set aside my genetics project and hack my way into the mainframe of the World Health Organization instead. Molecular genetics happens to be my special field of study, and that's one of the best places to visit if you like such things.

It was nothing but a whim; I wasn't looking for anything in particular. But we have a saying in science, about how the most interesting discoveries are almost always the accidental ones. It's called serendipity, and it ended up saving my life that day.

At any given time, the World Health Organization kept tabs on a dozen or more disease outbreaks in local areas around the world to make sure they didn't become an epidemic. Nothing unusual about that, and the one I chose to read about that afternoon was called the Orion Strain. I picked that one mostly because the file was classified, and it amused me to break through the security system and find out what they were being so secretive about. I certainly didn't think it would end up radically changing my life. But that's what I mean about serendipity; a little bit of whimsical curiosity can change *everything*.

The Orion Strain turned out to be a low level bacterium which had popped up for the first time in Calcutta, India, about a week earlier, and the only mildly interesting thing about it was the high death rate. So far at least, it seemed to have killed pretty much a hundred percent of the people who caught it, within no more than thirty-six hours after exposure. It was a viciously deadly bug, to be sure, but then of course there are a lot of viciously deadly bugs in the world and most of them never amount to anything much. It made me wonder why the file had been classified at all.

Then I saw what the reason was, and I gasped out loud without thinking, nearly dropping my pencil on the floor.

Dr. Weiss crumpled his *Tampa Tribune* for a second to frown at me, and I quickly made it look like I was totally absorbed in mouse DNA. But as soon as he went back to reading his article, I completely forgot about my genetics assignment.

Because it wasn't the deadliness of the Orion Strain that caused the blood to drain from my face and made me feel like a lump of ice had suddenly come to rest right in the pit of my stomach. It was the interspecies infection rate.

That may sound technical, but all it means is whether some other animal can catch a disease or not. Like pigs can sometimes catch human flu, for example. The scary thing about the Orion Strain was that it was highly contagious to any warm-blooded animal. Any bird or mammal, basically. There was no way you could ever contain something like that; a rat or a bird or some such thing would always slip through any barrier you tried to set up and they'd carry the infection elsewhere. There'd be no stopping it.

I quickly set up a simulation on my computer to analyze how fast the bacteria might spread, using the most conservative estimates. And that's when I *really* got scared.

"Drew, come look at this," I finally managed to croak. Drew Breyer was my lab partner and one of my few actual friends. He was fiddling with the electrophoresis unit at the moment, pretending to accomplish something useful. He was actually supposed to be helping me with the mouse analysis, but I didn't much care. Finishing the work myself was easier anyway.

Nevertheless, he was still technically my lab partner, so he yawned and then ambled over to my workstation to have a look.

"What is it?" he asked in a low voice, staring at the numbers on the screen.

"It's a statistical analysis of the progress of a bacterium called the Orion Strain on the Indian subcontinent over the past week. Infection rate compared to kill rate, speed of transmission, that kind of thing," I managed to say. That was good; focusing on data was an easy way to divert my mind from the terrible implications.

"And?" Drew asked, raising one eyebrow.

"Don't you see it?" I asked, astonished at his thick-headedness.

"See what, Tyke?" Drew asked, with a touch of irritation.

Oh, my name is Tycho, by the way, after Tycho Brahe the famous astronomer. Tyke, for short. Which I guess might have been cute when I was three years old, but it was definitely a liability at the John Brooke Academy for Math and Science. I hated the nickname, but I was so used to it that I barely noticed anymore.

But I digress.

Drew's question frustrated me, mostly because it meant I wasn't explaining myself very well. I must have been more rattled than I thought I was. I made an effort to calm down and be reasonably logical.

"Look here. I got these records from the World Health Organization in Geneva. This germ is spreading *fast,* and so far there's been a kill rate of a hundred percent. Everybody that catches it dies," I explained.

"Yeah, I know how to read stats, Tyke," Drew said dryly.

"You're not the least bit worried about that?" I asked.

"About what? A nasty little disease in Calcutta? Why should I be worried about that? There are nasty new diseases all the time and they never amount to anything. They kill some people and then they disappear, which is exactly what this one will do. The very fact that it's so deadly only means it'll flame out sooner, because it'll kill all the available hosts. It says right here that they've already sealed off the city to keep it from spreading. Even if they don't find a cure, it'll be over in a week. Worse comes to worst, it'll wipe out Calcutta, maybe even a few other cities if they're sloppy about their quarantine. Bad, yes, but it's not like it's the whole world or anything," he said.

"No, Drew. Look here," I said, pointing at the section that dealt with interspecies crossovers. This time he didn't need to ask me what the numbers meant. He drew in his breath sharply, just like I had.

"Are you sure those numbers are right?" he asked, actually looking worried for the first time.

"Yeah, I'm sure. The interspecies crossover rate is *also* close to a hundred percent among birds and mammals. They can't close borders against birds and mice, now can they? And besides that, look here; it says the bacterium can also form spores which are estimated to survive in the environment for at least twenty years," I said.

Drew looked ill, and I could hardly blame him. If that data was correct, then we were staring at the end of the world.

"Where'd you get this?" he asked.

"I told you, I got it from the World Health Organization. I hacked their computer," I said, allowing myself a touch of pride in spite of everything. The administration of the Academy would have had a hissy fit if they'd known I was using school computers for hacking into government databases, but in the meantime what they didn't know wouldn't hurt them.

"But surely they'll find a vaccine, or some kind of treatment," he objected.

"Drew, you're not thinking. It'll be a week till the first wave of infections gets *here*. Maybe even less than that if a bird flies in from one of the affected areas. In ten days, at most, everybody in Tampa will be dead. I give it two weeks for the whole world, and that's being generous. That's not enough time to find a cure for anything. You should know that," I reminded him. Drew was a medical science student; he of all people ought to know how long it took to find treatments for disease.

"But there's always a chance," he insisted.

"Yeah, I guess there's always a chance, but I wouldn't bet on it," I said.

Drew was silent, thinking. He might be a slacker when it came to assignments, but he was still one of the most brilliant kids in the state of Florida; he could analyze the situation as well as anybody, and I watched as despair slowly clouded his eyes. Even if we told the administrators and even if they believed us, there was absolutely nothing to be done about it.

"You don't think there's anywhere we could go to ride it out?" he asked hopefully. I considered it, and then shook my head.

"No. There're nowhere in the world that birds don't go, not even the most remote islands you can think of. We'd have to find somewhere sealed up *tight* if we wanted to hide out, with enough food and supplies to last us twenty years or more. There's no place on Earth like that, unless it was already built and ready by now," I said dejectedly.

"So you're saying unless somebody miraculously finds a cure sometime in the next week or so, then we're toast. Is that it?" he asked.

"Yeah, that's pretty much it," I admitted.

"I can't believe there's nothing we can do," he insisted.

"I'm open to suggestions," I said.

There was silence for a long time, and then I could have sworn I saw the glint of a smile on Drew's face.

"There's no place on Earth we'd be safe, huh?" he asked, and then I was sure of it. Drew was actually *excited*.

"Nope, none at all. Maybe somewhere out in the middle of the ice cap in Antarctica where no animals ever go. But we don't have time or money to build a fortress out there and stock it with supplies," I agreed.

"What about somewhere else besides Earth, then?" Drew suggested. My first impulse was to call him an idiot, but then I reconsidered.

"You mean the space stations?" I asked.

"No, there's no way they'll last twenty years without fresh supplies from Earth. They'll run out of food, and spare parts, and things like that. Not a good option," he said.

"What are you talking about, then?" I asked.

"The Moon, buddy, the Moon!" he cried excitedly. In fact he let his voice rise just a little too high, and Dr. Weiss frowned at us again from behind his newspaper. Both of us were quick to take a sudden fascination with the numbers on my computer, and after a few seconds Dr. Weiss went back to ignoring us.

I chewed on my lip, thinking. I didn't know all that much about the Moon, but I remembered it had always been one of Drew's pet hobbies. His grandfather had been a member of the original survey team for the Lunar Terraform Project, fifty years ago or more, but he'd been killed in a storm that destroyed the research compound where he was working. Barnaby Station, if I remembered right. If I'd heard that story once, I'd heard it a million times.

Anyway, the idea hadn't worked out quite the way they'd planned, for some reason. All I could remember was that they'd wasted huge sums of money and then ended up never finishing the Project anyway. The only interesting thing about the whole boondoggle was a couple of footnotes in our genetics textbooks about *Macrocystis tranquilitatis,* a type of kelp, and *Makaira caeruleus,* a variety of blue marlin, both of which had been developed for the lunar environment right there at the Academy. I remembered vaguely that there was no salt in the seas of the Moon, so saltwater organisms had had to be modified to live in fresh water. I couldn't remember much else.

"I didn't think people could survive up there," I said skeptically, and Drew wrinkled his nose.

"Well. . . yes and no," he said.

"What's that supposed to mean?" I asked.

"It means there's breathable air, and drinkable water, and a somewhat functioning ecosystem. It's survivable," he said.

"I hear a 'but' in there somewhere," I said.

"*But*. . . it gets up to about 140 degrees during the day, minus 20 at night, there are incredible storms all the time, the radiation level is fairly high, and there's not much to eat," he said.

"I see. So instead of the Orion Strain, it's better to die from starvation, or heat stroke, or freezing to death, or maybe cancer? Not to mention the fact that we don't have a way to get there in the first place," I scoffed.

"There's still the old research compound at Lakeside Station. It's probably run down and ragged out after all this time sitting there empty, but we could knock it back into shape, I'm sure. It'll have heat and air conditioning, probably a hydroponics lab to grow food, maybe some radiation shielding. It's a *chance*, anyway. Better than sitting here twiddling our thumbs and then dying from the Orion Strain next week, don't you think?" Drew said.

I couldn't very well argue with that assessment, so I shifted my defense. Truthfully, I was desperate for Drew to convince me. When you're staring death in the face, you'll give just about anything for a plan that offers even the barest scrap of hope. Even an utterly stupid one like running off to the Moon.

"Doesn't matter anyway, since there's no way for us to get there," I reminded him.

"I'll have to think about that one," Drew finally admitted.

"Yeah, well. . . we got precious little time to think about it, buddy boy," I said.

"Yeah, I know. I'll talk to some people, see what we can come up with," he said.

"I'd be careful who I said anything to," I warned.

"Oh, come on, Tyke; give me a little credit. I know who's trustworthy and who's not," he said, shaking his head.

I shrugged and started to say something else, but just then the bell rang and I had to sign out of my workstation before the next class came in. There was no way I wanted anybody to see what I'd been working on.

I was preoccupied for the rest of the day and paid no attention to my classes. There didn't seem to be any point, when you thought about it. Biochemistry was interesting, sure, but two weeks from now what difference would it make to anybody?

After school was over at three, I didn't have the heart to get involved with any of the extracurricular things which the school offered, or even to go to the library like I usually did. I just trudged slowly back to the dorm room to lie down on my bed and stare blankly at the ceiling. The Academy was a residential school, and except during holidays all students lived on campus unless our families were close enough to drive us every day.

My parents passed away a long time ago, in a boating accident on Tampa Bay when I was four years old. I don't really remember very much about them, honestly. My dad was an astronomer and my mother was a math professor, and I know they named me Tycho because they hoped I'd grow up to become a famous scientist someday. I'm not sure if biology was exactly what they had in mind, but that's what I've always loved.

Anyway, ever since they died I've lived with my aunt and uncle, Joan and Philip Carpenter, and my four cousins out in Clearwater Beach. Their names were Chris, Jesse, Callum, and Veronica, and it so happened that Jesse and I were born just two weeks apart. We'd been best friends ever since preschool, and one of the things I'd always liked about the Academy was that I got to share a room with him.

People were always a little surprised that we both went to school together; the Academy isn't such an easy place to get into. You have to score really high on your placement exams in eighth grade, and then you have to apply and have an interview and all kinds of things. It's a very prestigious place, and by the time we graduate high school we'll already have a Master's degree in our chosen field. There were a lot of programs to choose from, some of them better than others, of course. The advanced genetics program was one of the very best, along with marine science and aerospace engineering. Those were our top three programs, and sometimes it humbled me to think I was a part of one of them. There have been a lot of famous people who went to this place, and a lot of famous teachers, too. Dr. Weiss had a Nobel prize for his work in genetics, and he was far from the only one.

Jesse and I had shared the same room for two and a half years, ever since we started ninth grade, and all that time together had made us tighter than ever.

That's why in spite of what I said to Drew about being careful who he talked to, I'd already decided to tell Jesse everything.

He came in about four-thirty, covered in sweat from running. He always ran five miles around the dirt track after school every day, rain or shine, hot or cold. It was unusually warm for January, and he flopped down on his bed with a sigh of contentment wearing nothing but his running shorts.

"A thousand blessings on the head of whoever invented air-conditioning!" he said with a theatrical flourish to no one in particular, and I couldn't help smiling a little. Jesse is nearly impossible not to like.

"I think that was Charles Carrier," I told him, sitting up and leaning my back against the cinderblock wall.

"Well, then, a thousand blessings on the head of Saint Charles Carrier!" Jesse said, grinning.

"Whatever, dude," I said, rolling my eyes.

"You'd say the same thing if you knew how warm it was out there today. Track was so hot I bet you could fry an egg on the dirt," Jesse said.

"Nobody put a gun to your head and forced you to go out there running today, Jesse," I pointed out.

"True, but I wouldn't want to get all weak and pale and flabby like some people I could mention, now would I?" he said, laughing. I shook my head at the good-natured dig; Jesse was always trying to get me to run or swim or get involved in some kind of athletic activity. I wouldn't go so far as to call myself weak and pale and flabby, but sometimes I did envy Jesse a little bit for his chiseled muscles and his careless good looks. He's big and tall and blond, like my Uncle Philip, and I'm small and dark-haired like my mother and Aunt Joan. No one who saw us together would ever have guessed we were related at all. He also loves athletics, and sports just aren't my thing, not by a long shot. I'm a pretty good swimmer, but that's about as far as it goes.

I was about to say so when there came a knock on the door. I got up to answer it and saw that it was Drew.

"Hey, Drew Dog, what's up?" Jesse called from the bed.

"Um. . . just need to talk to Tyke for a minute, that's all," he said.

"I'm guessing that means you want me to trot off and leave y'all alone, huh?" he asked, smiling.

That was another thing about Jesse; he's always enjoyed playing the redneck country boy role, ever since I can remember. We have a saying in Florida, that the farther north you go, the more South you get. It's nothing unusual to hear a drawly voice around Tampa, but Jesse definitely plays it up to the fullest. His middle name is James, so I think he was doomed to be a rebel ever since the day he was born.

"Well, yeah, it's kinda private. Sorry, Jesse," Drew said.

"Oh, it's okay. I needed to hit the showers before suppertime, anyway. I'll see you in a little while, Tyke," Jesse said. He took a minute to gather up some clothes and a towel, and then headed down the hall toward the bathroom, whistling.

Chapter Two

Drew came inside to sit down on my bed, and I went back to leaning against the wall.

"What's up?" I asked, as soon as the door was shut.

"I think I found a way to get there, man," he said eagerly, eyes shining.

"Are you still hung up on that stupid moon idea?" I asked, and Drew looked a little hurt.

"Yeah, I am. And you ought to be, too, if you care about saving your own sorry hide," he said. I sighed.

"Sorry. . . I'm just stressed out to the max, I guess," I apologized.

"Well, yeah, no doubt. But listen. Like I said, I think I found a way to get us there," he repeated.

"I'm all ears," I said.

"Okay, so I was talking to Dr. Weiss this afternoon, and- " he began, and my jaw dropped.

"You told Dr. Weiss!" I exclaimed, horrified.

"No, no, I just had a hypothetical discussion with him, that's all. I didn't really tell him anything," Drew explained hastily.

"Okay, go on, then," I said.

"He told me about one of the new space planes they're working on out at MacDill, the XR-339's. His wife works out there with my dad, you know," he said.

"Yeah, I know. What about it?" I asked.

"Okay, well, he said the XR-339 could take off from a runway just like a plane and enter low-Earth orbit without needing any rocket boosters. It's got a thorium-228 nuclear reactor for power instead and it's got a good enough range to reach the space stations and make it back. They've tested it several times and it's come through with flying colors," Drew explained.

"And?" I asked.

"So then I went home and asked my dad about it, and he told me pretty much the same thing. He said a trip to the moon was a lot farther than it was rated for, but he couldn't think of any reason why it wouldn't make it," Drew explained, smugly.

"I'm surprised they told you all that," I asked, skeptically.

"It's not like it's classified information or anything, Tyke. They've had XR's forever. They used to have old clunky ones even back when the Terraform Project was still going on. It's just that nobody uses them anymore because rockets are so much safer and cheaper. That's what Dad and Mrs. Weiss are working on; trying to build an XR plane which is safe and cost-competitive," he said.

For the first time, I started to feel the first twinges of hope.

"Are they hard to fly?" I asked guardedly.

"Nope, not at all. Anybody who knows how to pilot a plane can fly one, no sweat," Drew said.

"Yeah, but I bet they guard that place like Fort Knox, Drew. We'd never get in there to *see* one of those planes, much less leave with one," I pointed out.

"Most people, yeah, that's probably true. But we got *connections*, buddy. Peggy Weiss can get in there any time she wants to, and so can my dad. They could slip the rest of us in there, and then we can pinch that ship like taking candy from a baby. No sweat," Drew explained.

"Maybe," I said, doubtfully.

"I'm telling you, it'll work. We just have to convince my dad and the Weisses, that's all. That's where you come in, Tyke. You're the one who hacked that computer and got the data. You'll have to explain everything to my dad first, and then he can help with the Weisses; they've been friends forever. Then we're good to go!" Drew said confidently.

"How many people are we talking about taking along on this trip?" I asked. I still couldn't believe I was letting myself get sucked into his whole crazy Moon scheme, although I had to admit I couldn't think of anything else to try. When there's only one option on the table, then all you can do is go along with it. No matter how crazy it is.

""Dad said they've got thirty-one seats, and that's including the pilot and copilot chairs. There would have been thirty-two but they had to leave extra space on one side for part of the airlock," he said soberly.

"So we can only take thirty-one people?" I asked.

"That's about the size of it," he agreed reluctantly.

That bothered me. How do you pick just thirty-one people and offer them a slim-but-real chance to survive a catastrophe, and then leave the rest behind? That's a hard choice to have to make.

I didn't want to think about it right then, so I changed the subject.

"Have you talked to anybody except Dr. Weiss and your dad?" I asked.

"I talked to Tabby and Aron, that's all," he said, and I nodded. Tabby was his sister and Aron Anderson was his best friend, so I would have expected those two, at least. I knew Aron pretty well myself since his parents were good friends with Philip and Joan, but I couldn't exactly say that I liked the boy all that much.

"Nobody else? They won't talk to anybody, will they?" I asked.

"Nope. I told them to keep their mouths shut. Aron's got no friends to tell, anyway, and Tab wouldn't talk if I told her not to," he said.

I thought about that.

"I have to tell Jesse, though," I said abruptly.

"Well. . . whatever you think. Anyway, I told Mom I invited you over for supper tonight at seven o'clock. I didn't tell her why, but that's your chance to convince Dad, so you better have all your ducks in a row. Me and Tab will do our best to help you out, but this'll mostly be your thing, Tyke," he said.

"Gee, thanks," I murmured, and Drew sighed.

"It was the best I could do, buddy. You know that, right?" he asked earnestly, and I nodded.

"I know, Drew. I'm sorry. I'll be there at six-thirty and then we'll see what happens," I said.

"All right, see you then!" he said, and a few minutes later he was gone.

It was already almost five, so I went to one of the computer labs in the dormitory and signed on. It took me almost forty-five minutes to download my data and organize it in such a way that it looked respectable, and then I took a few minutes to shave and comb my hair. Drew's parents had seen me often enough that I knew they wouldn't be impressed just because I gussied up before I came to supper, but I was nervous and it helped me calm down a little bit.

Drew lived about six or seven blocks from the Academy, in a little brown bungalow down by the river. There were a couple of sickly-looking palm trees in the front yard and it was nothing special as far as houses go, but I think they stayed there mostly so Drew and Tabby could live at home while they went to high school. As soon as those two graduated, I was pretty sure the Breyers would move out to Citrus Park or Treasure Island or one of the other nicer suburbs. I'd heard them mention it a time or two.

There was a sea breeze blowing in off the Gulf, and it was cool enough by then that I didn't mind the walk. Drew and Tabby were sitting on the front deck when I showed up, and I waved to them. Drew waved back, and Tabby, as usual, did not. She seemed to live with a permanent grudge against the whole world in general and other human beings in particular, and she was close to the most unlikable individual I'd ever met in my life. Her only redeeming features were that she adored Drew and she was incredibly smart.

She was the only girl in the aerospace engineering program at the Academy, and she well deserved her spot.

She said nothing as I climbed the steps, even while Drew clapped me on the back and ushered me into the house.

Mr. Breyer was sitting in the living room watching the news, and Mrs. Breyer was in the kitchen cooking. It smelled like meatloaf, which was just fine with me. They both said hi when we entered the house.

"When do you think I should talk to him?" I whispered.

"Wait till after supper; that's always the best time to tell him anything," Drew whispered back.

So in the meantime we sat down at the kitchen table and chatted about school and computers and unimportant things, with Mr. and Mrs. Breyer throwing in a comment or two now and then when they weren't too involved with the cooking or the news. I enjoyed myself, just like I always did; that house had always felt like a second home to me, almost since the first day I came to the Academy. Besides Jesse, Drew was my best friend.

The meatloaf was tender and delicious when we finally got to eat, and even the salad was good. I always liked to say that I hated rabbit food, but Gina Breyer could whip up a salad even I enjoyed.

But all good things end eventually, and after the plates were loaded into the dishwasher and the five of us were sitting together in the living room, I knew the moment of truth had come. I waited for a commercial break, and then cleared my throat.

"Um, Mr. Breyer, there was something I wanted to talk to you about, if you've got a little time," I said.

"Sure, sport. What's on your mind?" he asked, glancing at me.

"I guess you heard about what's been going on in India, right?" I began carefully. I didn't really think he would have heard anything yet, but it seemed like a good way to break the ice.

"No, can't say that I have. What do you mean?" he asked.

"I heard about a new kind of bacteria this morning, over there in Calcutta. It's called the Orion Strain," I said.

"Really?" he asked, like he wasn't too interested. I needed to get his undivided attention, so I decided this was no time to be delicate.

"The reason I mention it is because I think that bacteria is about to wipe out the whole human race," I said bluntly.

"Surely that's a bit much, don't you think?" he said, laughing a little.

"No, sir, I really don't think it is. In fact, I know it's not. I hacked into the World Health Organization computers today and found out all about it. I've got the data right here," I said, pulling out my papers.

Mr. Breyer furrowed his brow and clicked off the TV with his remote. He knew me well enough to know that I could certainly have hacked into a government computer if I'd wanted to. Any other time he might have lectured me about how irresponsible it was to break into other people's databases and so forth, but not that night.

"I see," he said.

"So far, it's been a hundred percent fatal, and not just to humans, either. It's deadly to all birds and mammals, too. So far the only cases have been in Calcutta, but I ran an analysis this morning and it'll spread exponentially. If nothing changes, then it'll be here in Tampa no later than a week from now, and all over the world within two weeks. I don't think we can stop it," I said neutrally, doing my very best to stay calm and reasonable. If you get upset then people stop listening, and I desperately needed him to believe me.

"I've looked at the data myself, Dad; I think he's right," Drew chimed in.

"Can I see that booklet, please?" Mr. Breyer asked expressionlessly, and I wordlessly handed him the data I'd printed earlier.

"Come here, honey; help me look at this," he said to his wife, and she moved closer beside him so she could see. She was a social director at one of the ritzy retirement communities in Citrus Park, so I'm not sure why he thought she'd know much about biology or even statistics, but I didn't say a word. Both of them read the papers silently, and I watched them grow pale as they grasped the significance.

"Have you told anyone else about this?" he asked suddenly, looking back and forth between me and Drew.

"No, just Tabby," Drew said, and I shook my head.

"Have *you* told anybody, Tab?" Mr. Breyer asked, looking at his daughter.

"No, Dad," she said.

Mr. Breyer rubbed his temples and thought hard.

"This is pretty serious stuff, kids. I won't lie to you; I hope you're wrong. I hope we all missed something, because if not. . . " he shook his head, leaving the rest unspoken. We all knew what he meant.

"We should ask Rob and Peggy about this," Gina said, referring to Dr. Weiss and his wife. That was exactly what I'd hoped one of them would say, because if we were to have any chance at all of getting ourselves a ticket to the Moon, then we'd have to get Peggy Weiss on our side first.

She went to the phone to call them, and after a hurried conversation the Weisses agreed to come over. In the meantime, Mr. Breyer kept on rubbing his temples and thinking.

"If this is true, then there's nothing we can do. *Nothing.* We might as well quit our jobs and enjoy the time we've got left," he said after a while. It sounded like the ideal time to mention the escape plan, and I glanced meaningfully at Drew.

"Dad, we did think of one possible solution," he said, and Jason Breyer looked at his son.

"What is it, Drew?" he asked, as if his mind were a thousand miles away.

"We could always go to the Moon," Drew said.

For a second, it was almost like the idea didn't register in Mr. Breyer's mind, but when it did he smiled.

"You mean the XR-339. That's why you asked me if it could make it to the Moon earlier!" he cried.

"And you said yes, it probably could," Drew reminded him, smiling himself. Mr. Breyer must have been almost as much of a Moon fanatic as his son, because he didn't ask any questions about whether or not we could survive up there for twenty years or what the conditions might be like or anything else like that. And of course, I'm sure he already knew all there was to know about the XR-339 and what it might be capable of. He had the kind of look on his face that a man gets when he's just won a million dollar lottery.

Then his smile faded.

"There are only thirty-one seats on that plane, Drew. That's enough for me and you and Mom and Tab, and Tycho, and the Weisses and their two kids, maybe a few other people. What happens to everybody else?" he asked.

It was the same question I'd been thinking about earlier, and there was no good answer for it, of course. Then Tabby spoke up.

"Dad, you always told us we should do everything we can for humanity, didn't you?" she said gruffly.

"Yes, Tab, and that's exactly what concerns me right now; escaping to safety ourselves and abandoning all these other people to die," he said.

"Would it save them, if we stayed behind?" she asked.

"No," he admitted.

"Can we take them with us?" she asked.

"No," he said.

"Then we haven't done them any harm, by trying to save ourselves if we can," she pointed out. It sounded harsh, but there was no way we could argue with her.

"But how do we *choose* who to save and who to leave behind, Tab? That's what worries me," he said.

I never got to hear Tabby's answer to that, because just then Dr. and Mrs. Weiss arrived, with Johnny and Bethany in tow. Neither of them were students at the Academy, so I didn't know them all that well even though we were all roughly the same age. I knew Johnny went to school at the music conservatory downtown because I'd heard Drew mention it before, but I wasn't sure about Bethany.

I was braced to have a tough time convincing Dr. Weiss of anything because I knew how demanding he could be in class. The way he grilled his students over every tiny step in their research was legendary. You never made a careless statement in front of that man unless you were prepared to back it up, that was for sure. It made my palms sweaty just remembering some of the sessions I'd endured with him.

But surprisingly, it didn't take all that long to convince him. He just read the data report and listened to Drew's idea, and then immediately started making plans to put it into effect. Maybe it helped that he was such a brilliant and logical man; he could read the data and figure out instantly what had to be done, without the slightest hesitation. Most people in a situation like that would have been tempted to sit back and take a wait-and-see attitude about things, to find out whether the threat was real or not before they acted. But there are occasions when waiting too long to take action will get you killed, and Dr. Weiss was smart enough to see the writing on the wall while there was still time.

Peggy Weiss agreed that she and Mr. Breyer could probably find a way to smuggle a group of people into the hangar where the XR-339 was kept, and then come up with some excuse to get us inside the plane. She could fly it, once they managed that.

They were busily hashing out all the details when Mr. Breyer finally broached the delicate subject of who should be taken along. But Dr. Weiss had an immediate answer for that, too.

"We have to take people who can repopulate the human race. We need as many healthy young people as we can find; hopefully some intelligent ones," he declared, and Peggy Weiss quickly nodded her agreement.

That seemed like a distasteful way of choosing people, at least to my way of thinking. I like to think I'm worth something besides just breeding stock. If that's all human beings were good for, then why bother to preserve the human race at all?

But I kept my thoughts to myself and said nothing. Dr. Weiss wouldn't have listened to me, anyway.

After several hours of discussion, it was decided that the best source of people to take would be students from the Academy, if we could find any, and that me and Drew and Tabby should discreetly approach some of our friends to get a feel for who might be willing and able to join such a desperate mission for survival.

I honestly couldn't think of anyone at school that I liked and trusted enough to ask, other than Jesse. Drew had already talked to Aron, and maybe those two would be able to think of more. Dr. Weiss also insisted that there had to be equal numbers of boys and girls; more of his breeding regimen, I guess.

It was agreed that we'd all keep in touch and that all potential recruits would have to be personally approved by Dr. Weiss. I didn't like that part of the plan, either, but since he was the one with the keys to the ship, I didn't have a lot of say-so. We also agreed that if all went well, we'd try to launch the ship no later than the day after tomorrow.

Time was running short.

Tycho
is available now from your favorite retailer!

Author's Note

Nightfall is in some ways very unlike the other books in the *Tyke McGrath Series*. It does involve Tyke himself, of course, but it's primarily about his parents and several other characters who are important later on in the series.

Micah himself is not only Tycho's father but also Cody and Lisa's son, two characters whom readers may already be familiar with from *Many Waters*. Nevertheless, I didn't want Mike to be simply a link in a chain, a way of connecting Cody and Lisa to Tycho. I wanted him to be his own character, with his own interesting story and his own unique way of looking at things. I think *Nightfall* succeeded in that.

But this isn't simply the story of the McGrath family. It's also a substantial chunk of Cameron and Joan's adventures immediately following *Truesilver*. It deals with Josiah Wilder, and the Doucet family, and several other characters from *The Last Werewolf Hunter* series. So there were actually lots of existing threads to play with in this story, and that always makes writing easier.

It also takes place in locales which have been important in other books, including Arkadelphia, Arkansas; Natchitoches, Louisiana; and Tampa, Florida. And though I love all those places, I hope the residents will excuse me for visiting so much destruction on them in this book. Stephen King reportedly said once that there's nothing quite like the feeling of vicariously killing off all your friends and neighbors and bombing your hometown to ashes. I think I'd have to agree with him.

Most of the details mentioned are real. The Gum Tree really exists (although it's inaccessible now, alas), and the locations of businesses, street names, and so forth would be instantly recognizable to anyone familiar with Arkadelphia.

The name of this book, *Nightfall*, refers to the time in which Mike and Annabelle's story takes place, the last few twilight years of the existing world before the Orion Strain destroys it. But even though nightfall implies ending, it's also the time when people come home and are reunited with their families after being gone all day. Readers may notice that theme in the book, also.

This is a tale of one possible future among many, a not-unlikely scenario in many ways but certainly not my prediction of how things will actually develop. The only sure and certain thing one can say about the future is that it will end up surprising almost everybody.

That said, science and technology continually place more and more power into the hands of a flawed and sinful human race. Sooner or later, that's a recipe for absolute catastrophe. It takes no great amount of wisdom to see *that* much. Nor is there anything to be done about it, unfortunately. Most everyone sees this; it's one reason why apocalyptic fiction is so popular nowadays. A few decades ago the mood was very different. Back then people talked and wrote as if they expected science to be our salvation, the thing that would solve all our problems and create a heaven on earth. One rarely if ever reads books like that anymore.

In any case, *Nightfall* is primarily intended for entertainment, and if it contains a few thought-provoking ideas then so much the better.

Mike and Annabelle will be out of the picture for a while, since they won't reappear until 2157 and there are quite a few things that need to happen in the series before then. The next several books will be about Tycho, the real hero of our series. That's not to say his parents don't still have an important part to play later on; they certainly do. But in the meantime everyone thinks they perished in the Gulf; even Tyke himself.

A big thanks to all my fans who loved these books; y'all are the best!

William Woodall
November 12, 2013

Discussion Questions

1. Mike ends up in the future accidentally and then can't get back home, an event which radically changes his life. Has there ever been something which permanently changed your life either for better or for worse? Discuss that event and how your life might have been different if it hadn't happened.

2. Joey holds the opinion that worry is a sinful and ungodly thing to do because it shows lack of trust in God. Discuss this idea. Do you agree or disagree with his conclusion? Explain your reasoning.

3. Philip says that one way or another the world will die for lack of love. Explain what you think he meant by this. Do you agree or disagree with Philip's prediction?

4. Joan says at one point that your circumstances are only as hard as you think they are, and don't really have much to do with whether you're happy or not. Do you think this is true? In what ways might a person who had very few material things still feel blessed and happy? In what ways might a very wealthy person lead a life of misery?

5. Mike's mother says that God is good in all things, and that we should trust in His love and do whatever He asks of us, even when we don't understand the reason. Has there ever been a time when God asked you to do something you didn't understand? Discuss that experience and what the results of it were.

6. As Mike discovers, there's often a difference between knowing the right thing and actually doing the right thing. Discuss this idea. Has there ever been a time when you knew the right thing but found it hard to do? How did that experience work out for you?

7. Annabelle says that human beings always have a choice. What exactly do you think she meant by this? Do you believe that human beings still have a choice to make, even in circumstances which may seem impossible? Discuss a time when you had a very hard choice to make.

8. Who was your favorite character from Nightfall? Discuss why you especially liked this person.

9. Philip asks the question: *"So if we're only like the curve in a waterfall, and there's not a shred of matter that we could ever put a finger on and say that that's really us, then what are we?"* Since this is actually a proven fact, what do you think the answer to Philip's question might be? What is it that makes a human being a human being?

10. Joey says that there's no such thing as a normal life, and that even the most ordinary-looking people have their own burdens and issues to deal with, most of which you'd never guess. Has there ever been a time when you suddenly discovered that a friend or family member was struggling with a problem you never suspected they had? Discuss that experience.

11. The future world described in this story is very different in some ways. What aspect of the future in *Nightfall* did you think was most interesting? How likely do you think it is that a future like this might really happen?

12. Joan says at one point that it feels too much like a straitjacket if you know too much about future events. What do you think she meant? Do you agree, or do you think it might be fun to know the future ahead of time? If so, what things would you want to know and what things might you prefer not to know? Explain why.

13. Philip says that a man is only the sum of his memories. Discuss this idea. Do you think this is true? In what ways have your experiences made you into the person you are today?

14. One reason Mike likes Annabelle so well at first is because she's so different from anyone he's ever met before. Do you know any truly unique individuals? If so, describe that person and what it is that makes them so unusual.

15. There are several unanswered questions at the end of *Nightfall,* such as what will happen to Mike and Annabelle or what happens to Lieutenant Bartow. What are some of the things you still wonder about, and how would you like to see them turn out?

16. Mike's decisions aren't always wise. What are some things you think he should have done differently? How might things have turned out in that case?

The Curse-Breaker Books
By *William Woodall*

Long ago, there was a Godly woman named Marybeth Trewick, who for various reasons found herself married to a rich but wicked man named Daniel who practiced all kinds of evil. She could only watch helplessly as her five sons grew up to become just as wicked as their father, and as her only daughter was forced to flee for her life lest she be killed.

But in the midst of her despair, God sent Marybeth a dream that after seven generations had passed, there would be five boys born to replace and redeem the ones that she had lost. These five would be breakers of curses and fighters against all things wicked and evil, and each of them would have the same vividly blue eyes, the same color as Marybeth's.

And even though the Curse-Breakers are each called to very different tasks in the world, the basic goal of fighting evil and loving God is always the same. These are their names and stories.

Brian Stone: The oldest curse-breaker, Brian's task is to save his brother's life and to remind men of Heaven by showing them the beauty of what could have been if the world had never fallen.

Cody McGrath: Two years younger than Brian, Cody is called to break the power of a dangerous sorceress. He's a dreamer of true dreams and a healer of the lost and broken-hearted.

Zachary Trewick: Four years younger than Cody, Zach is called to destroy one of the worst remaining aspects of his ancestor's wickedness; the werewolf curse which most of his family still embrace wholeheartedly.

Cameron Parker: Cameron and Zach are the same age, not to mention third cousins and best friends. Cameron has a big role to play in the struggle against the wolves, and later becomes the leader of all the survivors of Earth.

Brandon Stone: Brian's little brother, Brandon is three years younger than Cameron and Zach. He has a gift to know the meaning of dreams, and he is called to defend the weak and to uphold all that is righteous and true.

The Curse-Breaker Books form a collection of related stories about these five boys and sometimes their children. Each series tells the tale of a different Curse-Breaker (or sometimes more than one), but they also fit together in ways you wouldn't expect, in order to form a single unified storyline. It's helpful to read the books in order if possible, but it's not strictly necessary. You can read more about each series on the following pages.

The Stones of Song Series
By William Woodall

"There's a thing called magnanimity, or greatness of heart, and to me it's the most beautiful thing that ever there was. It means courage, but it's more than that. It means to cast aside all thought of yourself for the sake of another, like Moses in Gilead or the martyrs who died with a smile on their face. In its own small way it's a reflection of the Lord Jesus at Calvary, and therefore of God, the Light so beautiful that no one who sees it can ever turn away."

So says Cody McGrath, and in many ways that statement is the central theme of this series; the casting away of self for love of another, the scorning of selfishness in all its forms.

These are the stories of the Stone family: Brian, Jenny, Lisa, and Brandon, and some of the people they know and love, most notably Cody. All of them were called for great and glorious things, though sometimes only after great suffering and many mistakes.

<u>Unclouded Day:</u> Brian's life isn't easy. Abandoned by his father, abused by his alcoholic mother, and mocked by his classmates, his only treasures are his beloved little brother and his old guitar. This is the tale of his journey to find the Fountain of Youth, and perhaps to save the world.

<u>Many Waters:</u> Lisa is a small-town waitress with heavy burdens to bear. Cody is a young cowboy with big dreams and some very dangerous enemies. But when the two of them must face down an evil witch who tries to destroy their very lives, it seems that only a miracle can save them.

<u>Bran the Blessed:</u> Brandon hasn't always made the right choices in life, but he's never found himself in quite such deep trouble as this. But even though his life seems ruined forever, Bran still has a high calling to answer. . . if he can find the courage.

* * * * * * *

"I would absolutely, without reservation, encourage you to read this wonderful novel, even if you aren't the fantasy genre type. It was a blessing."
-Sue, Reflections and Reviews

"There are so many nuggets of truth in this book. It's about Heaven. It's about bad things happening for a reason. It's about deciding for yourself what truly matters most in life. It's a really good book!"
-Tattie, Christian Fiction Ebooks

The Last Werewolf Hunter Series
By *William Woodall*

Zach Trewick always thought he'd become a writer someday, or maybe play baseball for the Texas Rangers. What he never imagined in his craziest dreams was that he'd find himself dodging bullets and crashing cars off mountainsides, let alone that he'd ever be expected to break the ancient werewolf curse which hangs over his family.

But Zach is the last of the werewolf hunters, the long-foretold Curse-Breaker who can wipe out the wolves forever, and he's not the type to give up just because of a few minor setbacks. . .

Cry for the Moon: What would you do, if your family wanted you to become a monster? What if they wouldn't take no for an answer? When 12 year old Zach faces questions like these, he seems to have only one choice; *run*. Thus begins a long search for refuge, and perhaps redemption also.

Behind Blue Eyes: When a stranger kidnaps him from his own back yard, Zach soon finds that the past isn't quite as dead as he might wish. For the time has come at last for him to break the werewolf curse forever; and his family has no intention of letting that happen.

More Golden Than Day: When his girlfriend and then his cousin fall into the hands of the wolves, Zach has no choice but to take on his enemies for a second round. Only this time the stakes are horribly high, and if he fails he may end up losing everything he's ever loved.

Truesilver: When a family of wicked ex-wolves is accidentally awakened, Zach soon finds himself locked in a desperate fight for survival that he never anticipated. And even though he's sworn an oath to fight evil to the utmost of his power, there are times when courage is awfully hard to come by.

* * * * * * *

"If you are looking for a story about a boy who learns valuable lessons about family, love, friendship and God this is the book for you. I recommend this book to a pre-teen or adult. I truly enjoyed this book."
-Rae, *My Book Addiction Reviews*

"I found myself captivated with the story and could not stop reading until I reached the final page. Everything about this story is thought-provoking. Readers of all ages will appreciate this wonderfully told story,"
-Jancy, Kansas

The Tyke McGrath Series
By William Woodall

In the year 2154, the world has become a dangerous place. Extremist groups would like nothing better than to wipe out humanity completely, and even the people sworn to defend civilization against such threats have become deeply corrupt and untrustworthy.

When a virulent plague destroys all warm-blooded life on Earth, a small band of survivors clings to life on the partially-terraformed Moon. But fresh dangers lie in wait for the unwary; nor have they left behind all the wickedness in the hearts of men.

Nightfall: When Micah McGrath suddenly finds himself thrust into a dangerous and ugly future after a lab accident, his only choice is to make the best life for himself that he can. But when the secret police get wind of his research into time travel, he soon finds himself in deep trouble indeed.

Tycho: Tycho McGrath is a high school honor student in Florida when he discovers a terrifying secret: a man-made bacterium is about to wipe out all warm-blooded life on Earth within days. The only hope for survival is to flee at once, a plan which carries its own set of unexpected dangers.

Avenger: After spotting an SOS coming from the abandoned Moon, the survivors must organize a rescue mission. But the expedition quickly becomes far more complicated, leading them to the icy world of Titan in search of a holy mountain that no human eye has ever seen.

Freedom: When a cruel and power-hungry military commander on Venus decides to reconquer Earth, the only thing he needs is the formula for Tyke's Orion vaccine. The survivors soon find themselves locked into a bitter battle over the future of mankind, and who will inherit the Earth after all.

Elysium: What began as a simple mission to recover lost comrades in the Martian desert quickly turns deadly when Tyke and the others find *themselves* stranded on the Red Planet, with only the slimmest of chances to make it home again, or to fulfill the destiny which God has in store for them.

* * * * * * *

"Reminiscent of Freedom's Landing, by Anne McCaffrey, Tycho combines the best of traditional space-exploration sci-fi with modern apocalyptic fiction. For any fans of hard science fiction, it doesn't get much better than this." **- Liz, OH2 Reviews**

Trewick Family Tree

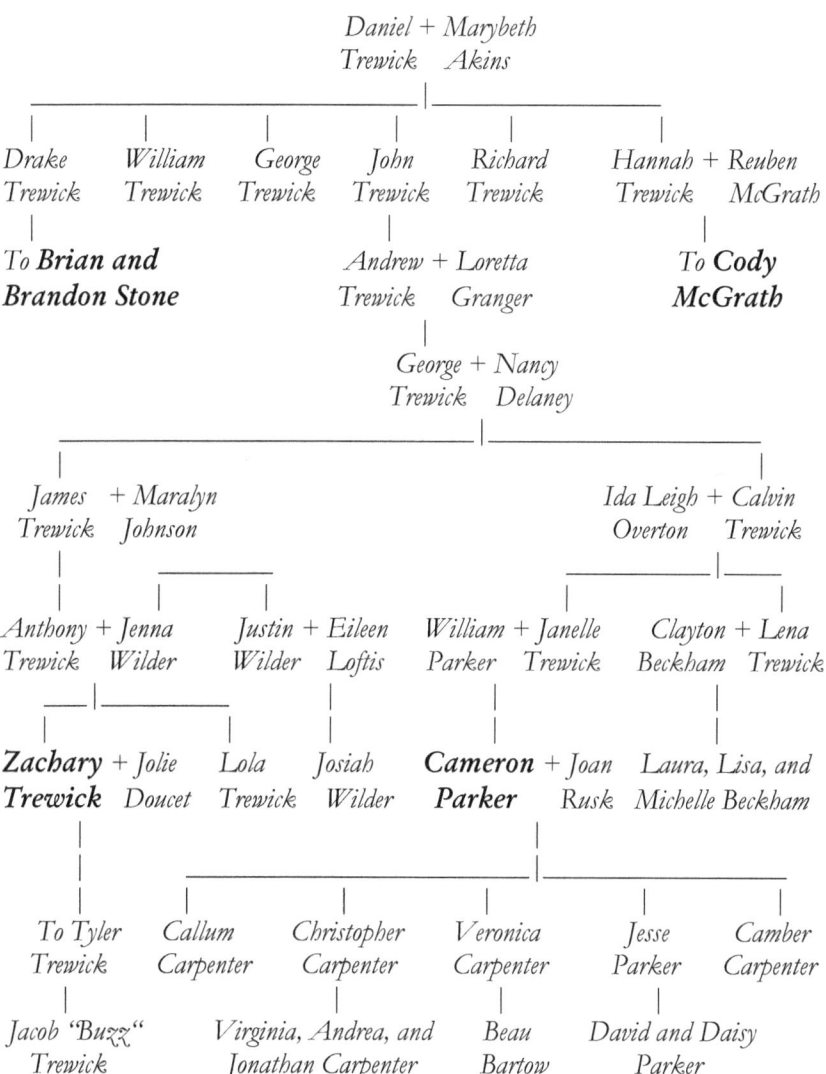

1. Curse-Breakers are in bold.
2. Cameron Parker later changed his name to Philip Carpenter.
3. Tyler Trewick is Zach's great-grandson.
4. Lisa Beckham's husband is Logan Tygart.
5. Laura Beckham's husband is Heath Coates, son of Albert Coates.

Trewick Family Tree

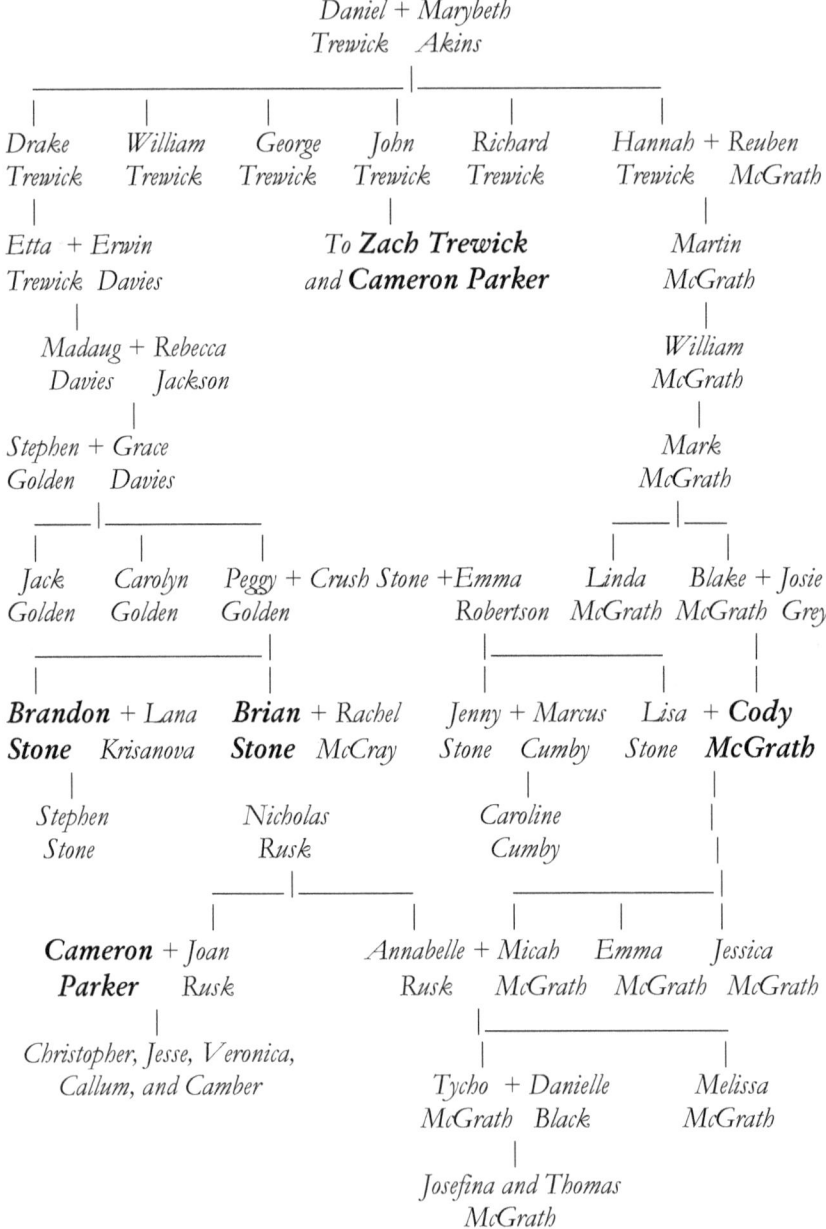

Daniel + Marybeth
Trewick   Akins

Drake	William	George	John	Richard	Hannah + Reuben
Trewick	Trewick	Trewick	Trewick	Trewick	Trewick McGrath

Etta + Erwin
Trewick   Davies

To **Zach Trewick**
and **Cameron Parker**

Martin
McGrath

Madaug + Rebecca
Davies   Jackson

William
McGrath

Stephen + Grace
Golden   Davies

Mark
McGrath

Jack	Carolyn	Peggy + Crush Stone +Emma		Linda	Blake + Josie
Golden	Golden	Golden Robertson		McGrath	McGrath Grey

Brandon + Lana   **Brian** + Rachel   Jenny + Marcus   Lisa   + **Cody**
Stone   Krisanova   **Stone**   McCray   Stone   Cumby   Stone   **McGrath**

Stephen
Stone

Nicholas
Rusk

Caroline
Cumby

Cameron + Joan   Annabelle + Micah   Emma   Jessica
Parker   Rusk   Rusk   McGrath   McGrath   McGrath

Christopher, Jesse, Veronica,
Callum, and Camber

Tycho + Danielle   Melissa
McGrath   Black   McGrath

Josefina and Thomas
McGrath

Doucet Family Tree

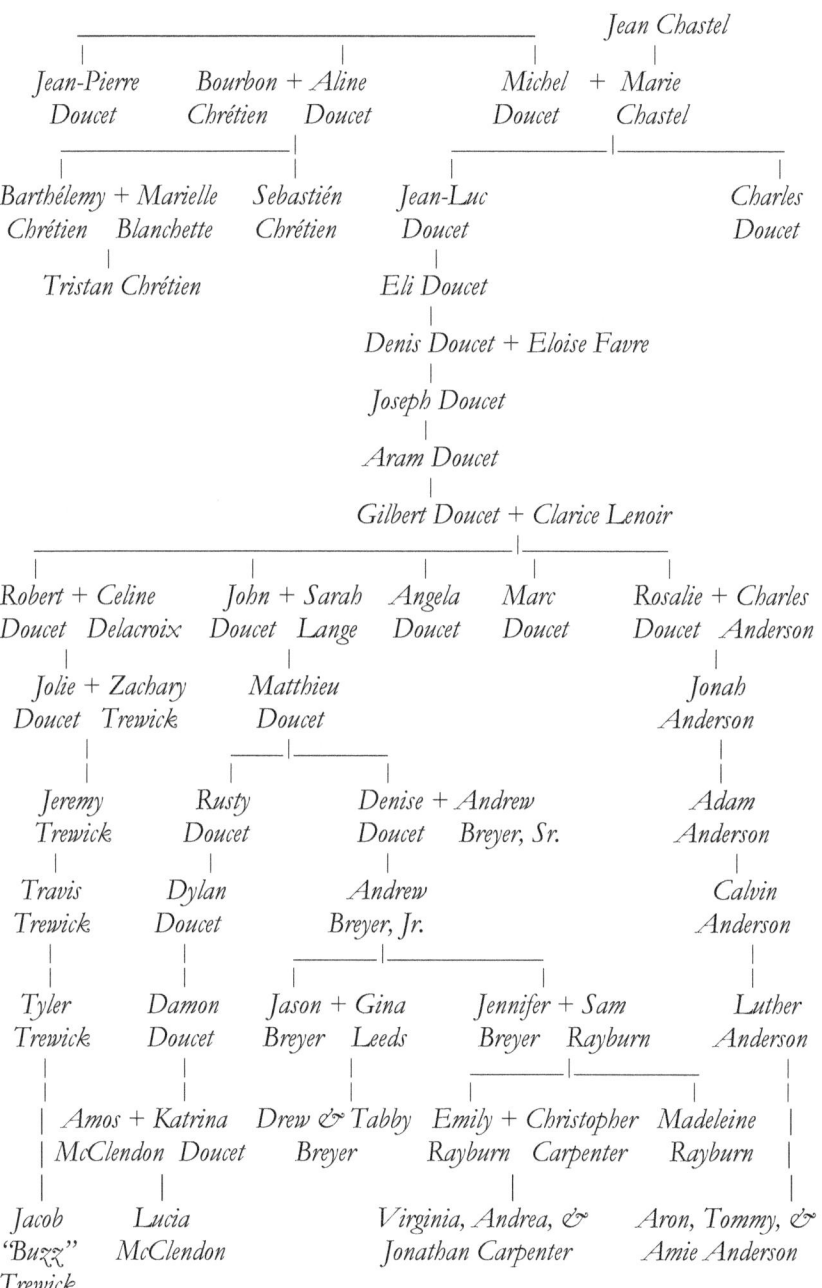

Bartow Family Tree

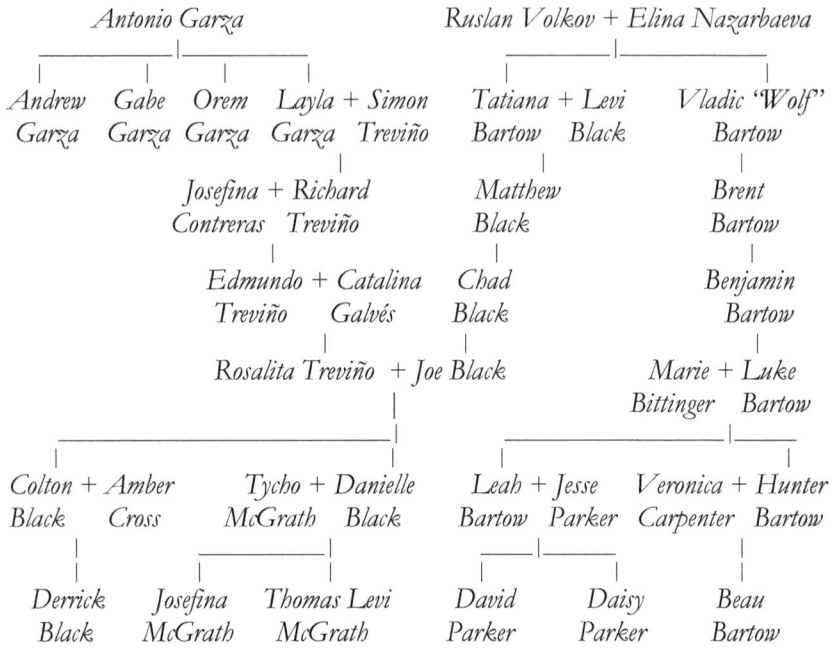

Jones and Golden Family Trees

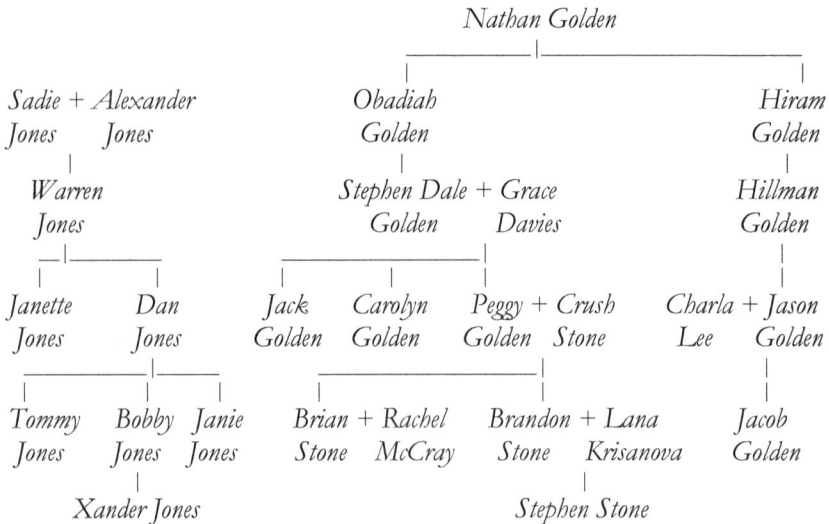

If you'd like to find out more about
The Tyke McGrath Series
and other books, please visit:

William Woodall's
Official Author Website

www.williamwoodall.org

Here you will find:

Free short stories
Discussion questions for teachers and book clubs
Free sample chapters of all my books
Photos of characters and locations for each story
Articles
Interviews
Quotable Quotes
Contact Information
And much, much more!

www.ingramcontent.com/pod-product-compliance
Lightning Source LLC
Chambersburg PA
CBHW050928120626
46552CB00001B/101